Judit Berg

ALMA

and the Dark Dominion

With a contribution from Judit Polgár,
the best woman chess player of all time

First English edition 2019 by Quality Chess UK Ltd
Copyright © 2019 Judit Berg

Alma and the Dark Dominion by Judit Berg

Hardcover ISBN 978-1-78483-066-3

All sales or enquiries should be directed to Quality Chess UK Ltd,
Suite 247, Central Chambers, 11 Bothwell Street,
Glasgow G2 6LY, United Kingdom
Phone +44 141 204 2073
e-mail: info@qualitychess.co.uk
website: www.qualitychess.co.uk

Distributed by Quality Chess UK Ltd through
Sunrise Handicrafts, ul. Szarugi 59, 21-002 Marysin, Poland

Published in 2013 by Ecovit as
ALMA-A sötét birodalom
Translated from Hungarian by Ralf Berkin
Typeset by Kallia Kleisarchaki
Proofreading by John Shaw
Illustrations by Barbara Bernát
Original cover design by Barbara Bernát
Cover adaptation for the English version by Kallia Kleisarchaki

Printed in Estonia by Tallinna Raamatutrükikoja LLC

Contents

I. A Curious Coincidence

The day had felt strange since early that morning. At first it seemed that nothing was going to work out, but then more and more peculiar things happened as morning moved to afternoon. Perhaps the most improbable thing of all had been the three of them meeting like that. They never normally spoke to each other at school, so the fact that they all ended up somewhere they would never normally go, and all at the same time, was a minor miracle in itself. Yet coincidence, or perhaps a series of coincidences, had gathered them together, as if someone had intentionally twisted the strands of time and space into the kind of knot that takes ages to untangle.

Felix didn't have the faintest intention of going to the park that afternoon. They'd played a basketball match against the Lakeside Leviathans that morning, and Coach Cochran had promised them a trip to the cinema as a reward for their well-earned victory. He was a tough trainer, but with a soft centre. Then, despite their plans to meet at a particular time, and regardless of Felix's stunning performance on the court, a crazy coincidence managed to mess everything up. His mum and dad had been invited to a posh wedding that would probably go on until dawn the following day, and so they thought it best their son stay at home. Gran said she'd come over and look after her abandoned grandchild even though Felix had turned twelve and was quite able to look after himself, thank you very much! But he'd still have been happy to see Gran, and not only because she'd probably make pancakes for tea and he could talk to her about absolutely anything, but because his kid sister Bella wouldn't spend the whole afternoon following him around like a lost puppy.

His parents had their coats on ready to leave, when Gran called to say that a blackbird had flown into her flat and was flapping about from one room to another in a desperate attempt to escape. Gran said she'd opened all the windows but the poor bird simply couldn't find the way out. There was no way she could come away for the night with a frantic bird about the place: it had made an awful mess already, and even managed to fly right into the mirror and nearly knock itself out. Gran was waiting for the boy next door to come and give her a helping hand to drive it out. She'd be over the minute it had found its way out, and she'd had time to tidy up again. She'd definitely be there by teatime. So there was no need to worry about the pancakes or anything absurd like spending the night on their own, but Felix would just have to look after Bella until she showed up.

Felix simply could not believe that a brainless blackbird had stopped him going to the pictures with his pals. He was fuming inside, and with a bitter look on his face he took tight hold of Bella's hand and dragged her down to "play" in the park. Bella insisted on riding her bike so Felix decided to watch from a safe distance, because there was no way he was going to be seen out with a girl who still had stabilizers.

Drifter hadn't planned to go to the park either. He was the weird one in the class, who spent all his time glued to his computer screen playing some kind of strategy game that involved guns and bombs and points and plans and loads of complicated stuff you only understood if you knew the software inside out. He loved his computer, but he also loved his skateboard, and so he'd organised to meet his mate Saller. They were going to practise some new moves in Market Square. Saller was a streetwise kid. He'd once come second at the local skateboard championships, and he knew the kind of tricks that made even the pros stop and stare. Drifter had decided it was time to catch up, and Saller had said he was willing to teach him all he knew.

The pair of them had agreed to meet in the afternoon, because the market traders had normally cleared their stalls away by then and the square was pretty empty. A few old cabbage leaves and broken crates couldn't stop two such devotees determined to perfect their flips on the bottom step of the battered fountain. Drifter was the first to arrive, and his head was buzzing after several solid hours of gaming. In fact, he was feeling pretty weird all round. A handful of fat pigeons pecked at the few edible things they could find on the ground, while two magpies hogged the spot where the hotdog van normally stood. Drifter went on a quick spin around the square to scare the pigeons and aimed for a grand finish with the magpies. Those birds were brave! They didn't as much as ruffle a feather when they saw him coming, and he had to swerve to avoid hitting them. Magpies are bigger than you think! The board turned, Drifter jumped, and the magpies hopped onto the top of a stall that had been left standing. Drifter could feel their eyes burning into his back like they were planning their revenge or something.

"Okay, sorry!" he muttered, then he reached for his mobile to check the time. Saller should have been there ages ago. He'd just got it out of his pocket, when it rang and made him jump. It was Saller to say that their plans were most definitely off. He was stuck in the cranky lift between the sixth and the seventh floors, and that thing wasn't going anywhere in a hurry. So he was sitting in the dark waiting for someone to come and set him free. Drifter said he was sorry and all that, then he made for the park because the plinth under the statue of a soldier was just the right height to jump from with little risk of a broken leg. Saller could always come and find him if he got out in daylight. Drifter was sure he could hear the magpies laugh as he left.

Alma was the third child to find herself by chance in Sycamore Park that afternoon. She was actually halfway through her fifth match by the time Felix appeared with his kid sis, and Drifter turned up with his skateboard. The trees sheltered a number of old concrete tables where old men in hats and a handful of young dads gathered to play chess on the warmer afternoons. Some of them treated this forgotten corner of the park like their second home and spent all their free time there when it wasn't raining.

The tables were one thing, but the best bit was a giant chessboard marked out on the grass, where the squares were big enough to stand on and the chunky wooden pieces were the size of toddlers. Next to the playground, it was a pretty popular place with the local kids. But everything was quiet that afternoon. The kids must have been off somewhere else, and the grown-ups were busy concentrating on their precious chess.

Alma had been playing chess since she was five, and she'd entered loads of competitions. Today, a warm afternoon in May, she'd been on her way to the place at the end of the road to buy her first ice cream of the season. She liked it best with extra sprinkles on the top. It was incredibly sunny for that time of year, and Alma didn't feel like walking the whole way in the heat, so she decided to take the route through the leafy park. Her family had only moved there a couple of months ago, and, what with school and chess, she hadn't really had any time to get to know that part of town. She'd only ever ridden through the other part of the park on her bike before, so she was delighted to discover the cool shade of the ancient sycamores and the winding path through a patchwork of colourful flowerbeds.

And then she walked right into what looked like an open-air chess festival! It only took a minute and she was already standing watching the closing moments of a game. The men were in the middle of an annual championship held between the real regulars. It was blitz chess, where the players weren't allowed to ponder for hours on end, and the whole game had to be over in

under five minutes. This kind of chess takes a lot of attention, concentration and speed, and it makes a great spectator sport. The minute a place became free, Alma forgot all about her ice cream with the sprinkles, and announced that she'd love to have a go herself. The men in the crowd – they were all men – didn't seem too keen to let a twelve-year-old girl join in the fun they were having, but seeing as they were a player short, they decided to let her play this once. Young Alma romped through the first game, and then she was in. Quite a little crowd had gathered by the time she stood facing her fifth opponent, and the onlookers whispered to each other about her daring challenges and unusual moves.

Alma was completely absorbed in her passion for chess and so she never noticed the man dressed all in black with a hat, who had his dark eyes fixed on her from the very first minute. The dappled shade of the sycamore trees masked the reaction on the dark figure's face as he watched Alma win one game after the other. As the furrows on his brow deepened with every victory, a shadow seemed to flitter over the tables. The only person in the park who had an eye for this sort of thing was still busy doing something else. That particular person was Drifter, who was hard at work perfecting his jump from the plinth of the soldier statue.

He bunny-hopped to the top, and took a look around as he stopped to catch his breath. Crows and blackbirds were pecking at the grass on the left, a clutch of confused seagulls bobbed on the surface of the pond to the right. Drifter's eyes then roamed further afield until they spotted something very odd in the branches of the sycamore trees that stood next to the path that ran down the side of the park. One branch in particular was packed with birds huddled close up next to each other. The peculiar part about it was that they were arranged crow, seagull, crow, seagull. Black, white, black, white. And there must have been at least eight of them standing like this.

"That's impossible!" he thought to himself, and he gave his eyes a good rub. "Crows and seagulls don't get on. They don't even have stuff like that in a circus. Perhaps they're all just magpies and I'm seeing funny," he went on. "Mum might be right about me staring at my screen too much."

Drifter kicked and flipped his board, and popped it under his arm before setting off to take a better look at this feathery phenomenon. He glanced up again as he made his way over, and was stunned to see that the branch was bare! Had he been seeing things? He decided to take a good look around and try to discover what had tricked him quite so convincingly. But when he got there, he couldn't find a single feather of evidence of crows and seagulls having been there, let alone making friends and standing in line like that.

Drifter's gaze wondered over to the chess pieces arranged on the grass by the park path. He looked over just in time to see a black shadow sweep down the path as one of the pieces moved forwards. Drifter gave his eyes the second good rub of the day. He'd slowly grown used to the sensation that animals were looking at him with human expressions, but a giant chess piece that could move itself was too much even for his rich imagination.

"Could it be sunstroke?" Drifter thought for a second, but he was quick to dismiss this. May sunshine really wasn't that strong and, anyway, he never went out without his baseball cap on. He had to wear it to keep his curly hair back when he was on his board.

Drifter wandered over to the grass. All was calm down by the path, where the players were still deep in concentration. A brown-haired girl with a ponytail came pedalling towards him on her bike. She looked familiar somehow, and Drifter squinted to focus on her face as she came closer.

"That's bighead Felix's baby sister."

Felix and Drifter had been sworn enemies since the first year at infants school. Felix hated the fact that Drifter never really took part in class activities, was always forgetting his homework, and spent all his time on his computer or his skateboard. He thought the baggy rags he called clothes looked pathetic, and he just couldn't understand someone who had the kind of long hair that was always in his eyes. For his part, Drifter really wasn't into anyone who was good at school, good at sport, and good-looking all at the same time. He thought that Felix's success had made him arrogant, and he did his best to avoid him whenever he could. He turned away. The girl on the bike bore a disturbing resemblance to her big brother, and he didn't really want to bump into either of them.

A cold breeze blew down the tree-lined path. Drifter was sure he could see a long line of crows and seagulls marching along in perfect black-white-black-white succession. Then on the other side – and there was no doubt about it this time – another of the wooden chess pieces made a move. Drifter was just starting to fear for his sanity when the girl wobbled and rode into a bin. Drifter ran straight over and right into Felix, who had appeared from further back. Her big brother was quick to pick his kid sister up. He treated Drifter to a cool nod and then took a look at the bike.

"You should be more careful!" he scolded Bella. "Why go so fast when you can't even use your brakes properly?"

"That's not true! I use my brakes all the time! But one of the black pieces moved and it made me jump!" Bella bawled, and pointed to the giant chess set on the grass.

"Sure it did! And the litter bin just leapt out in front of you!" Felix barked.

"I saw it move, too!" Drifter butted in, suddenly overcome with curiosity to work out what this was all about. If the girl had seen it, it must have happened. He suddenly felt so much saner! Felix got back to his feet and stared at his longhaired, skateboarding classmate. He pulled a face.

"I always thought that you were on about the same level as my sister!"

This was a bit too much for Drifter, who drew a deep breath and took a definite step closer to his famous rival. Rather than back off, the school's best basketball player stood his ground and held Drifter's stare. Bella glanced nervously from one boy to the other, then she had an idea and pointed to the crowd clustered around the chess championship.

"There's that new girl in your class! She's playing chess with those old men!"

Felix and Drifter both turned to look over at the same time. Felix immediately recognised Alma, and he pulled the sides of his mouth down in a grimace. He really didn't like that girl and her chess prowess didn't impress him one bit. He was outraged by the idea that they called it a sport when all the players did was sit on their backsides all day and move little men around a board. Four sessions of basketball training a week – now that was what he called proper sport, with real running and jumping, stretching and sweat!

Drifter was slow to spot Alma because the man dressed all in black caught his eye first of all. The dark figure was staring hard at the girl, but then he looked up for a second and looked right back at Drifter. A cold shiver ran down Drifter's spine and he got goosebumps despite the mild weather. He had the sudden sense that Alma was in some sort of danger. He hadn't said a word to the girl since she'd started at their school, but he somehow knew that she shouldn't be left alone.

"Look at that bloke in the black hat!" he said as he nudged Felix. "There's something not right about him!"

Felix stared at Drifter as if to say "what are you talking about?" before turning back to take a better look for himself. Alma then gave mate, and the crowd murmured in admiration, some even applauded. Another dark shadow swept down the path. And the man in the hat was gone! Perhaps he was blocked from view by the rest of the players around the table, or perhaps he'd left the minute the match ended. Anyway, there was no time left to look, because there was a clap of thunder so loud that perhaps a bolt of lightning had struck a sycamore tree. The people in the park all looked up to see that the spring sunshine had suddenly been replaced by black clouds. There was a second rumble and the battle in the skies commenced, bringing gusts of wind and buckets of rain that sent everyone running for cover.

Alma took a step back from the table and stared around for a second or two. She'd been so deep in concentration that she couldn't immediately recall where she was. She didn't recognize the park, and the sight of people dashing from the rain confused her completely. She stood hopping from one foot onto the other as she tried to fathom out which way she should run. Then she caught sight of her new classmates and made a beeline for them.

"The old bus shelter!" Drifter shouted, because that was the closest dry place he could think of. The four of them ran as fast as they could and came out at the main road that ran around three-quarters of the park. All they had to do was get over the zebra crossing and they would be out of the pouring rain and under the shelter on the other side. The same idea had occurred to plenty of other people, because running any further in that kind of storm seemed too risky for most folk.

The rain beat down so hard that the stripes painted on the wet road seemed to slide around and Drifter was convinced he could see black and white squares rather than the usual broad lines. None of them had any time to think about this though, because they had their sights set firmly on the shelter. Drifter was the first off the kerb with Alma, Felix and Bella hot on his trail. They got halfway across and all four of them stopped dead in their tracks.

It was impossible to explain, but it felt like the spring storm ended right in the middle of the main road. Black, white, black, white and then suddenly the wind, rain, and road, zebra crossing, and houses on the other side all vanished. The four children found themselves standing in a completely unfamiliar place with no sign of the bus stop, no sign of the town, and no sign to show them where to go.

II. KATALINA

They just stood and stared. The suburban street and raging thunderstorm had been replaced by a grassy meadow bathed in silky sunshine. The houses had gone, the pavements had gone, the lampposts had gone, and so had the flocks of people running from the rain, and the cars with their wipers battling against the downpour. The children's wet faces were now kissed by a warm breeze, and clumps of leafy trees rustled nearby. The only signs of any human presence were a couple of ploughed fields and a handful of cows grazing lazily on the hill opposite.

The sun might have been shining at its brightest and best, but the children were frozen to the spot. They stood motionless as if they feared the slightest step would take them into yet another unknown land. Bella began to pull at her big brother's arm, and Felix was so frightened that he forgot to tell her to stop. Still fresh from the chess, and shocked by the rain, Alma felt like she had slipped into a bad dream that had come to life.

"Wake up! Wake up, Alma!" she said to herself, repeating it over and over.

Drifter was the only one of them to keep his head. He took the whole thing in his stride because now he knew that the odd events of the day had all been leading up to this: Saller getting stuck in the lift like that, the menacing magpies, and all the mad stuff in the park had made him think he'd lost it for good. But when the road melted into a meadow, it somehow put the rest of events into perspective.

"Wake up! Wake up!" Alma continued to repeat, and looked more terrified by the moment.

"It'll all be some sort of silly dream," Felix began, as he squeezed Bella's hand even tighter.

"Well, if you ask me, I think we're all pretty wide awake!" Drifter cut in.

The others shuddered at his words.

"You can all hear my voice, we're all standing in the same meadow, the sun's shining down on all of us, and we can all see the same things. Does anyone feel anything different?" Drifter asked, but when no one answered, he continued confidently:

"All four of us can't possibly be dreaming the same thing at the same time! We all set off together, and something has happened to all of us. I don't know what caused it, but we've all crossed into another dimension."

"That's impossible!" Felix tutted.

"It seems impossible," Drifter replied in part agreement, "but it's still true. It's just like a computer game, when you finish one level and then enter a whole new world."

"But that doesn't happen in real life!" Felix protested.

"And do chess pieces move on their own in real life?" Drifter sliced back.

"Nope!"

"They do, because I saw them move! That's why I fell off my bike!" Bella chimed in.

"Now I think about it, weird things have been happening all day. Something was out of joint in the world."

"Come off it! What weird things?" Felix said heatedly. "It was a perfectly normal day: basketball game, lunch, family."

"And I ended up in the park completely by chance. I hadn't meant to go there," Alma mused.

"I'd planned to go somewhere else, too," Drifter added.

"Well, now you mention it, it's not exactly how I'd planned to spend my afternoon either. There was no way that I wanted to take my kid sister out on her bike," Felix nodded. "But I still say it's pretty normal to go to the park."

"But we only went to the park because a blackbird flew into Gran's flat, and she couldn't shoo it out, so she had to stay at home!" said Bella. "Would you call that normal?"

"Did you say a blackbird?" Drifter asked. "I've had several run-ins with birds today, too. It was as if all the magpies, crows and seagulls had gone completely berserk. Perhaps it was the birds that caused all of this!"

"Well, I haven't seen a single bird all day," Alma said with a shake of her head.

"And didn't you see that strange man staring at you either?" Drifter asked. The thought of the dark figure watching Alma made Drifter feel strangely uncomfortable. The last thing he remembered thinking before the storm broke was that he had to take care of her, because that man looked capable of all kinds of evil.

"Weird birds, chess pieces that move themselves, and now a prowler!" Felix summed up, and shook his head. "Do you believe in werewolves, too?"

"It's no good you making fun of me, I pointed him out to you, but then he disappeared. He looked really scary. He was up to no good, for sure."

"I didn't see him," Alma shrugged.

"Doesn't matter now. Let's try and find a road home," Drifter said. "If we managed to get here, we should be able to find our way back."

The others thought this sounded convincing enough, and so they all started to search. The first thing they did was to stand exactly where they had stood when this new world appeared around them. They felt and stamped around to see if they could find a trapdoor that would lead them back home, or some kind of portal that linked the meadow to the world they had left behind. Because all four of them agreed that this wasn't a dream, and if it wasn't a dream, they must have fallen through into a parallel dimension. None of them had ever believed such a thing existed, but they'd seen it in films and read about it in plenty of books. Alma suggested that they should try to repeat in reverse everything they'd done in the storm, in the hope that, just like in a film, they could wind time right back to the point that they stepped onto the zebra crossing. The four of them jumped, walked backwards, and looked around, but they couldn't find the slightest sign of a path back home or anything else that might explain their sudden arrival in this strange land.

Bella suddenly remembered her bike, and she started to cry. It had either been left behind in the old world, or disappeared without trace. Whatever the case, it wasn't with them now and Bella was afraid that she'd lost it forever.

"My skateboard's gone, too!" Drifter clapped his hand to his forehead. "If..."

"Don't say it!" Alma said as she raised a finger. "We're sure to find it if we get back."

"And if we don't?"

"If we don't get back, you won't need it anyway."

"I meant, what if we don't find it," Drifter grumbled resentfully, but then he looked at Bella, and he said no more. The tears were still rolling from her eyes.

"I want to go home to Mummy," she sniffed, and for once Felix didn't bark at her for being a whining baby.

Alma didn't have her mobile with her, so the boys got their phones out to call for help, but it was no use. They waved them around all over the place but there was no network, no internet, no GPS, and nothing that looked even remotely like a Wi-Fi connection. Felix eventually ended up sending a text to his dad, and Drifter sent one to his mate Saller, asking them to call them back if they could. The messages got stuck in their outboxes, so their only hope was that their phones would bleep in a minute or two, and they'd have coverage again.

After a quick chat, they soon decided that there was little more they could do here. They thought it best to explore their surroundings and see if they could ask someone for help. All the excitement had made them hungry, and the sudden warmth was making them thirsty, so they set out to find a village or a spring or a water pump. Felix loved any kind of physical exercise, so he shinned up the nearest tree to get a clear view of the surrounding countryside.

If they hadn't been so full of uncertainty, they would have certainly spent a minute or two taking in the beauty of the meadow in full bloom, the bright green bushes rustling in the breeze, and the regimented rows of fruit trees in a number of orderly orchards. But instead of seeing a genuinely picturesque landscape, they had the sense that they were surrounded by endless forest, prickly undergrowth, and wilting weeds. A line of trees led off in a westerly direction with a stream or path meandering in their shade, so that's the direction they took. A stream would mean water, and a path might hopefully lead to civilization.

Their first challenge was to make their way down the side of the hill, scrabble across a rocky outcrop, and cut through a field filled with purple flowers. It was not until they started to cross a strip of scrubland that Drifter began to look uncomfortable. It wasn't the terrain that troubled him, but an increasingly strong sensation that something wasn't right. It was the same feeling that he'd had in the park, when he'd spotted the birds arranged in line on the branch of a sycamore tree.

The scrubby field was followed by a mass of elderberry bushes in full bloom, that splattered the green canvas of undergrowth with white. The others began to sense something strange, too. An unsettling aura filled the air, and the closer they came to the bushes, the more they were sure that they could hear a rumbling somewhere in the distance. Felix scanned the horizon to see if a second storm was approaching, but there wasn't a cloud in the sky. The rumbling got louder and louder, and it soon became clear that it couldn't be thunder, because it was more of a pounding noise made by a mighty machine, or a herd of wild beasts racing across a vast expanse of land.

The noise was approaching from the base of the slope beyond the elderberry bushes. They still couldn't see what was making the din, but the whole hillside came to life. A flock of birds flew up, flapping and twittering loudly, and the bushes rustled as wildlife rushed for cover. The children froze for a second time. They couldn't decide whether to hide, or if they ran, which way to go. Could the damp shadows of the bushes possibly hold greater danger than whatever was heading their way? Luckily enough, they didn't have too much time to think, because a strangely dressed young girl leapt out of the greenery, and yelled at them to move.

"Quick! Hide!"

The children all looked around, and ran towards the helpful stranger. They panted as they pushed their way into the dense undergrowth, and sat crouched on the ground. Staring back at the open grassland from the cover of tangled branches, they were shocked to see a dark knight in shining armour galloping at the head of an army on horseback, all clad in black, brandishing billowing flags and gleaming weapons. It looked like a scene from one of those mediaeval tournaments, where men dress up and perform for the crowds outside a castle in the country. The difference was that these knights looked much more convincing than a bunch of dads playing soldiers in the spring sunshine.

The mounted army galloped past like the wind, rode to the brow of the hill, and vanished over the horizon. The dust churned up by the hoofs slowly settled, the thudding sound receded into the distance, and the countryside was calm once more. A breeze blew through the trees, restoring perfect peace to the picturesque setting.

"Who were they?" Bella said with a definite tremble in her voice.

"Warriors. There's going to be another war," the girl said sadly.

Felix had so many questions that he didn't really know where to start.

"When? Who are they fighting? And where are we? And... who are you?"

The girl looked them up and down, her eyes both curious and concerned as she inspected the boys' trainers, Drifter's baseball cap, and the tight jeans that the girls were wearing. She, on the other hand, looked like a picture in a school history book: embroidered blouse, long skirt, and her hair in plaits.

"You're outlanders," she finally announced.

Her voice sounded distant but in no way unfriendly.

"We'd really like to go home, but we can't seem to find the way back," Alma told her.

The girl scrutinized them now for a second time. Although she was slightly smaller in stature than Alma, the contours of her face suggested that she must have been about twelve or thirteen. The tough skin on her hands was a sure sign that she worked on the land, and her open expression suggested that she was a friendly sort. She stood and scanned the new arrivals, and her eyes lingered for a second on Felix's face before she eventually spoke with a shy smile.

"My name's Katalina, and I live here in Fianchetto. I know the place like the back of my hand, and I'm happy to help you in any way I can."

After a rushed introduction, the kids quickly explained how they had found themselves in this other world, and told Katalina all about the storm on the zebra crossing. They hoped she would be able to offer them an explanation, because perhaps she had heard of similar incidents in the past and knew what they had to do to get back to Sycamore Park. But the more she heard, the more surprised she appeared, and so by the time they came to the end of their tale, all four knew that nothing like this had happened before. And if a time gate or secret portal did exist, Katalina had no idea what it looked like or where to find it. She waited for them to finish, and she threw her hands apart.

"Travellers never come to these parts, and the locals never go very far. People live their little lives in the village where they were born, and that's where they die, if they're not called up to the castle first.

"Why, what's in the castle?"

"That's where His Highness Lord Dharma lives, and we are all his humble subjects. If he calls you to go to war, you have to go. His command is the highest law in all the land."

"Do girls have to fight, too?"

"If need be, yes."

"But that's not fair!" Bella protested. She was starting to sound quite upset. "And if someone doesn't want to play wars?"

"You still have to go. There are plenty of people who can hardly wait to be called to the castle," Katalina added before leaning in closer and saying in a whisper:

"The old folks say that Lord Dharma rewards those who do well in battle. It makes no difference if you're a peasant or you've got blue blood, if you prove your worth, a new life awaits you! My grandma told me about one peasant girl, who was called to the castle during the Great War. She did so well that they made her queen!"

"That's right. If a poor girl stands the test, she'll become queen!" Bella nodded, but Felix just laughed.

"Yeah, in fairytales!"

"Not just in fairytales!" Katalina contested.

"Look, it's quite possible that we've landed in a fairytale," Drifter pondered, "and everything that's real here only ever appears in books back home. You know: wicked witch, prince turned into a frog, goblins."

"It's not like that at all! Why are you making fun?" Katalina said with a flushed face. "Can't you see that everything around you is very real? The wars are tough, and we struggle to survive as best we can. And if I hadn't shouted to you when I did, you'd have all been trampled to death by those horses!"

"We're grateful you warned us, we really are," Felix said in his serious voice. Drifter also did his best to calm Katalina, who really seemed to take offence at the suggestion that she lived in a fairytale world. As usual, he thought he'd try a joke.

"Are you sure you don't have dragons here as well?" he asked with a cheeky grin, hoping that Katalina would see the funny side and laugh a little. But, to his surprise, the young peasant girl appeared disturbed by the question, and answered a little uncertainly.

"There could well be dragons..."

When she saw the shock on Drifter's face, she gathered her thoughts and spoke directly to Felix as if none of the others were standing there.

"Grandma sometimes tells tales of a dragon that lives high up in the hills, but she says that no one has ever seen it with their own eyes. I think it's just a scary story made up by grown-ups to frighten young children, but you can never be sure with these kinds of things. Grandma says that it's just as true as all the other stories she's told me about this troubled land."

"Well it seems that we're in no immediate danger of bumping into one, so let's just say that there are no dragons," Felix said convincingly, getting a shy smile from Katalina.

Now they were all agreed, Katalina offered to take them back to her home in Fianchetto. They could all have a rest in her grandma's cottage, and perhaps she could give them advice on how to return home. That was, of course, after they all had something proper to eat and drink.

III. THE BEES

Fianchetto sat nestled below nearby hills, and it would take them no more than an hour to get there by foot. With Katalina leading the way, the trials and tribulations of the past few hours began to look like thrilling adventures that could only end in the best possible fashion. The children were soon all smiling as they made their way along the winding path, and were less concerned about the risks that awaited them, and more excited to discover what Katalina's grandma would give them to eat when they eventually arrived.

Katalina strode out confidently at the front of the pack, and she happily answered Felix's questions as they marched along. He was interested to learn about everything from local customs and the style of architecture, to the wars Katalina had mentioned and even the way the locals farmed the land. He was trying as hard as he could to work out where they were in the history of the world. He nodded and "uhummed" at Katalina's responses, and then worked out what he needed to ask next to get closer to the solution. Alma was walking no more than a couple of paces behind, and so she managed to get the gist of their conversation.

She soon realized that Katalina's world was a considerable way behind the twenty-first century. They had never heard of electricity, factories or vaccinations, and there were definitely no cars, motorways, computers, credit cards or mobiles. They used oxen and horses to plough the land, lit their homes with tallow candles, and fought wars with swords and cannons.

"It really does seem that we've landed somewhere back in the Middle Ages," Alma thought to herself, but she got no nearer to the truth than that. No matter how many questions Felix asked Katalina about the names of towns and rivers in the area, none of her answers matched anything that Alma could recall from geography lessons. It was impossible to say where or when they were.

"At least tell me the year we're in," Felix asked, hoping to solve at least that problem, but Katalina's answer was of very little help.

"Grandma says that the castle where Lord Dharma lives was built five hundred and thirty-two years ago," she said as simply as she'd told them that the year was 1487. But she hadn't said anything as reassuring as that. Felix glanced sadly back to Alma.

"Are you any good at history?"

"I got an A, and the same in geography," she said with a shrug. "But I've still got no idea when or where we are."

"I can't work it out either," Felix said with a shake of his head, and he carried on plying Katalina with questions.

Bella was walking not far behind Alma, and she wasn't at all pleased about trudging this far on her own. She slowly caught up with the bigger girl, and slipped her hand into Alma's. Alma smiled and wrapped her fingers around Bella's much smaller hand. Bella felt better now she was part of the gang, and started to happily chatter away. She told Alma all about her class at school, all her friends, and especially about the riding lessons she'd been taking for the last two years.

"The boys say that horses are smelly and boring," she said in a whisper with a glance in Felix's direction. But when her big brother didn't turn back, she carried on with confidence. "I think they're the most intelligent animals in the whole wide world. You can tell them everything."

"And they understand what you say?" Alma asked with a look

of mild surprise.

"There are some words they understand," Bella nodded, "but I didn't really mean talking. If I concentrate really hard, they seem to know what I want and I don't have to say a word. It's almost as if they know what's in my mind by the way I stroke them."

It was at this point that Felix thought he should cut in. He shouted back over his shoulder with a cold shrug:

"All little girls are nuts about ponies. It's just another of their stupid crazes like playing with Barbies. Ponies are really smelly and boring!"

"What did I tell you?" Bella pulled a face. Alma couldn't help laughing.

"Horses are my favourite animals, too, although I suppose I only ever meet them on the chessboard, and then they're called knights."

"And you can't sit on their backs either," Bella chuckled.

"Sure enough, but I can launch loads of attacks with them. It sometimes even feels like I'm galloping into battle. They move in such a weird way, too: one to the side and then two forwards or backwards."

"That adds up to three," Bella counted, then her eyes twinkled. "Then it must really be like galloping into battle, because did you know that proper horses gallop three steps at a time?"

Felix looked back for a second time but he didn't say anything. He was fascinated by the sight of a little lake as it emerged from behind a clump of bushes and a band of rushes that lined its shores. He was sure that the locals used these to thatch their roofs. Drifter was now tagging along at the back of the gang. He was half listening to what the girls were saying but his thoughts were somewhere else entirely. Unlike Felix and Alma, who seemed convinced they had landed somewhere lost in time, he still thought that this must be some sort of fairytale world, where nothing happens like it should or would in reality. However many times he turned it over in his mind, the only answer that made any sort of sense was that they'd been caught in some kind of magical trap. So it was no wonder that he started to feel uncomfortable again, as if something bad was about to happen. Drifter tutted to himself as he tried to shake the funny feeling off. There was no way that they'd be faced with danger every half an hour! But, try as he might, the odd sensation lingered.

"I'm either going to go completely nuts, or I could get a job as a fortune-teller, who sees disasters just before they happen," he muttered to himself as he continued to scour the horizon for the next mishap waiting to happen.

Well, he didn't have long to wait. Katalina had just turned back to tell the others that they'd soon be in her village, when a boy appeared running right towards them.

"The bees are coming!" he yelled from a distance.

The kids stopped in their tracks as Bella looked to Katalina for reassurance.

"The bees have gone mad!" the boy bellowed as he continued to run as fast as he possibly could.

Drifter was the first to catch on. He knew that there was only one place they could go to escape the unwanted attention of raging bees – under the water.

"Katalina! Jump in the lake!" he shrieked.

Now the boy was getting closer, they could see the cloud of buzzing bees that were pursuing him with such determined speed. The others knew what to do now, too. They ran towards the lake so fast that they didn't even have time to slip off their shoes, and they threw themselves fully clothed into the water. No sooner were they in than the swarm of bees was above them, and they only just had time to take a deep breath and duck under the surface. They were so scared that they never gave a thought about how cold the water actually was. All they could think about was holding their breath as long as it took for the angry bees to fly past. Alma still had hold of Bella's hand, and when she felt that the little girl couldn't keep it up any longer, she guided her back up to take a hurried gasp of air before ducking

down again. It all happened so fast that they couldn't quite tell if the bees had gone or not.

They all carried on like this for a couple of minutes before Katalina eventually took the brave step of staying out in the air for long enough to have a good look around. The swarm had gone, and so with cold wet clothes clinging to them, they made their way out of the water.

"What happened, Jack?" Katalina asked the boy, as they both stood shivering on the shore.

"It's your grandpa, Kat! His bees have gone berserk! We need to hurry to the village!" Jack stuttered as his whole body shook with cold and shock. "He got really badly stung!"

This news was all it took to set Katalina running fast to Fianchetto. She shouted back over her shoulder:

"Follow me!"

Jack and the others were soon hot on her heels as they ran at top speed across a grassy meadow, through an apple orchard and over a deep ditch. Soon they could hear their racing steps echoing off the walls of country cottages. Katalina's grandparents lived on the outskirts of the village, and so they soon stood panting outside their front gate. People had crowded into the beekeeper's garden to see for themselves what had happened to the old man.

The honeybees had attacked Katalina's grandpa with such unexpected ferocity that he'd been stung at least a hundred times before he could even think of defending himself. And it wasn't just his hands. The poor old soul had been stung on every square inch of exposed skin. Katalina's grandma stood rubbing him all over with half an onion and a bunch of crushed parsley to try and draw some of the poison, while the village womenfolk dabbed at him with rags soaked in cold milk to cool him down. Katalina could see that her beloved grandpa was in very bad shape, and no one could tell if he'd survive such an attack. She fell sobbing at the old man's feet, while all the other kids could do was stand and stare in numbed silence.

"That number of stings can give you a fit even if you're not allergic to bees!" Drifter whispered.

"Do you think he's allergic?" Bella asked with a wobble in her voice. "I am, and that's why Mum makes me take my medicine with me everywhere I go!"

"Why didn't I think of that? Calcium!" Felix said as he slapped his head. "Get it out, Bella, quickly!"

The little girl slipped the pouch from around her neck. Alma had thought that it was just a pretty embroidered purse, and had no idea that it contained a substance powerful enough to save a life.

"'If a bee stings your lip while you're eating an ice cream, this tiny ampoule of calcium will help until the doctor arrives,' that's what Mum says."

Bella pressed the bubble of glass into Felix's hand. Her brother snapped the top clean off and knelt down by Grandpa's side.

"Open your mouth!" he said, and he spoke with such force that the old man instantly did as he was asked. Katalina's grandfather didn't give a thought about who this unexpected stranger could be, and none of the villagers protested either. They all stood around with bated breath as they waited to see if the serum would slow the old man's deteriorating condition. Felix let the liquid drip into the old man's mouth one drop at a time until the ampoule was empty.

"It might not be enough, but it should work for a while," he said with a warm tone of hope in his voice.

The old beekeeper looked back at the boy with gratitude, and then he turned to his granddaughter and said in a voice that could hardly be heard:

"Fetch the small stone jar from the pantry! And rub royal jelly into the stings!"

Katalina leapt to her feet and sprinted into the house, while a couple of the stronger village men picked her grandpa up, and, under strict instruction from her fretting grandmother, carefully carried the old man into the cool house. They lay him gently down on a bed directly under the window, and Grandma propped his head up with a firm pillow. They were busy placing fresh slices of red onion on the swelling stings when Katalina reappeared carrying the little jar of royal jelly. Grandma got quickly to work dabbing it on the old man's burning skin and then sent Katalina to collect cold water from the well to soak a sheet. Grandpa's breathing began to slowly ease.

"This really is marvellous medicine," he said to Felix. "I got just as badly stung some fifty years back, and very nearly died. What manner of healer are you, my child, that you should have such a serum?"

"It's only calcium, and you can buy at any pharmacy. But I don't suppose you have pharmacies here..."

Felix suddenly got all muddled up because he realized halfway through that what he was saying probably sounded like gobbledygook to the local peasant people. He decided to try and explain.

"I know it might sound incredible, but we actually come from another world. We ended up here totally by accident, and we still don't know how we're going to get back. Katalina suggested that you might be able to help us."

Felix was surprised to see that no one laughed at this, and neither did they accuse him of telling tall tales. A couple of villagers started to whisper, and Grandma puffed herself up and spoke in the triumphant tone of someone who had at last found proof to support her common claim.

"You see that? I always said that sorcery upsets the animals! Nature has gone wild again, the bees have gone mad, and new outlanders have arrived at the very same time!"

"New outlanders?" Katalina asked her Grandma sounding quite surprised.

"Outlanders appeared in Fianchetto a great many years ago, and they too claimed to have been transported here from a world beyond. They all wore the oddest attire, they behaved in the most peculiar way, and they brought disaster and calamity with them," Grandma continued, who was beginning to find a rhythm to her words. "You remember, my darling girl, I told you about the hordes of locusts that very nearly ate folks alive in their homes? And then there were the starlings that lay waste to our finest fruit crop. And then there were the ants..."

"Don't mention those tiny brutes!" an old lady said as she clutched her hand to her heart. "The whole village was overrun by them. They swarmed through my cellar, crawled up my walls, and I even found them in my best linen drawer!"

"Now that's what I'm saying!" Katalina's grandmother added as she carried on the tale. "And if you all recall, these terrible times always happened when an outlander set foot in Fianchetto. That bearded fellow appeared. You know the one. He was the fool who claimed to be a knight! Then those two men appeared wearing glass before their eyes!"

"Yes, I know the men you mean. One of them told us all he was a matted matician!" the previous old lady chuckled out loud.

"Mathematician," Katalina's grandpa corrected, but his weak whisper was heard only by Drifter, who was standing by the old man's head.

"And what happened to all these 'outlander' people?" Alma asked with concern

The villagers responded to this with stony silence.

"Well... they left," Grandma muttered. "I suppose they found their way home."

"How do you know that?" Katalina asked with a curious frown.

"I just do, my darling girl, I just do. We would have heard if it hadn't been so. They all of them went to the castle, and we saw the gates open before them. Someone from the village always followed them there in secret, so that we could be sure, but Lord Dharma always allowed them to enter, and they would be safe inside there."

"And how do you know that?" Katalina repeated.

"My darling girl, if His Highness Lord Dharma takes somebody into his castle, he is sure to treat them well. He takes the very best care of guests, because that is our way here. I know full well that he helped those poor people back to their own worlds."

"And how do you know that?" Katalina asked for what was now the third time, and she said it with such sharpness that the smile froze on her grandma's mouth.

"Why, because that is how it must have happened. They couldn't have stayed there for all this time."

"Does that mean that no outlanders have ever been seen leaving the castle?" Alma quietly asked.

The kindly old lady swallowed hard and turned to look at Alma. Her eyes lost their twinkle for a second as she looked sharply at Alma, but then she again became the cheery Grandma, who loved to tell stories to an eager audience.

"They didn't come out, my child, for how would they, when Lord Dharma has sent them back to where they came from? He is the highest of high, and lord of man, beast, land and water. Some even say he can control the very elements themselves!"

"Can he stir up a storm?" Drifter asked with obvious doubt.

"Why he can that!" the old lady cut back knowingly. "And I can tell you, my child, that the water of life itself flows from the castle well, because His Highness has ruled this land for five hundred and thirty-two years. He has lived in that castle since the day it was built!"

"So what's going to happen to us now?" Bella asked, looking to Alma for an answer. The youngest of the four had not understood much of what had been said, but she could clearly see that Grandma's words had hardly reassured them.

"Why what do you think, my child?" Katalina's grandmother answered on Alma's behalf. "You will eat a fine supper and spend the night with us here in our house. Then, fresh and early tomorrow morning, you'll make your way to Lord Dharma in the castle and ask him to help you travel back to your own land!"

IV. Fools in the Forest

The mysterious castle and the lord whom they'd been told had been in residence for more than half a millennium hardly seemed an inviting prospect, but the children were forced to accept that they had no other option. They tucked into the supper that Katalina's grandmother laid before them, and listened to the old woman's string of stories. Soon they all began to blink a little too often, and when Bella yawned loudly for the third time, Grandma sent them all to their beds for the night. Alma and Bella slept in the best room, while they boys were set up with bags of straw in the stables. Everything felt a little strange to begin with but then the sun-kissed scent of the straw and the chirruping of cicadas soon lulled them into a deep, peaceful sleep.

They were greeted at breakfast with a spread of goat cheese and bread with honey. Being a city kid, Drifter had never had the chance to taste milk so fresh that it was still warm, and so he pulled a face when he sniffed the suspicious liquid. Felix gave him a firm kick under the table.

"Don't make such a fuss, just drink it! You'll offend them!" he hissed.

"Can't I even smell it? I'm not drinking anything before I know what it is!" Drifter groaned.

The girls ate their breakfast with gusto. It was only Katalina who sat lost in her own thoughts. Then the friends thanked Grandma for breakfast and said their goodbyes. The old lady suggested they had best leave Grandpa because he was still fast asleep and the rest would do him good.

"Do you, by chance, have any of that serum left, my child?" she asked Felix as he stood in the doorway, while she hooked a back of bread buns over his shoulder.

"I'm afraid we only had one ampoule with us," he said with a shake of his head.

Katalina didn't say farewell to the others quite yet because they had agreed that she would go with them as far as the castle gate.

"The castle's not far from here, I'll have your lunch waiting for you when you get back, my darling girl," Grandma said as she waved them all off.

They came across Jack grazing his herd of goats on the outskirts of the village. Katalina skipped over to him.

"Can I ask you to do something for me, Jack?"

The country boy blushed to the roots of his hair.

"I told Grandma that I'm only escorting our visitors, but I've got business at the castle, too. I have to get in there somehow. I won't be home for lunch, so could you tell them, so that they don't start to worry?"

"Oh, don't go into the castle, Kat! You know how dangerous that place is!" Jack stammered, and then he blushed again as he clamped his hand to his mouth and glanced at Katalina's pals. "What I meant was..."

"Why is it dangerous?" Felix cut in. "Until now everyone's been saying how helpful Lord Dharma is to those in need."

"But we don't really know if that's true or not," Katalina admitted with a sigh. "It's true that there is none as powerful as him in all the land and that he can do things that no one else would dare attempt. If anybody can help you, it's definitely him. But I can't promise that he'll be friendly. And it's far from guaranteed that the gate will open when we get there. We've never seen it happen, we've only heard it in tales told in the village. And they... Well, you've heard them yourselves. No one really knows what truth lies in Grandma's stories. And she's never made mention of outlanders before."

"Do you think he might hurt us and never let us leave the castle?" Bella asked, and squeezing close to Alma.

"We have to hope that he will help," Katalina said with forced determination.

"But why are you going with them? You surely don't want to travel to their world, do you?" Jack asked.

"I think my Grandpa might be dying," Katalina said as she lowered her head. "This morning Grandma told me that we should leave him to sleep, but I slipped into his room to see for myself. He's been stung so very badly that the medicine he took won't be enough. The only thing that can save him now is the water of life."

"If such a thing even exists," Felix added.

"But I have to try!" Katalina said as she looked him straight in the eye. "I have to try even if it's dangerous and even if it does turn out to be nothing more than a fable, and there's no such well in the castle. But then Lord Dharma might have a cure, or perhaps he really can do magic! I'll ask him myself!"

"Your grandmother's stories are all very entertaining, but my father always claims that the castle is the most evil place in all the land and should be avoided at all costs!" Jack warned. "Promise me that you'll all be very careful!"

"We promise!" Katalina nodded.

They all said goodbye to Jack and carried on their way. They walked in silence for a while as each of them thought about Jack's warning. The path led slowly into a forest, where the morning dew glistened on green blades of grass in the light filtering down through the leaves. Now, surrounded as they were by the gentle rustle of the breeze through the trees and birdsong floating down from what seemed like every branch, it seemed impossible to imagine that they had left an old man dying from vicious bee-stings behind them and were preparing to confront an almighty lord, who may turn out to be evil.

They were nearly halfway through the dense forest, when Katalina stopped as they approached a small glade. She lifted a single finger to her lips and beckoned the others to follow as she hid behind a thick tree trunk. They could hear what sounded like happy chatter from behind a couple of bushes, when two figures appeared in view. At first glance it was hard to tell if it was the similarities or differences in their appearance that were more striking. One was a skinny thing with a hooked nose, unkempt hair and dressed from head to foot in ruby red. The other had a rather squat, rounded form with a button nose, bald head and wore only sky blue. Even though their appearance differed in every way and their clothes were cut and shaped in diverse fashion, it was plain to see that they somehow belonged together as they walked, talked and moved through the forest in a way that only two very close friends could.

Although they had obviously seen better days, their clothes suggested that they were servants of some kind, who, for some reason, were strolling deep in a dark forest. They didn't appear threatening in the slightest, and even Drifter's sixth sense didn't pick up any obvious warning signs. Their happy chatter continued as they walked out into the opening and only stopped when the one in red robes glanced over his companion's shoulder and spotted the children attempting to hide behind a mighty oak. He stopped, and stood there staring. The one in blue halted too, and following his friend's eyeline, spotted the children, too. The minute they realized that they hadn't walked into an ambush, and that it was simply a collection of kids huddled behind a tree, they smiled and, like puppets on the same string, waved together in friendly greeting.

The children were relieved and walked cautiously towards the two strangers to see if they might give them better directions to the castle.

"Who are you?" Bella asked as she came eye to eye with the thin and the fat figures.

"Oh, we're just two poor fools!" the one in red said.

"Speak for yourself! I'm no fool!" blurted the one in blue.

"You'll have trouble convincing anyone of that!" the red one laughed.

"Lies!" the blue one spat.

"Let's not go into that now."

"Do you two always argue?" Bella asked in astonishment.

"Yes! No!" they said together.

"We fit together like pieces of a puzzle."

"We're each other's opposite."

Katalina frowned for a second as she listened to the duo before turning to her companions.

"I know who they are now. You need to take care with these two! One only ever speaks the truth and the other does nothing but lie."

"Is that true?" Bella asked.

"We won't answer that..." the blue one said.

"Because then you would know right away which one of us tells the truth and which one doesn't," the red one concluded.

"It's naughty to tell lies!" Bella informed them.

"But that's how it is between us. At least one of us is always lying," the red one laughed.

"At least one of you?" Felix quizzed them.

"That's right," the red one replied. "That's how we protect our lord and master.

"Or more precisely: ourselves."

"Do they really protect their master, Katalina?" Alma asked. "Because if they do, we now know which one is telling the truth!"

"I really don't know. We are afraid of Lord Dharma, because we know that our peace and safety depend on him. There are some who look on him as a god and would risk their life for him, while others despise him for the power that he has over us all. They are the ones who defy his decrees, fight against him, and are forced to defend themselves against his soldiers."

"So we don't know which group these two belong to," Felix summed up.

"That's right!" the fools chortled.

"I think we should leave them and keep on going. We'll never get to the castle if we stand around here all day," Drifter interrupted.

"Are you on your way to see Lord Dharma?" the one in blue enquired.

"We want to ask for his help," Katalina explained.

"So that we can find our way home to another land," Bella added.

"It's certain that no one can leave our country against his will," the red one announced.

"It is not!" the blue one added.

"Really?" Drifter asked with a glint in his eye. He happened to be the one least enthusiastic about their trip to the castle.

"Of course."

"Are you telling the truth or a lie?" Alma asked.

"The truth," said Blue.

"He's lying," corrected Red.

"Oh, it doesn't really matter," Alma muttered. "Lord Dharma might be the only one who can help us or he might not, but we still have to get into the castle to get medicine for Katalina's grandpa. We have to get into that castle even if its owner might try to kill us!"

"Not might, definitely!" said Red.

"Not definitely, might!" said Blue, correcting him.

"Oh, stop it! No one asked you two!" Drifter snapped.

"You've realized at last! It's pointless asking us anything, because you'll never know which of our answers to believe!" laughed the one in blue clothes.

"That's right," Drifter agreed, and looked questioningly at the figure in blue.

"But you might work it out," the other one said with a shrug.

"You're very naughty, and you want us to make a mistake. You're deliberately not helping us!" Bella bawled, and if Alma hadn't stopped her, she would have run right at the man dressed in red.

The two characters didn't appear at all surprised by this reaction because they were obviously familiar with how their responses could irritate everyone.

"Oh, no, we wish you no ill! We don't really care what happens to you. The only important thing for us is that one should tell the truth and the other tell lies," Red said with a calm shake of the head.

"That's not true, because I mean well by what I say!" Blue interjected.

"And is that why you lie?" Drifter grilled.

"No, that's why I tell the truth!"

"Don't believe a word he says!" Red giggled. "Go to the castle if you want, but don't forget that it's a dangerous place!"

"It is not dangerous! I'd be lying if I said it was dangerous!" Blue butted in.

"Stop!" yelled Drifter, who had heard just about as much as he could take from these terrible twins.

The duo looked at each other and burst into laughter.

"All the best, we'll be on our way!" they hailed.

"One minute, I've just got one question that I'd like you to answer!" said Felix, who'd been pondering something for a while.

"What's the point?" Drifter asked shaking his head, but Felix didn't bother to respond. He looked first at the figure in blue, then at the one in red, then back at the one in blue.

"I would like to know if Lord Dharma is the only one who can help us get home again."

"Who are you asking?" the two of them asked together.

Felix looked at Blue.

"I want to ask you what you think your friend will say in answer to that question."

The blue one pulled a funny face, chuckled to himself and

then cleared his throat to speak.

"He will say no."

Now Felix turned to Red.

"And what do you think your friend will say if I ask him the same question?"

"He will say no!" the red one laughed then waved before walking off with his blue companion.

"Then we'll have to look for someone else who can help us," Drifter said with relief. "If we don't have to then don't let's go to the castle. Or at least, only to get the medicine, if we really must."

"We have to go," Felix shook his head. "They just said, no one else can help us."

"That's not what they said!" Bella piped up.

Drifter didn't know if he could stand this any longer. First there had been the banter between the two fools and now even Felix was starting to twist his words.

"What do you think the red one would say if I asked him if the blue one knew if I knew that you're not normal?" he asked with audible agitation.

"He'd say that you're not normal," Felix responded with perfect calm. "And you can believe me when I tell you: he was the one telling the truth."

"And what makes you think that?" Drifter snorted.

"Logic, and the fact that I stay awake in maths class."

"Oh, you're so pleased with yourself, aren't you?" Drifter grimaced. "Logic and maths, hey?"

"Oh, and a bit of hard work. That kind of thing," Felix added with a grin.

"I'm not interested in the opinion of a big-headed maths monkey!" Drifter turned his back.

"Can you two drop it for a minute?" Alma scolded the boys. "All this arguing isn't getting us anywhere. We need to concentrate on the task in hand! We need to get into that castle just as quickly as we can because it's starting to look like Lord

Dharma might have a few surprises up his sleeve. We've only got ourselves to count on, and bickering won't do anything to improve our chances."

"That's right," Bella nodded, and Felix turned on her in an instant.

"And who asked you?"

Katalina put her hand on his arm.

"We should be going!" she said in a faint but firm voice. "And on the way you can tell us how you worked it out."

Felix muttered something between his teeth but didn't raise his voice again. He followed Katalina down the path and they were soon back to chatting like the friends they had become. Felix was shy to explain his thinking at first but soon warmed up when he took Katalina back through the logical steps and she listened to his words with keen fascination.

"The fact that only Lord Dharma can help us would have still turned out even if I hadn't worked out which one of them was lying and which one wasn't. The important thing was that I didn't ask them for their own answer, but what they thought the other would say. If Lord Dharma really was the only one who could help us, then the truth-teller would respond truthfully and say 'yes'. But seeing as I asked the liar what he would say, he automatically responded by saying 'no'. When I asked the truth-teller what the liar would say, he answered honestly and also replied with 'no'. Because he knew the other would tell a lie. So, being as they both said 'no', the answer was obviously 'yes', and Lord Dharma really is the only one who can help us."

"But how did you work out that the one dressed in red was the one who told the truth?" Katalina questioned. "The other one was much friendlier."

"They let the cat out of the bag at the very beginning," Felix smiled. "Do you remember that the one in red said that at least one of them was lying?"

"Of course," Katalina shrugged. "Because I said the same."

"Not entirely!" Felix said and fixed her with a stare. "You said that one of them lied and the other would tell the truth. But the red one said that at least one of them was lying."

"And?"

"And that's the point, when he said 'at least'. Because that means that either both would lie or only one."

"I'm with you so far," Katalina nodded.

"And if he's the truth-teller, then the situation's simple: he told the truth, because it's certain that his companion would always lie, because at least one of them would lie."

"And if the liar had said that at least one of them would lie?" Katalina asked.

"Then we could definitely say that the whole sentence was a lie. Because if it's a lie that one or both of them would lie, then the truth must be that they are both telling the truth. But that's impossible, because we started from the premise that he was telling a lie."

Alma and Bella were walking hand in hand behind Felix and Katalina. Alma nodded in agreement with what Felix was saying and then she tried to recollect what the one in red had said about the castle and this Lord Dharma they had heard so much about. "We have to get into that castle even if its owner tries to kill us!" she recalled to herself with a shudder. "It would be good to know a few things about the place first so that we don't get trapped in there. We need to form a strategy of how best to defend ourselves."

Drifter, who, as usual, was tagging along at the end of the line, couldn't avoid commenting on all of this to Alma:

"Did you understand any of that logic garbage? None of it made any sense to me at all!"

"It's not easy to follow through from beginning to end, but if you apply yourself, it makes perfect sense."

"I can't stand all this convoluted thinking thing! Why should I bother applying myself to something that doesn't interest me?"

"The fact that it doesn't interest you doesn't stop it being useful," Alma announced. "We wouldn't have got very far on this one without Felix's logical thinking, now, would we?"

Drifter fell silent. Alma was worried that she had upset him, but she really hadn't meant to. She'd meant what she'd said. Her experience with chess had taught her that she often had to force herself to think a move through and work out what consequences it might have. And the same was true when it came to retracing her steps and seeing what decisions had led to what outcomes. This situation was just the same, even though it had nothing to do with chess. Alma had learnt that it made sense in all areas of life to see what the consequences of her decisions were.

Drifter carried on fuming inside for a minute or two but soon decided to let the anger and insult subside, and by the time they were walking out of the forest, he also found himself rewinding the conversation they'd had with the fools and trying to figure out what would be waiting for them when they eventually arrived at the castle.

He was only shaken out of his train of thought when they eventually stepped out of the forest and stood facing the castle. With turrets and towers, the mighty castle stood imposingly on top of a huge hill. It didn't look the least bit inviting. The kids stood uncertainly at the foot of the hill as they accustomed their eyes to the sight, and tried to instil themselves with the courage to climb up.

V. The Secret Doors

The castle was completely intact. Flags billowed over the tiled towers, the rugged stonework wasn't crumbling, and they couldn't see the slightest sign of war on the walls, though they were built five centuries before. Here and there a brave ivy vine traced the sides of the massive fortress, and in places moss had managed to soften the rigid lines of masonry, but the castle still stood strong and proud, looking out over the land it ruled. The sturdy stone walls had windows cut into them at regular intervals, and Bella started to count them in an attempt to work out how many rooms the castle might contain. She stopped when she got to forty-two.

The boys scanned the battlements to see if they could spot a cannon aimed down at them or a watchman's helmet glinting in the sun. With no sign of a single guard, the kids walked up the hill with a feeling of considerable relief. Alma wondered what could be the possible function of a band that ran around the base of the walls, about as tall as a person. This band was fairly wide, appeared grey from a distance, and Alma thought that it might be decoration, although this would be unusual for a fortress.

Katalina was the only one who blinked at the castle with a look of worry on her face. She dared not say anything to the others but she felt uncertain that they had come to the right place. She clearly recalled that the last time she had travelled past the castle with her grandparents, the path running up the castle hill had led directly to an enormous wooden door with a drawbridge that could be lifted or lowered with heavy metal chains. But now there was no sign of a door or a drawbridge, as if the castle had turned its back on its visitors. And she had no recollection of any grey stripe, either.

"Perhaps we took a wrong turn in the forest," she thought, "and we've come out around the back of the castle. The main entrance must be on the other side," she reassured herself, but she knew perfectly well that they had taken no wrong turns, and she had emerged from the forest at exactly the same point as the last time she'd been here with Grandma and Grandpa.

Even though none of them was in a hurry to meet Lord Dharma, and they walked with considerable caution, they soon found themselves at the top of the hill, where the path ran right into the castle wall. The weather-beaten wall showed no signs of recent work, and it was impossible to imagine that a gate or entrance of any kind had ever been here. Katalina stood staring while the others hurried off following the walls to see if they could locate the missing gateway. As Alma got closer, she now saw that the strip she had thought was grey from a distance was actually patterned with black and white squares.

The castle was so massive that it took them a good half an hour to walk right around it. They didn't bump into anyone or spot anything, let alone a guard, and the whole place felt abandoned. The oddest thing of all was that the chequered band that ran around the walls wasn't broken by a single nook or cranny, let alone a door. When they got back to the path, they stood staring in disbelief. They were all quite sure that they had completely circumnavigated the castle and failed to find anything resembling an entrance.

"A lot of mediaeval castles were built with secret tunnels that led to a nearby forest or cave, so that soldiers could come and go when the place was under attack," Felix reflected, "but I have never heard of one that had no gateway, and no way in at all."

"But this castle used to have one!" Katalina blurted out, and then she went on to quickly explain what she remembered seeing.

"And your grandma also told us how other outlanders were let into the castle," Alma added. "And if they were allowed in, there must have been a gate for them to pass through."

"This happens all the time in video games. You can only get in to a place if you have enough points, or you've picked up a key or something that will help you open a secret door," Drifter pondered. "Maybe we should have picked something up or perhaps there's a puzzle that we need to work out now we're here."

"Yeah right. And then we can win an extra life!" Felix added sarcastically. "When are you going to realize that this isn't one of your games?"

"But why couldn't this world have different rules?" Drifter snapped back. "Up until now it's been a bit like a computer game with different challenges and all in such a strange setting. If this really is an evil castle ruled by an evil lord, then he could have easily made the entrance invisible."

"But that doesn't happen in reality!"

"You might be sharp on maths and logic but you seem to have forgotten everything they told us in history. Real castles have real gates!" Drifter insisted.

"Let's say for a minute that Drifter's right," Alma interjected, who was starting to worry about the constant conflict between the two boys. "There has to be an entrance somewhere because Katalina said she saw one. Our first challenge is to find it."

"I don't know any caves in the forest or any other entrances to what might be an underground tunnel," Katalina said sadly.

"The first thing we need to do is take a closer look at the wall," Alma suggested.

"We're looking for anything that seems odd or out of place," Drifter told the others.

Felix clamped his mouth tight shut to show that he was going to keep his thoughts to himself They all set off and scoured the walls for tiny cracks and odd angles, and even pulled some strands of ivy back to inspect the surface underneath, but they couldn't find a thing. Drifter insisted that they should try pushing any block of stone that stuck out or looked a different shade in case that would reveal a trapdoor of some kind, but nothing budged an inch. They had very nearly made their way all around the castle for a second time, when Alma noticed that the chequered pattern was a little mixed up in one particular spot. The eight lines of alternating black and white squares suddenly ran out of sync as if the stonemason had run out of patience just as he got to the end and he had applied the mosaic to the wall in any pattern he fancied.

"And there's one block missing!" Bella spotted. Felix came down on her like a ton of bricks.

"I bet it just fell away. This castle is so old, it's a miracle it's still standing at all!"

Drifter immediately set about pushing and prodding the empty square but still nothing happened. Bella felt around the area and suddenly shouted:

"The square next to it moves!"

The young girl carefully pushed the block to one side until it suddenly slipped into the empty space. Bella then put her hands on the next square and wiggled it a bit until it slid to replace the last square.

"It's just like one of those little toy puzzles!" she laughed. "You know, the ones where you have to move the little squares around until you make the whole picture!"

"Then let's try and get back to the original pattern," Alma suggested.

She quickly calculated the area they needed to reorganize. A total of sixty-four squares were out of sequence, measuring eight squares by eight squares.

"It's exactly the same size as a chess board," Alma laughed to herself.

"Can I move them around?" Bella asked in an excited gasp.

The others were happy to let her. The smallest of the group deftly manoeuvred the black and white tiles from side to side and up and down until the proper mosaic pattern had been perfectly restored. They all stood for a second and admired her nifty handiwork.

"Odd that it should all revolve around black and white again," Drifter commented. "Everything strange that happened before we landed in this world was connected to the same two colours."

"Okay, so it's all been about black and white again," Felix repeated, "but could someone tell me why that's important? What difference does it make? Has anything actually happened?"

Felix didn't even bother to turn around but simply pointed angrily at the chequered strip on the wall. The others automatically looked in the same direction. They were all stunned by what they saw. As soon as he saw their reaction, Felix also turned to take a look and his eyes opened wide with surprise. The chessboard block that Bella had just put back in place now appeared to have faint figures on some of the squares. The closer they looked, the more obvious it became that the shapes resembled chess pieces. It looked like a chess game that had stopped halfway through.

Alma carefully raised a hand to touch one of the pieces. It felt like it had been carved in relief on the stone square it sat on. There was no way she could either lift it off or move it around.

"I'm sure these weren't here before," Felix muttered to himself.

"It looks a lot like we've found our entrance," Drifter announced. "Now all we have to do is work out how to open it!"

"Alma, you can play chess. What is it?" Felix said as he turned to her.

Alma looked for a while and thought.

"It looks to me," she said eventually, "like a simple chess puzzle. My coach gets me to do loads of these. There's a position and I have to take White and mate in as few moves as possible."

"Why is it White to play?" Bella asked, sounding surprised.

"I don't know. That's how they always do it. Unless it says

different, White always has to give mate to Black."

"And could you do that now?"

"I could," Alma smiled, "and in one move. Look, let's say that this is the chessboard," Alma said as she ran her finger around the sixty-four squares. "That means that White's rook is on h7. If we move it to d7, it means we've given checkmate to Black."

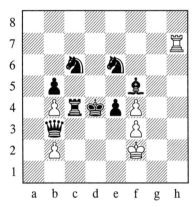

And with that Alma gently touched the white rook and drew her finger across the board to where she wanted it to be. The others couldn't believe their eyes when the chess piece suddenly jumped from the first square to its new position, as if Alma's finger had just dragged it across a touch screen. Katalina took a quick step forward to see if she could move a piece in the same way but was saddened to find that they were all once again fixed in place. She couldn't even manage to move the white rook that Alma had just sent in a straight line across the board.

"Okay, so we've solved that, but now what?" Drifter thought aloud.

By the time he had finished speaking, there was a fresh surprise: a new chess position had appeared on the adjacent sixty-four squares on the castle wall.

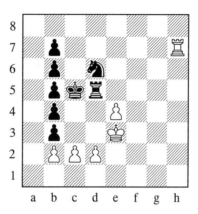

The kids gathered puzzled around the stone chessboard.

"It's another one-move problem," Alma explained, "and the white rook will give mate in this one, too. I wonder if I'll be able to move it to c7."

"Let me have a go," Bella appealed.

Alma stayed where she was and simply pointed to where the rook should be placed. And the rook moved the moment Bella put her small hand on it.

"It worked! I did it!" the young girl cheered.

The gang of friends stared at the wall again, in case a new problem appeared. They didn't have to wait long because a new puzzle appeared on the set of sixty-four squares next to the last.

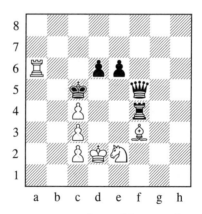

"I bet we have to move the white castle to a new position again!" Bella enthused.

"That's right!" Alma nodded. "But in chess the castle is called a rook. It's not that difficult to solve."

Alma had only just moved the white rook to c6 when the fourth problem appeared on the wall. Felix was beginning to run out of patience.

"It's going to take us ages to work our way around the whole wall. Do you know how many chessboards would fit along this strip? At least a thousand or maybe more. I really don't feel like pushing rooks around all day."

"It might be enough to solve five, or ten problems, and then the castle wall will open up," Drifter hoped.

"It must be good to be such an optimist," Felix grumbled. But the girls paid him no attention and moved up to the wall to take a closer look at the latest exercise.

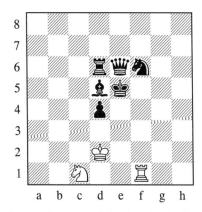

"Can I move the rook again this time?" Bella said as she hopped from one foot to the other, as if she knew exactly what to do to solve the problem. Alma shook her head.

"Hang on a minute, this one's not that simple. We can't do this in one move."

"I bet someone is about to say that the castle is toughening up!" Felix grunted.

"That's what it looks like," Alma responded. "Just when we were starting to get cocky, this is what happens."

"Can't you solve it?" Katalina asked as she stepped closer and looked more worried than someone trapped in a cage of tigers who couldn't find the emergency exit.

"Relax, it hasn't beaten us yet," Alma smiled in reply. "But we could see this problem as a message. If you look, you'll see that Black has a lot of officers and a pawn on the board, while the white king has only got a knight and a rook."

"What officers? Which ones are the officers?" Bella asked.

"Knight, bishop, rook, general."

"Which one's the general?" Katalina asked in obvious surprise.

"Well, the queen of course. It's the one with the crown. The queen can move just like the rook, but it can also move diagonally like a bishop. It's the most dangerous of all the pieces."

"The wicked black queen," Bella whispered to herself, and glanced admiringly at Alma. "Can you defeat her?"

"This is the solution," Alma announced with a happy smile. "Watch this! The first thing we do is attack with the knight and give check to the black king from d3. The king will have to escape, but it can only move to e4. And now you can move the rook, Bella! Push it to f4! Mate!"

"Fabulous!" Felix added angrily, and lay theatrically on the grass. "I bet we'll get the fifth problem next," he said. "Wake me up the day after tomorrow when you've finished playing your silly games!"

He shut his eyes and pretended to be fast asleep. Of course, he was wide awake and listening to hear what happened next. So he was surprised when nothing happened at all. The others stood around for a minute or two and also waited for the next problem to appear but when the wall stayed the same, none of them knew what to do.

"Do you think it got upset with Felix because he shouted?" Bella asked with a slight sob.

"I don't think that a castle wall can actually get upset," Drifter said as he shook his head. "Maybe it's simply run out of problems. Maybe we need to move on from here. Maybe I'm supposed to try and push this chessboard now."

As he said this, Drifter placed his palms on the board nearest to him, the one from the third problem, and he pushed hard at it with all the muscle he could muster. Katalina screamed in surprise when the chessboard receded into the wall and a small door appeared in its place. Drifter was just as shocked, but he masked his surprise by triumphantly dusting his hands off and making a grand announcement.

"Ladies and gents! The entrance!"

Felix immediately sprang to his feet and joined the others as they huddled around the narrow opening. At last they had found a way into the mysterious castle! They all stood shuffling from one foot to another, but no one seemed too keen to step inside.

"Listen, you lot," Alma said eventually. "We know that there are all kinds of dangers waiting for us in there. We need to stick close together and keep our eyes peeled! If we take care and concentrate, I'm sure we'll be fine. After all, we found the secret door!"

"I can go first if you like!" Drifter offered.

No one argued with him and so Drifter stepped gingerly through the gap. Absolutely nothing happened.

"Follow me, it's fine. It leads into a long passageway that's all!" he shouted out from beyond the stone wall.

Alma was next. At least she would have been next to follow Drifter in, but the door wouldn't let her. It felt like she was faced with an invisible barrier that was impossible to pass through. She tried for a while before eventually giving up and passing her place to Felix. The door seemed no keener to admit Felix, and none of the others could break through the invisible obstacle either. Drifter tried to walk back out to rejoin the others but now he ran into the same invisible screen but from the inside. They were all forced to realize that the cunning castle already had them in its grasp, because four of them were stuck outside, while Drifter was trapped behind something that none of them could actually see.

"Maybe there are more doors hidden behind the rest of the chess problems," Alma suddenly thought, and she pressed herself hard up against the preceding chessboard. But this time nothing happened except that everyone's temperature went up with the tension of the situation. Little Bella took a step back, sat down on the grass and stared hard at the open but impregnable entrance, as if she was trying to burn a hole through it. Her eyes then began to scan the other problems and for a moment she forgot her fear.

"Look, there's a letter 'B'!" she squealed.

"What?" Felix frowned.

"Look hard! The chess pieces in this problem are arranged in a letter 'B' shape. I used to call it the Bella letter when I was at playschool."

Felix peered at the chessboards then literally jumped for joy.

"And the other problems spell out letters, too! The first one is 'A', the second one 'B', and the last one's 'F'. And the third one... I can't see now. Drifter, is there a letter on your door, too?"

"Yes, a 'D'!" Drifter shouted from inside. "Could the doors be made to fit our names? You should all try the chessboard that spells your initial!"

"And me?" Katalina asked in a quivering voice.

"You can come with me!" Felix said confidently.

They all put their hands onto the stone wall and pressed hard against their particular letter. Alma pushed hers first and an entrance opened up in front of her. She wasted no time and walked straight in. She was genuinely relieved when she walked easily through and found herself standing next to Drifter in the same passageway. The two friends walked slowly towards each other, hands outstretched, certain that they would bump into an invisible barrier sooner or later, but a few uncertain steps and their palms met. The warmth of their fingers touching filled them both with happiness and relief that, even though the castle had tried to trick them several times already, it didn't plan to split them up.

Bella and Felix were soon to join them. Bella pushed her chessboard in with such stern determination that her door opened several seconds before her bigger and stronger but still doubting brother's.

"Come on in!" Alma shouted. "All the doors lead to the same passageway. We'll all be together on the inside, too."

Bella summoned all her courage and ran bravely through her doorway straight into Alma's welcoming arms. Felix was slower in his step as he strode through the narrow gap. Katalina walked right behind him. But the door that had willingly admitted Felix blocked Katalina's path just as Drifter's had for the others before. Felix still had a step to take and tried to reach back for Katalina's hand, but the secret doorway was a split second quicker. The castle definitely didn't want to let Katalina in. She ran in panic to Bella's doorway, and then tried the others but they were all blocked by an invisible barrier.

"Don't leave me here! Take me with you!" she whimpered, and the first tears trickled from her eyes.

It made no difference. The ones who were in weren't coming out, and the wall refused to let young Katalina walk through. As if that wasn't enough, the children soon spotted that the stone openings were starting to narrow as if a hidden machine was cranking them shut.

"Run around the wall again and study the pattern!" Felix shouted. "There's still a chance you'll find your own secret door!"

"And if I don't?" Katalina sobbed.

"We'll get the cure for your grandpa, I promise!" Alma reassured her.

"If I don't find an entrance, I'm going to sit down here and wait for you until..." Katalina told her friends, but they didn't hear the end of her sentence because with a rumble, the stone wall shut.

The four kids were left standing in the dimly lit passageway. With no other obvious option, they all took a careful step forward into the depths of the castle.

VI. War of the Gnomes

They proceeded for some minutes without anything of note happening. The wall was unbroken by doors or windows, yet they didn't have to grope in the darkness: the whole corridor was bathed in a mysterious half-light. The corridor rose slightly, and from time to time took a sharp turn, so no wonder the children soon lost their sense of direction. They had no idea where they were going. All they knew was that they were steadily going up into the interior of the castle.

As no obstacles blocked their path, their pulses returned to normal, and in a few minutes they even grew accustomed to the hollow echo of their footsteps. Gradually their fear was replaced by expectant curiosity. Perhaps they would meet the castle-dwellers, or be faced with some kind of choice, because so far the seemingly unending corridor had offered neither a fork, a crossroads, nor a door.

"Where are all those rooms we saw?" wondered Bella. "I'm fed up of all this walking."

"Don't forget, the windows were all high up," said Alma. "We'll probably have to climb up several storeys before we find any rooms."

Then, as if to affirm Alma's guess, the corridor suddenly led to a flight of steps which led steeply upwards then, after a sharp corner, into a winding spiral staircase. Felix was the only one not gasping for breath after a hundred steps: Coach Cochran regularly got the team doing steps during basketball training, so he was used to this kind of thing. Drifter and the girls were soon out of breath, and panted as they clambered up, though none of them were inclined to ask for a rest.

The seemingly hopelessly long climb brought its reward: the higher they got, the brighter the passageway around them, and after the three-hundredth step they came to a sunlit corridor intersecting their path. On the left was a series of iron-hinged wooden doors at regular intervals, while on the right open windows looked onto the outside world. Through the arched openings carved into the stone wall the sun shone warmly onto all the dust particles dancing in the beams of light. Not a soul was to be seen, and all was silent and deserted. Bella immediately ran to the closest window, hoping that through it she would see Katalina, who was probably moping at the foot of the castle.

But there was no sign of her, only a varied landscape spreading out down below. For sure, the view over the countryside was stunning. Bella gazed admiringly at the hillside flecked with clumps of bushes, ponds, and plough-land. Alma stood behind her, and they tried to guess which side of the castle they were on. The two boys looked out of the window next to them.

"Look at that church steeple. Is that Katalina's village?" said Bella, pointing.

Alma squinted to try and locate the tip of the distant building.

"What church steeple are you babbling on about?" said Felix angrily from the next window. "There's only a hunter's high-stand among the trees."

"No there isn't. Can't you see it?" retorted Bella. "Look, a troop of horsemen has come out. I reckon they've come from the village."

"Till now I thought you really did know about horses!" laughed Drifter. "Because that, Bella, is a herd of grazing cows!"

Bella stared wide-eyed at Alma, and quietly tapped her forehead with her index finger, to signal that the boys gazing out the other window were utterly daft. Alma stepped beside Drifter to teach him the difference between a grazing herd of cows and a troop of galloping horsemen, but when she looked out the boys' window, she was lost for words. Indeed, three brinded cows were grazing at the foot of a high-stand. There was no sign of a church or horsemen.

"That's impossible," she murmured, and went back to Bella. After all, the two windows were only a few steps away from each other, and faced the same direction! But from Bella's window the dust kicked up in the wake of the horses could clearly be seen, as well as another troop in pursuit as they broke out from the trees. Yet from the boys' window the landscape was completely different!

"Look at this! Come here!" shouted Alma in amazement.

Now it was the others' turn to be astonished. After taking in the view, they ran to the next window, and the one after that. The windows were positioned a regular distance apart, on the same side of the corridor, yet behind each slit a completely different scene met the eyes of the group. One window showed a forest and reeds by a pond, all blazing with fire; another showed well-tended homesteads alongside ploughed land. In some places they saw villages, towers, and even a crowd at a fair, while elsewhere they saw horsemen, marching peasants, and peacefully grazing flocks. Through the fifth window they glimpsed a nobleman's coach, as the over-ornamented carriage left the castle accompanied by horsemen in black.

"Might that be Lord Dharma just leaving?" worried Bella, but instead of answering the others raced to the next window. The countryside here was divided by a wide river, and across a massive wooden bridge a coach similar to the previous one made its way to the castle. In the background the charred remains of a burned town smoked away.

This sight was too much for all of them. They turned their backs on the window and looked at each other helplessly.

"I wouldn't fancy being a map-maker in this castle," said

Drifter, with an easy-going grin.

"Something isn't right," said Alma shaking her head.

"We'd better go back," said Felix. "I can't stand mystical things that can't be explained."

Drifter looked back, then gave an ironic laugh.

"Have a good journey back, Felix!"

Felix turned back with sense of foreboding, then cried out in shock. Where a few minutes ago the spiral staircase had led up to the corridor, now there was a thick oak door, just like the ones opposite the windows. There was no sign of the stairway.

"It must be here! It was here just a moment ago," snapped Felix, and set off towards the door. "We looked through seven or eight windows, if I'm not mistaken. The stairway must be behind this door!"

The others ran close behind him, so they were all huddled together as Felix pressed the doorhandle. But when they looked through the door they recoiled in horror. The door opened not to a spiral staircase or a dusty drawing room, but to a seemingly infinite plain, where wild horses raced. The boisterous herd suddenly changed direction and galloped towards the children, who stared in fright.

"Wild horses," whispered Bella with a sparkle in her eye.

But she couldn't admire the herd rumbling over the prairie, because as the horses came nearer, Felix slammed the door shut before them. The wild thumping of hooves was immediately cut off, as if the door had perfect sound insulation.

"I don't understand. I mean, we're upstairs," said Felix, scratching his head.

"Do the other doors also open to a place outside the castle?" said Alma looking down the corridor.

"Let's see!" suggested Drifter – he was already opening the next door.

With time you can grow accustomed to unexpected events, and after the happenings so far the children would have been surprised to see wild horses again, or even a normally furnished room. But there was nothing of the sort. The room revealed best resembled a nicely-designed nursery. Through knee-high trees, bushes no bigger than cabbages, and houses as big as Lego castles, there wound roads a palm's-breadth wide. The miniworld stretched in every direction, with fingernail-sized birds singing in the trees, while from a small distant forest tiny voices could be heard.

The children entered the room smiling in amazement. At the enthralling sight they left caution behind them, and falteringly, trying not to tread on the button-sized flowers on the lawn, they set off in the direction of the voices. The thick wooden door slammed shut behind them. They halted at the noise, looked at each other puzzled, then Felix angrily went back to open it again. But the door handle wouldn't budge. The door was shut fast. Drifter joined him, and the two of them tugged at the stiff lock, but in vain. Apparently, the way back had been cut off behind them.

But the slam of the door had been noticed by the beings running riot beyond the trees, and now they flooded out of the thick of the forest. Tiny little gnomes dressed in gold and turquoise appeared. Some were rather shabbily clothed, others more ornately. Gnome women carrying baskets, armed soldiers, and haughty little lords came out of the trees, then a gnome king in turquoise came to the fore. Close behind came a pageboy in blue-green velvet, followed by two horsemen. The armour of the gnome soldiers sparkled in cobalt blue, and the horses in their decorative tack were hardly larger than kittens.

"What are you outsiders doing in my empire?" bawled the wee monarch at the children. His beard bristled so fiercely on his tiny chin that Bella couldn't help laughing.

"Oh, how cute they are, Alma!" she giggled.

But the little king was anything but kind and friendly. Especially when another gnome with a crown stepped out of the forest. The two kings were as alike as two peas, with perhaps the only difference being in the cut of the precious stones ornamenting their crowns. On seeing his double, the first king began to angrily stamp and jump around.

"Be off, be off with you, bane of my life!" he screeched.

"Hold your tongue, you wretched upstart!" retorted the second king.

More and more gnomes flocked to hear the shouting match, and soon a sizeable throng had formed round the children on the meadow. Now and again kings with crowns appeared in the crowd, and they were angrier than anyone, even though most of the gnomes were shouting aggressively and shaking their fists at the others. All were wearing either gold or turquoise clothes, as if they belonged to two enemy armies, but to the children's surprise instead of arguing with each other they decried their own companions. Amid the chaos and shouting Bella managed to count eight identical gnome kings in turquoise, but as far as she could see there were at least as many kings wearing gold.

"The giants will bring peace!" hollered an old woman. At this, the hubbub died down, and the host of gnomes began to chant in unison:

"Let the giants decide, let the giants decide!"

"What giants?" asked Bella, huddling alarmed beside Alma.

"I'm afraid they might mean us," whispered Alma. "Compared to them even you seem like a giant."

Surprised, but with a satisfied smile, Bella stood upright. The gnome kings separated from the mass and gathered in front of the children. Alma squatted down so they wouldn't need to look up, because most of them reached only as far as her ankles. The others followed her example, and Bella, Felix, and Drifter all knelt in the grass.

"We ask for your help, great outsiders!" began the first king in turquoise. "My empire is in dire peril. A gaggle of pretenders to the throne has invaded my country."

"What do you mean, your country, dumbo?" another turquoise king snarled at him. "You and your ilk have occupied my homeland!"

"So you must be enemies, right?" asked Bella in astonishment.

The eight little kings were so alike they could even have been octuplets if they hadn't hated each other so much.

"Of course we're not enemies," said the first unexpectedly. Then with a gentler expression, almost smiling, he pointed to the closest king in a golden cloak. "Dear Albert here is my enemy."

Albert, wearing gold, nodded in agreement, and added indignantly:

"It's no use Arthur and I being perfect enemies, if all these roguish pretenders to the throne won't even let us make war."

"Clear off then! We have the right to make war with each other!" shouted another gold-coated solder.

"That's right, that's right!" said the kings.

"Do you know Lord Dharma?" interrupted Drifter.

The gnomes suddenly fell silent, but their terror-stricken, humble nodding showed that they knew the all-powerful lord of the castle very well.

"Why don't you ask him to help? He lives here, as far as I know. We're looking for him too," continued Drifter, not noticing the worried looks on the gnomes' faces.

The eight turquoise and eight golden kings put their heads together, even forgetting their shouting match. They pondered for a while, then in surprisingly unanimous agreement they let Arthur, the turquoise king, speak for them.

"His Lordship cannot abide being disturbed with trifling matters. You are the ones that must help us! In return we can give directions and good advice how to come before Lord Dharma."

"If, on the other hand, you do not help us, you will die an excruciating death!" threatened Albert dressed in gold, raising his club.

"That's all we need! I won't let myself be blackmailed!" Drifter burst out. "We can find our own way out, thanks very much."

He leapt up and angrily made for the closed door, but then something unexpected happened. As the gnomes grouped in a circle, the two groups of eight kings signalled to them, and they rushed on the children, shouting furiously. As nimble as squirrels, they climbed up their legs, three of them clambered into Alma's hair, and some of them pulled the screaming Bella onto the ground. The fighters had a cannon too, which they used to shoot at the boys. Although the cannonballs were only as big as walnuts, one of them struck Felix's forehead. He reeled from the blow, and by the time he came round he was lying in the grass, bound by gold chains. Drifter's foot got caught in a hidden net, which a group of gold-clothed gnomes hoisted up high, so after the second step he too fell headlong.

In just five minutes, the four children were bound hand and foot, crouching in the midst of a ring of gnomes.

"There's no room for disobedience!" announced King Albert. "Now we stand before you and explain how things stand. Either you find a solution to this conflict, and leave as heroes, or you won't live to see the morrow. Get it?"

"Thanks, Drifter," hissed Felix bitterly. "Your heroics really paid off!"

"Tough. I won't be blackmailed," whispered back Drifter sharply.

Fortunately the angry host of gnomes had ears for nobody but Arthur, who to make his point climbed onto a rock to address the captives.

"So, as you know, in this country I, King Arthur, am the lawful monarch. King Albert, my sworn enemy, and I were just about to fight a great decisive battle, when the battlefield was overrun by pretenders to my throne. Here in front of you stand my seven likenesses: Balthazar, Centurio, Donald, Ervin, Fritz, Gerald, and Hector. They too claim that this is their kingdom, and are preparing to fight to the death with the kings in gold, who in turn are likenesses of Albert. Look at them! Bruno, Cecil, Derek, Eric, Frank, George and Henry. But according to the law, a country can have only one king, and only he has the right to wage war against his enemy."

"We're not likenesses! We are real kings!" shouted Balthazar, Centurio, Donald, Ervin, Fritz, Gerald, Hector, Bruno, Cecil, Derek, Eric, Frank, George and Henry. "We have the right to wage war!"

"But you should make peace!" whimpered Bella, but the sixteen monarchs gave her such a round rebuff that she started to sob.

"Wait, let's try to think through the situation logically," interrupted Alma. "We got into this castle by solving chess problems. Now let's imagine we've stumbled into a game of chess."

"Come on, these aren't chess pieces!" Felix brushed her aside, or he would have done if his hands hadn't been tied behind his back. "At least if they were black and white..."

"That doesn't matter. Two different colours are in opposition. It doesn't actually matter whether the opposing sides are dressed in black and white, or blue and gold. But chess is played to fixed rules, and the essence of the whole thing is war. In fact, it's a war where only two opposing kings can take part at once. Perhaps we can find the solution using similar logic," said Alma, and turned to face the kings.

"Had you reached any kind of fighting position when the others turned up?"

"Oh, for sure!" Battle was in full swing!" nodded Albert. "What's more, I was winning!"

"Show us who was where," asked Alma.

Kings Albert and Arthur blew into their horns, and stepped haughtily onto the field. Arthur called loudly for his commander, a large muscular figure in a turquoise fur-trimmed jacket, to stand in front of him, and ordered the group of peasants and a rolling contraption resembling a siege engine. Albert gave orders only to his commander, but at his word another siege machine was pulled onto the field.

"Who came next?" asked Alma.

"I, Balthazar, did," announced the second king in turquoise, "with Bruno, my enemy."

"Show us what your positions were!"

The two kings took up their positions on the battlefield. In front of Bruno were two complete cavalry divisions dressed in gold. Balthazar faced the horsemen with a somewhat depleted army. The next pair were Cecil and Centurio.

"See, Felix, even the first letters match up! The kings stand on the file given by their initials," said Alma under her breath.

After the kings and the opposing armies had all occupied their places, there was enormous commotion on the battlefield. Most of the kings in turquoise stood in one rank, and some of the monarchs in gold crowded into the same place.

"We don't know who we're supposed to be defending!" shouted the soldiers. When hell breaks loose, even we won't recognize who the real king is! We can only shed our blood for one king!"

"Wait, wait!" said Alma, hushing the gnomes. "I have to stand up to get an overview of the situation."

Because she couldn't budge because of the chains, a few gnomes ran to help her and stood her up. Alma narrowed her eyes to survey the gnomes swashbuckling at her feet, then broke into a smile.

"I think I've got the answer. Let's try to partition the battlefield in our minds. We could divide it into squares, like a large grid, or even better, a chessboard!"

"You are wise, golden-haired giant," nodded King Albert eagerly. "I too like to plan the course of battle like this. I and my commander often plan the attack on squared paper."

"Right, Alma, okay. I get that you want to draw a chessboard under them at all costs. But what's the point?" said Felix, perplexed. "Whoever heard of a game of chess where there was a piece on every single one of the sixty-four squares? That doesn't exist for real."

"But gnomes with turquoise clothes exist, do they, Felix?" said Drifter scathingly.

Alma laughed.

"Well of course, the chessboard is never actually full. But

eight different positions, say eight checkmate puzzles would fit onto one board. You just have to tease them apart, and solve them one by one. If we imagine that everyone corresponds to one chess piece, you can see the classic starting position:

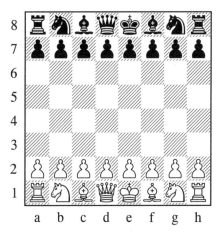

It looks to me like we have a separate mate-in-one chess problem on each file. Eight different positions, eight valid battles. And, logically, eight pairs of opposing kings. On file 'a' Arthur and Albert stand opposite one another, on file 'b' Bruno and Balthazar, and so on with the others. Everyone here is genuine, nobody is a phony or a pretender to the throne, just that through some mishap they've all come to the same location."

"So what should we do now?" asked Arthur, somewhat at a loss.

"First of all, untie us! Then you can fight each other, if you've nothing better to do. First fight your battle with Albert, then on file 'b' come the two kings with the initial B. When they're done, the C's can come, and so on. One by one, everyone will have a turn."

The host of gnomes in turquoise and gold weighed up the proposal for a few moments, then broke out in jubilant shouting. The poorer gnomes without a helmet threw their hats in the air, the women waved their kerchiefs, and the hussars raised their swords in honour of the children. The sixteen kings shook one another's hands in satisfaction. Not forgetting of course, to release their prisoners.

Albert and Arthur expressed their thanks to the four giants, then guided them towards the door.

"It's shut!" said Drifter grumpily.

"In this castle, every door is shut as long as the person inside has business there. You'll surely be able to open it now."

"And where do we find Lord Dharma?" asked Felix.

"Look everywhere for him! Sooner or later you're bound to find the path leading to him."

"But which path leads to him? You said you'd tell us!"

"We promised directions and good advice," stated Albert with dignity. "We cannot show you a sure path, because there is no route that is guaranteed to lead to him, but if you follow your own paths, and do so with honour, you will find what you are looking for. The good advice is just this: trust yourselves!"

"There is no better guide than your own selves," added Arthur.

"I'd have preferred a map," grumbled Drifter.

"Oh, if you want a map, then go to the map room!" said the two kings, shrugging.

"Is there one? Where?"

Albert reached resignedly into his pocket and produced a small folded scroll. He proffered it to Alma with the following words:

"Perhaps the wisest of the giants knows how to read a map!"

Alma took the small scroll, and the door opened of its own accord.

"Who would have thought. Photocell doors in the Middle Ages," mumbled Drifter to himself, but nobody heard, because the room was booming with the gnomes' cheers of farewell.

1. Qc5#

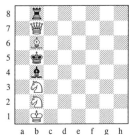

1. Nd4#

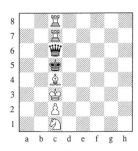

1. Rxc6#

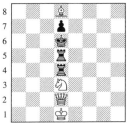

1. Qh6#

1. Qa7#

1. Qb4#

1. Be3#

1. Ng3#

VII. The Map

Although the door from gnomedom led to the castle corridor, the children soon noticed they hadn't returned to it at the same place they'd left it. The corridor seemed familiar, but on the walls between the doors hung weapons, and the windows were flanked by heavy velvet curtains. Just to be sure they peeked out of three or four windows to see the outside world, but they found the same as before: each window looked over a different landscape. The second window opened onto a vast plain where armies bristling with weapons and flags gathered opposite one another. The commander and officers of one set of troops could clearly be seen observing the preparations from a hilltop. The artillery of the other formation were occupied by setting up their cannons and catapults.

To see soldiers getting ready for war sent a shiver down Alma's spine. She would like to have known who was going to fight who and what for, just as she would have been reassured to have answers to other worrying questions. Alma took a deep breath. She truly hoped that finally light would be shed on every mystery, and she was quite convinced that until then they couldn't expect help from anyone. Even the kings had said as much: they could only trust in themselves. But in order to get through without external help, the others needed to be persuaded not to squabble, and instead to cooperate at last.

"Come on, Alma, show us that map!" sounded Felix's impatient voice. "Let's not waste time!"

"Wait a minute!" she said looking at Felix seriously. "I think before we go any further, we should talk over what's happened so far, to prepare for what comes next."

"What is there to talk over?" said Drifter, raising his eyebrows exasperatedly. "I'm not going to say sorry, if that's what you mean."

"It wouldn't do any harm though!" snapped Felix. "It was thanks to your ranting that the gnomes attacked us. If Alma hadn't solved the chess problem, we'd be dead by now."

"You might as well just call me a murderer!" said Drifter stepping closer with a spark in his eye.

"Stop it now!" interjected Alma angrily. "The important thing isn't to apologize. But we could draw a few conclusions that might be useful later."

The two boys looked in astonishment at the blonde girl's red, determined face. At school she mostly stood to one side, or chatted with the girls. They never imagined she could have such a strong will.

"What conclusions?" asked Drifter, easing up slightly.

"We should analyse our moves so far, to work out where we've gone wrong, and what we were good at."

"Drifter made an error, and you played some neat chess. Is that what you wanted to hear?" asked Felix antagonistically. "Or do you want us to analyse the chess games?"

Alma frowned and glanced at Felix disdainfully, but tried to keep herself in check. She knew how important it was in a tense situation to concentrate on the goal instead of arguing. At chess training they regularly talked over the moves in previous games. They didn't just analyse the losing positions, but rethought the winning games too. Alma's coach believed that even after winning a match she shouldn't rest on her laurels. It may be that the victory is thanks only to the opponent making a bad move, or overlooking an obvious mistake. It does no harm to know what our strengths are, and where our secret weaknesses and fears lurk.

"Listen, Felix! You play basketball. You must talk over things at the end of the match, like where you could have defended better, or what would be good to do the same next time."

"Sure, before and after the match there are team chats about tactics," nodded Felix reluctantly. "But we can't play chess, so if you want to analyse things, you'll be on your own. So why don't we set off instead?"

"But this isn't about chess!" explained Alma. "At least not just chess. We've got this castle where a whole bunch of apparently incomprehensible, dangerous and weird things keep happening. We don't understand the logic behind it yet, but perhaps that'll come to us later. But if we want to move forward and find Lord Dharma, we can't go on making mistakes. Now in real life we have to do the same thing as we do before a chess game or a basketball match: we have to think through what we want, work out a strategy, and then implement it as skilfully as possible. If we have a plan, and we know our strengths and weaknesses, we're more likely to reach our goal. It's true for everything, not just sport."

"I'm not weak," said Felix, sticking his chest out resentfully.

"I didn't say you were. Though so far you haven't once had the strength to control yourself. You run everyone down," retorted Alma. "Haven't you noticed we're always bickering?"

"All right, we bicker a lot. That's our weakness. Can we go now?" asked Felix impatiently. He didn't relish the idea of an analysis of errors and weaknesses one little bit. The others pondered on the idea. Drifter thought to himself, and Bella wondered out loud.

"What else are we weak in?" she asked. "Apart from you none of us knows how to play chess."

"That doesn't matter. It looks like it's enough for one person to know," said Alma smiling. "But we have to cooperate, and everyone must give their best, if we want to grapple our way out of this situation. And we could be a bit more cautious."

"Yes! For instance, if we go into a room, we leave the door open!" Bella realized. "If it hadn't slammed shut, we could have run away from the gnomes. I was so scared!"

"Me too," nodded Alma.

"Actually, even I prefer computer adventure games," added Drifter.

"So, we argue, we're reckless, and cowardly," interrupted Felix rattily. "What a great analysis. Marvellous. Now I really feel better about going forward."

"Wait Felix, there's good stuff too. Such as, our logic never let us down," asserted Alma. "In every situation, even when the wild bees attacked, we thought of the right solution. So perhaps we could trust ourselves a bit more, and that means there's no need to be so afraid. Right, Bella?"

"The gnomes said that too, that we should trust ourselves!" said the little girl, with a sparkle in her eye.

"Okay then. Let's see what else we are good at!" Drifter, who meanwhile had warmed to the idea of a talk-through, nodded his head.

"Felix is very strong!" stated Bella firmly.

"And he's good at maths and history as well as logic," added Alma.

"Alma is the best in the world at chess!" enthused Bella.

"If only I were!" laughed Alma. "But you are good with horses."

Felix had already opened his mouth to make a disdainful comment about his sister's knowledge of horses and the importance of horse-riding, but he changed his mind. Alma would be bound to point out that he was grouching again. Instead, he stayed quiet and limited the expression of his opinion to a pursing of his lips.

"And you, Drifter?" Alma turned to the droopy-haired boy, who hovered there with a slightly fazed expression.

"I'm no good at anything," he said, shrugging his shoulders.

"I just do skateboarding and computer games. Well, I know my way round the internet."

This time Felix couldn't resist making his opinion heard. He cast a pitiful glance at Drifter, and tutted. He might even have made a remark, but suddenly his ears pricked up to distant voices. He raised his hand to his lips to signal to the others to be quiet.

They heard people coming from the other end of the corridor and talking. The children blinked at one another in uncertainty. They didn't want to miss the chance of meeting a good-natured castle dweller, but neither could they risk running headlong into bad-tempered armed guards. They didn't dare hide in the rooms opening off the corridor, after all who knew what was waiting for them behind the thick oak doors. If they left the entrance open, the people coming would probably notice, and if they closed it... No. They weren't in the mood for another life-threatening adventure. They had no choice but to run in the opposite direction to where the voices were coming from.

"Follow me, on tip-toe!" instructed Felix, and set off silently. The others followed.

For a long time the corridor offered no escape route: on the left were identical doors, on the right were windows with velvet curtains, each one looking out somewhere else. They had passed about twenty-five rooms when the corridor opened into a spacious hall. From the hall other corridors led off, in fact opposite was a staircase which led both up and down. In the middle of the grand hall, on an enormous plinth, stood a statue of a soldier brandishing a flag on the back of a rearing horse. The children stopped dead. There wasn't much point in going on, because they might meet someone coming the other way in the other corridors. Who knew, perhaps there were regular patrols throughout the castle.

From the approaching voices they reckoned there must be only two or three people coming, so they decided to hide behind the statue pedestal, and wait until the unknown figures had passed. They stole silently behind the stone block and hid tight. The voices came closer and closer, and gave less and less the impression of a patrol. Rather it sounded like a stream of complaints and bitter whining, and it was clear now that two men were speaking.

After a while two stout, crestfallen men appeared. They were carrying a large wardrobe and moaning bitterly. Even though they'd put a plank and rollers under the wardrobe to make it easier to move, the massive furniture was still very heavy. The two men pushed and shoved it grumpily, and all the while complaints poured from their mouths.

"I tell you, we'll never reach the south-eastern turret."

"Wouldn't be any use if we did. Something would get in the way again."

"A stone barricade."

"An earthquake."

"A flood."

"A plague of rats."

"It won't work anyway."

"We are going to mess up again."

"Because we can't do anything right."

"And I can hardly move a limb now."

"My back is killing me."

"I've got an awful stitch."

"Lord Dharma will be furious."

"He'll punish us again."

"We'll never get free."

"Woe is us! Our lives are a misery!"

There was no end to their whining and moaning. When they got to the hall the two men stopped for a breath, but they carried on belly-aching. A dirty patched waistcoat covered their bodies, and their shirts and threadbare trousers could have done with a good wash. The first had greying locks that dangled in his eyes, while the other struggled to keep a battered straw hat on his balding head. Their movements and posture told volumes about their lack of purpose and lucklessness.

The children hid tight behind the pedestal. They were sure the two elderly men presented no danger to them, but they couldn't decide whether to leave their hiding place. If they were servants of Lord Dharma, they'd be sure to report to their master that they'd met outside intruders, though Lord Dharma would probably have learned of their arrival by now. But they might be able to give directions or advice, if they asked them nicely.

"I think we should say hello," whispered Alma to Felix.

Felix nodded. Drifter shrugged his shoulders, but obviously he had nothing against them talking to the bad-tempered wardrobe-shifters. Finally they came out of hiding, and greeted the men quietly, so as not to frighten them. All the same the greying man jumped as though he'd been caught robbing a bank, and the balding one jumped in fright. When the children assured them they meant no harm, in fact they needed help, the two old men started complaining again.

"Told you so! Lord Dharma could have sent a couple of muscular helpers."

"That's just typical, we have to put up with four children too."

"At least if they could carry stuff."

"Don't kid yourself! Who's interested in helping others these days?!"

Felix looked at Alma, who nodded silently and took out the map that Albert, the gnome king dressed in gold, had given her. These two weren't going to quit moaning of their own accord. Perhaps if the children asked them something, it would jolt them out of their self-pity. But first they had to work out what they wanted to ask, by looking at the map. Alma spread out the vellum scroll, and the others stood round it. The two old men leaned in over the children's shoulders, but when they saw they were looking at a map, they tutted all-knowingly.

"Maps aren't much use to you here. Apart from the castle walls everything's always changing. You'll never get out. Now be off with you!" they said, turning round to continue their moaning.

At first glance they thought they saw a rough ground plan

of the castle on the scroll. On the four corners of the square building stood four round turrets. Inside were small rooms and larger chambers, narrow corridors winding between them. The whole ground plan looked like a labyrinth.

"This won't help us work out where we are," frowned Drifter. "We don't even know which floor it is. Including the underground and overground, this castle must be at least ten storeys. Plus, if the rooms really do move around, it's hopeless trying to find our way."

"It must mean something! Anyone who makes a map does so for some purpose," said Felix, furrowing his brow. "Look, they've drawn in the turrets, perhaps because they are part of the castle walls, and therefore don't change. And there are two crowns here. Maybe one of them indicates Lord Dharma's throne room."

"Or his treasury," chipped in Bella.

"And this shape?" wondered Drifter. "Looks like it could be a person. Maybe that's where the guards have their quarters. Or that's the chamber the lord receives visitors."

"Where he holds audience," corrected Felix, cockily.

"Call it what you want. The question is, do we have to go there or not? And where is it anyway? The gnome kings spoke of a map room. Theoretically, this drawing is only a map leading to the map room."

Alma thought for a bit. "There's not much sense in a plan that doesn't indicate which floor it shows, especially in a castle where everything is always in flux. I reckon this is supposed to be another chessboard."

"Since when did they put rooms and corridors on a chessboard? It's obviously a map," concluded Felix.

"Why? It might even be both at the same time," Drifter realized suddenly. "After all, so far the solution was always chess. This could be a chess-castle, where maps are disguised as chess problems. Alma, look and see if there's a meaningful chess position on the diagram, and whether you can create checkmate. Perhaps this is how to find out where the map room is."

Alma's mind was racing.

"Well, if we take the faded figures to be White, and the sharp ones to be Black, then yes, it could be a chess position. The two crowns, say, aren't a throne room or a treasury. No, they're two kings. The round-headed figure isn't a guard, but judging by its shape, say, a pawn. The two towers aren't real towers either, but rooks from a chess set."

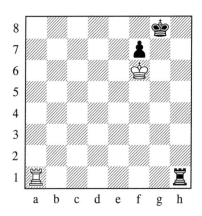

"If that's how it is, can you get to checkmate?" Bella drew closer.

"The first thing is definitely to take the black rook with the white rook," said Alma. "If Black didn't have to move, but could wait, we wouldn't be able to give him mate. But he's in zugzwang, I mean, he has to move somewhere, and there's only one place to go: f8. That way he walks into checkmate, because when we move the rook up to the other corner, h8, there's no way out. Checkmate."

"Great. But what does all that mean?" said Felix, perplexed. "Does any of that tell us where to go?"

Now it was Drifter's turn to come up with a good idea.

"Perhaps we have to take the same path that brought victory to White. The key thing is not which floor we're on, but which way to go. Look. The white rook started from one corner, or we might say, the bottom turret of the castle."

When he saw Felix's face he braced himself and rephrased

things:

"Let's say it's the south-western turret. It went over to the other corner, which we can call the south-eastern. From there it went up to another corner, the north-eastern one. Perhaps the map's message is to go round visiting each turret in turn."

"Wouldn't it be simpler to head right for the throne room?"

"Maybe these are tests. In adventure games you sometimes have to follow a path to find a key or a weapon at some point. Then later, you use that to defeat the enemy. Maybe hidden in the turrets is a key that opens the door to the throne room. Or maybe we'll find a message there."

"You're reading too much into it," said Felix.

"Not necessarily." Alma raised her finger. "We found the way in thanks to Drifter's gut feelings. Maybe instinct is one of your strengths?" she said, smiling at him.

Drifter felt a bit sheepish.

"Erm, I don't really know," he muttered. "But based on the map, all we can be certain of is the position of the four turrets, and that to win, we have to go round all four corners. So I vote that from now, we follow the path of the white rook, whether it leads to the map room or somewhere else."

"Me too!" said Alma, putting her hand up.

"Me too!" Bella joined Alma.

"I hope decision-making isn't one of our weaknesses," mumbled Felix, but even he nodded agreement. If everyone wanted to go round the turrets, he wasn't going to stop them.

Now they'd agreed, all they needed to do was work out which path led to the turrets. The two wretched men were still hanging around behind them. They shoved at the wardrobe reluctantly, obviously not really wanting to get started. With sour faces, they were just describing the difficulties of the work before them.

"Let's ask them!" suggested Alma.

The others nodded. Perhaps the two portly men would leave off complaining to answer a question. Their hope was not in vain: the two men knew exactly where the south-eastern turret was, in fact it turned out they were heading that way too. At the command of Lord Dharma, they had to deliver the heavy wardrobe to the guard-room located in the turret.

"You can come with us, although we're rather slow," said one of them.

"This heavy weight is almost too much for us," said the other, whining.

"We can help!" offered Alma. "It's bound to be easier together."

The portly old men stood there open-mouthed, staring at the four children in astonishment. They couldn't fathom why the children had offered to help, when it wasn't even their job to carry things.

VIII. The Dream

Katalina sobbed for some time at the foot of the castle. She couldn't understand why she had to stay outside. All her life she'd been an honest, hard-working girl. She'd always done the job assigned to her, and since the death of her parents she'd supported her grandparents. What was more, she always thought of Lord Dharma with the greatest respect. From the bottom of her heart she'd resolved hundreds of times that if the master called her to battle, she would fight to defend her homeland and her lord. But now she saw the castle and its proud lord ousted the faithful, devoted subject. She was the one the heartless stone walls would not allow in, she who for years had happily served her master with selfless work.

Katalina was in a whirl of anger, humiliation, and despair. She was hurt by the brusque rejection, the openings closing right in front of her, but even more troubled by worry. After all, it wasn't for fun or curiosity that she wanted to get into the castle. No, she wanted to get the life-saving medicine for her grandpa. The old beekeeper urgently needed the water of life that flowed in the castle well. Like his granddaughter, he too had been a faithful servant of Lord Dharma all his life.

When she'd cried herself dry, Katalina resolutely set off round the castle again. Not for nothing did she live close to nature. She wasn't in the habit of feeling sorry for herself. Like the woodland plants, she desired life and light. Just as hedges lining the fields, grasses along the path, and trees in the wood all incline to the light, so Katalina always searched for how she could best be happy. She made up her mind to explore until she found another irregularity in the castle wall, where perhaps she could adjust the stones, or until she found a crack through which she could squeeze into the castle.

She didn't know how to play chess, but she decided if she found a chess problem, she'd keep trying until she was lucky enough to hit on the right solution. But even though she walked round the castle three times, and thoroughly scrutinized every little crack, all was in vain: she found nothing at all. In fact, she noted with despair that the chequered band running round the walls was growing fainter, and by the time she'd been round three times the mosaics had faded so much she couldn't even have seen them with a magnifying glass. The castle had hidden the last trace of the place where the others had entered.

Katalina thought to herself. She tried to imagine what might have happened to her friends after they passed through the wall. It was possible they'd found Lord Dharma easily. Perhaps they had a friendly reception, and now were enjoying a tasty banquet in the lord's glorious dining hall. She thought longingly for a moment of the long table covered with good food, the crystal glasses, the silver or gold cutlery, but the pleasant images soon disappeared. Deep down she suspected that Felix and his friends were met not by a helpful host, but by countless difficulties and dangers. Perhaps their lives were at risk that very minute.

"If only I could help them!" she thought in desperation. "And if only I could help Grandpa. Instead, I'm stood here, doing nothing and helpless."

She would happily have gouged out an entrance for herself in the castle wall with her bare hands and nails. But since this seemed as senseless as all her other ideas, she suddenly lost heart, and felt utterly despondent. She thought it would make more sense to go home, and pick some medicinal herbs on the way, to see if an infusion of them might ease the swellings of the bee-stings on Grandpa's body.

But she didn't, in the end, set off for Fianchetto, because she remembered a story she had heard many times as a little girl from her grandma. The tale told of two friends who set off together to find the apple tree that bore happiness. They wandered for weeks and months, their path leading through bleak wilderness, baking deserts, and sultry swamps. They had to struggle with wild animals in the woods, evil dwarfs, and heartless people, and they suffered from cold, snow, and icy winds. But they were not ones to give up hope, and onward they went. Finally they came to a forest overgrown with nettles, trailing vines, and thorny bushes, and they had to cut their way through it with knives. Their strength was almost sapped, but they persevered.

Or rather, one of the friends strove on undaunted; the other lost hope in the thick scrub of the forest. He let his arm fall, put his knife away, turned his back on his companion, and set off back home, his head hung low. It was no use his friend calling him, encouraging him saying they would soon reach their goal; his reserves of strength were drained. Nothing interested him any more, not even the fruit of the apple tree of happiness. But the other boy didn't lose heart. Though his soul was brimming with sorrow, he didn't give up. He was already up at daybreak, and continued his way. Lo and behold, behind the next bush the thorny scrubland and nettles came to an end. The boy found himself on a sun-drenched meadow, in the middle of which was the miraculous apple tree, laden with fruit.

"Never give up hope, my love!"

Every time she told it, Grandma concluded the tale with these words.

"You never know whether the apple tree of happiness might not be just an arm's reach away."

Katalina felt reassured now she remembered the story. She mustn't lose heart. She couldn't go back, for who knows, perhaps five minutes after she left the castle gate might open, and she would be invited to the well of the water of life. Whatever happened, she would wait here just as she had promised.

She had nothing to do, and all the walking and worrying had tired her out, so she settled down in the grass. At first she sat and stared at the castle, but she soon leaned back and fell into a slumber.

In her dream Katalina started with fright, and tried at all costs to wake up, but she was unable to. Then, from the forest in her dreams, there flew a wonderfully beautiful, snow-white bird. Its shape was like that of a peacock's, but it was hardly any larger than a blackbird. It flew straight towards her, perched beside her, and spread its tail-feathers like frost flowers. Then it began to sing.

The completely unknown song sounded so sad, that her eyes began to fill with tears. When the first teardrop trickled down her cheek, she suddenly understood the song. The snow-white bird was singing that even if the water of life reached her grandpa, it would be too late. By the time the castle gate opened, Katalina plunged her flask into the well, and ran back to the village, her grandpa would be beyond help. The water of life would keep the living alive to the end of time, but it could not bring back the dead.

When the song came to an end, the snow-white bird flew back to the woods. Katalina woke up. Her face was stained with tears from her dream, and her heart was overtaken by dread. What if the bird had really sung the truth, and the miraculous water got to Grandpa too late? Who knew how long she would have to wait there idly? Time was getting on, and sooner or later it really would be too late.

Katalina suddenly realized what she had to do. She would bring Grandpa here, so that when Felix and the others opened the castle gate, she could pour the life-giving water straight into his mouth. Instead of idly waiting, she had to rush to Fianchetto, so that she could get back to the castle in time. Hesitating no longer, she sprang up, and began racing home for all she was worth. The road was long and tiring, but Katalina was driven by the hope that perhaps this help would be in time to save her grandpa. From time to time she stopped for a minute to get her breath, and drink a few draughts of water from the stream running beside the road, but then she ran on.

She reached the outskirts of the village by early afternoon. Jack the shepherd boy was still minding the goats grazing on the meadow. When he saw Katalina he started waving.

"I told your grandma you'd be late back. She's very worried but she's not angry. Will you explain what happened?"

"Thanks, Jack!" panted Katalina. "There's no time to explain now, I've got to take Grandpa to the castle right away."

"I'll help you! I'll harness the horses!" said Jack, jumping to.

"You can't leave your goats here!" said Katalina in amazement.

"The goats can find their way home. And you need help," he announced decisively. "Bring your grandpa out to the yard. Meanwhile I'll prepare the cart!"

Katalina gave him a smile of thanks, then ran on into the house. She found her grandma in the bedroom. With a worried look on her face, she was changing the cold packs on Grandpa's stings. Seeing Katalina, she jumped up with nervous expectation to assail her with a barrage of questions.

"Grandma, I'll explain everything later. Now we must hurry. I'm taking Grandpa to the castle to be cured by Lord Dharma. Can you get some pillows ready, the compacts, and some food and drink for the journey?"

Grandma saw that Katalina meant business, and understood she had to accept the girl's decisions. She asked only one question:

"Are you following Lord Dharma's orders?"

"No. But I know this is what I have to do. Do you remember the snow-white bird in the dreams, that appears to everyone at some time, to warn them of some imminent danger? It came and sang to me today. I have to take Grandpa with me!"

Grandma nodded silently, and set about packing supplies. She too had once seen the peacock-tailed snow-white bird in her dreams.

IX. The South-Eastern Turret

Fortunately the way to the turret was not up the stairs, because it would have been an impossible task to lug the enormous wardrobe up the steep staircase. The two old men set off up a winding steadily climbing corridor, puffing and panting bitterly as if they were carrying the furniture on their backs. But the children had almost completely relieved them of the burden. Felix and Drifter were holding and pushing the heavy furniture, and the girls positioned the rollers under the plank. When the corridor became really steep, the old men stepped in to help too, albeit half-heartedly and huffing and puffing. But at least they buckled down to work.

They'd been struggling for about half an hour when they came to another chamber. The layout was suspiciously similar to the previous one, but the statue in the centre was not of a horseman, but a beautiful, slender queen with an icy stare, bearing weapons. The two old men flopped down on the pedestal. They looked too tired even to complain. The children too were glad of a rest. Felix remembered the satchel on his shoulder. Inside it were the rolls and drink that Katalina's grandma had packed for them.

They didn't start talking until they'd taken the edge off their hunger. Quizzing the two old men about life in the castle, their work, and Lord Dharma, they learnt that the balding man with the hat was called Baker, and his tousled grey-haired companion's name was Farthing. They used to live in a village near the castle, but things didn't go too well for them. Baker was a baker by trade too, and Farthing worked as a goldsmith, or rather would have worked. Because both men were marked by boundless laziness. Fewer and fewer people went to Baker's shop, because he didn't like getting up at dawn. This meant the fresh bread was often not ready until about midday. As time went by, the women in the area began to prefer to bake their own bread and cakes at home, and lazy old Baker was soon reduced to begging.

Farthing's story was similar. At first he got by well enough, but he got fewer and fewer orders, because he didn't keep to his deadlines. What's more, he ran low on tools, because he was too lazy to pack them away after finishing work. For a while they lay around in the workshop, then one by one they all disappeared. In the end he could only take on the simplest of jobs, because all he had left was one pair of pliers and a hammer. When he hadn't had an order for weeks, and he'd cooked his last handful of peas, he went into the village to cadge some food for supper from the village folk.

On the way he met a steward of Lord Dharma, who was recruiting assistants for work in the castle. Because all the village folk were busy in the fields or in their workshops, the steward couldn't find anyone. They were better than nothing, so he collared the two roaming tradesmen, and steered them full throttle towards the castle. Lord Dharma put them both to work, but he was never satisfied with anything they did. In his anger he gave the two wretches increasingly difficult tasks, and since they were unable to complete any of them, as punishment he didn't let them go home.

"Our master is cruel and evil," whispered Farthing with a tear in his eye.

"He's tormenting us to shreds," added Baker.

"Many times we've approached him on bended knee, pleading with him to let us go home."

"But he just laughs, and says we can go when we've properly

finished the job given to us."

"So why don't you finish it for once?" said Alma, shaking her head.

"At first we didn't feel like it. We were too lazy and clumsy," sighed Farthing. "Later we pulled ourselves together. But by then Lord Dharma had become angry, and gave us impossible tasks."

"He ordered us to scoop the water out of the castle moat."

"To black-out the room with a skylight, in the middle of the day."

"To make a carriage that would carry him through the sky on the wings of the wind, with no horses."

"Other times he gives a job that seems easy: to make three hundred pancakes, or to carry the books from the library into another room. We perk up at the prospect of being able to finish the task and go home. But then it turns out there's no fire, no frying pan, and no eggs, and you can't make pancakes without them. And the books had disappeared from the library earlier, so there was nothing to take into the room next door. Then Lord Dharma laughs jeeringly and shrugs his shoulders, saying if we don't carry out his order, why should he let us go home."

"How long have you been in the castle?" asked Bella sympathetically.

"One hundred and eighty years," sighed Farthing.

"Oh, a hundred and ninety I should think," corrected Baker.

"Now that I find difficult to believe," smirked Felix.

"But it's true!" said the old men indignantly. "Every day Lord Dharma gives us a draught of water from the lion fountain, and we don't age."

"But we get no younger either."

"Why would we want to be younger? In fact, I don't even know why we want to go home. Think about it: all our friends and loved ones have been dead for a hundred years. We don't know anyone in the village now."

"We're beyond time."

"Timeless remnants."

"But at least we could relax."

"I bet something crops up this time too."

"A stone barricade."

"An earthquake."

"A flood."

"A plague of rats."

"It won't work anyway."

"We'll botch it again."

"Because we can't do anything right."

"And I can hardly move a limb now."

"My back is killing me."

"I've got an awful stitch."

"Hey, will you give it a rest?" snapped Drifter. "We've put up with that for an hour. How many times do you need to say it?"

"Let's get going," said Felix, getting up. "That turret can't be far now."

Baker and Farthing staggered to their feet, and the children sprang up. The south-eastern turret was indeed close, and from the windows they could see they must be on one of the upper storeys. The old men had caught some of the children's enthusiasm and eagerness, so they stopped complaining and carried on their way. Lord Dharma's order was that the wardrobe should be positioned in the south-eastern guardroom.

"Just five corners and a straight corridor, and we'll be there," said Baker.

"It's been easier than I expected," added Farthing happily.

Unfortunately, before long it turned out he had spoken too soon. They all sensed the path was winding its way through the interior of the turret, because round the five corners mentioned by Baker, the corridor floor rose steeply. Although it was far from an easy task to push and steer the great weight, the group's enthusiasm meant the wardrobe practically glided along. At first sight, the straight section leading to the guardroom at the end of the corridor seemed strikingly easy, because the constant incline in the floor changed to a descent, so the rollers carried the carved wardrobe by themselves. But less than ten metres before the end they came across an unexpected factor. They didn't notice the danger until the last minute, and had to use all their strength to stop the swiftly rolling shipment.

And stop it they had to, no doubt about it. Inexplicably, at one point the paved corridor floor simply disappeared, leaving a gaping bottomless hole. At first it looked as though a four-metre section of the floor had sunk. On the other side of the chasm the corridor continued. On the other side they could see the iron-hinged wooden door of the guardroom, next to which lances and shields were leaning on the wall and an iron chain lay coiled up on the floor. But it was impossible to reach the room, because the floor had sunk from wall to wall.

The children edged to the brink of the hole to see how deep it was. Because the steep winding path they had followed must have passed beneath the sunken floor, they took it for granted the sink-hole couldn't be too deep, because the corridor hadn't shown any trace of obstructions, rubble, or mounds of stone. All the greater was their astonishment when they looked into the hole: it seemed almost bottomless. The missing flooring seemed to have plunged into a huge chasm, from which rose the smell of cold, dank cellars.

"That's impossible!" mumbled Felix to himself. "That can't be for real."

"This can't be for real either," corrected Drifter. "If you think about it, not many of our experiences have been like real life."

"I knew it, I told you so!" whimpered Baker. "Lord Dharma sent us on a wild goose chase again. We'll never get across to the guardroom!"

"Just when we'd started to believe we could do it. But no, he's tricked us again. The path leads to a bottomless pit! Another mission impossible, all our work goes to waste," echoed Farthing.

"We've failed. We'll be here for ever!"

"There must be some solution!" said Alma decisively.

The two old men fell silent. The announcement was so unexpected their whining dried up.

"Yes. The solution is that we turn round and go back. Nobody's jumping across a chasm that wide, especially not with a wardrobe," said Felix. "We must have made a mistake. This wasn't the turret to come to. We misinterpreted the map."

"It's definitely the right place!" wailed Farthing. "And Lord Dharma has again prevented us from succeeding."

"That's exactly the point, don't you see?" Alma's eyes sparkled wilfully. "Another seemingly hopeless, impossible situation. Baker and Farthing get this all the time. And the same happens to us. Remember the castle wall with no entrance? And the apparently insoluble chess problem with the gnomes? The difficult thing is that it seems like there's no solution. Lord Dharma is obviously doing this to test you," she said looking at Farthing.

"Them and us too. Obviously," nodded Drifter.

"In other words, it's definitely a bad idea to go back," stated Alma.

"Well, I can think of some other bad ideas too," murmured Felix, peering into the gaping depth beneath their feet. "Hey, get away from the edge!" he shouted irritably at Bella, who was behind Alma and almost balancing on the edge of the void.

"Even if we could by some miracle get across, it wouldn't be any good to us," snivelled Baker. "It's no use us getting there without the wardrobe."

"What about going back to the chamber?" suggested Bella. "We're bound to find some old plank we could build a bridge with."

"Oh, you don't know this castle!" countered Farthing, disparagingly. "Each path leads to a given place only once. If you go back, you end up somewhere completely different. If we leave here, we're bound to get to Lord Dharma. We'll never find our way back."

"Actually, we're looking for Lord Dharma," interjected Felix.

"Then you'll end up somewhere else! Believe me, the castle

itself decides who to guide where."

"What I don't get is if each path always leads somewhere different, how did you know that from the resting place there were only five bends and a straight corridor left to go?" frowned Felix.

"You get to know your way around in a hundred and eighty years," sighed Farthing.

"A hundred and ninety," corrected Baker.

"If you set off with a purpose, the path is familiar as long as you're going in the right direction. If you pursue your goal, you find it, even if it takes a long time. But if you vacillate, turn back, or leave the right path, then everything conspires against you, and the castle becomes a labyrinth."

"The gnomes again," murmured Alma. "Remember what they said? If you follow your own paths, and do so with honour, you will find what you are looking for."

"If only my GPS was working," sighed Felix. "It's a bit more reliable a guide that these wise sayings."

"Whatever. We have no choice anyway. So on we go!" directed Drifter, and sniggered to himself over the impossibility of the situation.

They all felt it was worth thinking a while to find a solution, so they settled down to discuss what they should do. They didn't want to turn back, so the only way to go was onwards, across the chasm. While the others sat on the ground to rest their tired legs, Felix examined the other end of the corridor from the edge of the sunken part.

"If there's anyone in the guardroom, we could ask for help. If we shout they're bound to hear," he pondered. "They might have a plank or a ladder which spans the gap. And if they don't that iron chain on the ground would do."

"What chain?" The others suddenly looked up.

"In front of the door I can see a coiled chain, and judging from here it looks long enough. Above us there's a beam going crossways, so if we threw the chain across it we could swing over to the other side."

"We could even toss the wardrobe across, like on the playground swings," added Alma.

"We could sit in the wardrobe and swing across inside it," said Bella.

Now everyone was enthusiastic. The task didn't seem nearly as impossible now. All they needed was a little help from the other side. The guards were bound to be in the guard room. After all, it was their business to guard things. Nothing could be easier than to shout across to them. They confidently sprang to their feet and began yelling away. The thick stone walls added a fearsome echo to the shouts. The door opposite remained shut fast, so Felix got them to shout in chorus while he conducted them. "Hellooo!" They shouted at the top of their voices, but the guards didn't stir. After five minutes they were forced to admit there was no answer to their calls.

"But we still have to get over," Drifter fired up. "We must get that chain!"

"Jump over for it, if you can!" sneered Felix. "Even a grasshopper couldn't."

"I've jumped further than that on my skateboard," said Drifter proudly. "Pity it's not here. Wait a minute..."

Drifter mused over the plank supporting the wardrobe, and the rollers under it. It wasn't exactly safe. In fact, it was exceedingly risky, but if he got enough momentum before the jump, perhaps he'd manage it. Alma saw where Drifter was looking and almost screamed in fright.

"Absolutely not! That'd be suicide!"

The others, who hadn't been following Drifter's thinking, turned round to see what was happening. But he was already trying to persuade Alma.

"Look, the corridor slopes downwards, so the other side is a bit lower. I just have to pick up enough speed. The plank and rollers will fall into the pit, but the momentum will easily carry me across."

"Impossible," Alma shook her head in horror.

"Look, I wouldn't agree to a somersault in mid-air, but I can jump four metres easily!"

"You're out of your mind!"

"Maybe," laughed Drifter. "Skaters are never quite normal. Come on. The wardrobe's in the way. Let's move it!"

Felix, Alma, Farthing, and Baker joined forces to dissuade Drifter from his crazy plan, but he was steadfast: with sufficient speed he'd be able to get enough momentum to carry him across to the other side. Only Bella remained calm. When Drifter's gaze met hers, in her friendly eyes he saw trust and silent encouragement.

In the end his persistence paid off, and because there was no other solution in sight the others also agreed to let him try the seemingly impossible jump. They lifted the wardrobe off the plank, and stood it next to the wall. The corridor was wide enough for both the wardrobe and the plank on its rollers. But the main difficulty had yet to be overcome. While they were pushing the wardrobe, they'd placed the rollers under the plank one by one. But if Drifter wanted high acceleration, nobody would be able to feed in the rollers fast enough, so there was no chance of him rolling down the corridor at top speed. The only way to use the rollers was to accelerate in a short time over a short distance.

In the end, it was Felix who came up with a way to speed up the plank.

"What if two of us take our trouser belts and stand at the edge of the hole? Drifter could grab the two belts and with brute force we pull him forwards. If we get it right, we'll give him enough momentum to kick off."

"Fine by me," said Drifter after a moment's thought.

Baker's and Farthing's trouser belts seemed long and strong enough. But for acceleration muscle power was needed too, so instead of Baker, Felix stood on one side to help Drifter kick off. Alma was tense and nervous, but she'd caught some of the others' enthusiasm, and eyed the opposite bank of the chasm increasingly optimistically. Drifter made a few trial runs to get the feel of how to transfer his weight to give momentum to the plank, and then nodded confidently.

"It'll be fine!"

Baker wiped the sweat from his brow, and looked admiringly at Drifter, who had determination in his face and a sparkle in his eye. Drifter arranged the rollers under the plank so they would roll as far as possible under him. Then he adjusted his baseball cap, positioned himself on the plank and seized the two trouser belts.

"Off we go!"

Felix and Farthing took a deep breath. Felix counted to three, and together, with all of their might, they yanked the strong leather belts. Drifter braced himself, gripped onto the belts to get momentum, and kicked off. The plank rumbled as it glided over the rollers, but before it plunged into the chasm, Drifter shifted his bodyweight backwards and moved his supporting back leg forward, causing the tip of the plank to rise as it flew into the air. The rollers fell immediately into the depths, but the plank described a beautiful arc over the abyss. It didn't have enough power to land squarely on the other side. Only the first half reached the edge of the hole, and snapped on the brim before falling, but Drifter easily threw himself forward and made it to the other side with a loud grunt.

From the other bank there was relieved, happy cheering. Drifter stood up, dusted himself down, and waved to the others happily.

"Made it! Wait, I'll have a look around!"

He went straight to the guardroom door, knocked, and since there was no answer, he opened the door. Or he would have done, because the door was locked. Just to be sure he pulled at the door for a while, but as there was no answer, he went back to the edge of the chasm.

"It looks like nobody's there. What now?"

"If we've come this far, let's get the wardrobe into the room. After all, that was the task," said Felix.

"But it's locked," Bella chipped in.

"We take it to the other side, we go over too, then we pick the lock somehow. We can't let things like that stop us!" asserted Felix.

Drifter had already picked up the end of the iron chain on the ground, and carefully unwound a section of it. The links in the chain were strong and intact, and looked like they would be suitable for moving heavy weights. He braced himself, then tossed the end of the chain up in the air and got it to fly over the cross-beam. Felix deftly caught the swaying end of the chain and pulled it towards himself. The boys agreed that Drifter would swing the other end of the chain over to Felix too, so they could fasten it to both sides of the wardrobe.

Nobody had noticed until now that next to each hinge for the wardrobe doors the cabinet-maker had fixed one iron ring. These came in handy now. The two ends of the chain could be fixed relatively securely threaded through the four rings. Soon the wardrobe was waiting at the brink of the abyss to swing across to the other side. Felix counted to three, and Baker and Farthing gave a good shove to the wardrobe. Like a rectangular swing, it glided to the other side. Drifter grabbed it, held it for a couple of seconds, then let it swing back to Felix and the others.

"The chain can take it, this weight is nothing to it," he said. "Why don't you sit in it one by one, and use it to get across."

"So we are going to swing," laughed Bella. "But this is more exciting than at the playground."

Farthing volunteered to be the first to sit in the insecure vehicle, because he was the largest in the group. If the chain and beam could take his weight, the others were sure to be safe. The wardrobe swing worked brilliantly, and after the initial fright, Farthing admitted it had been a thrilling experience to swing over the bottomless depths. Second to sit in the wardrobe was Bella, then came Alma, Baker, and finally Felix. Nobody was left to hold the wardrobe for him, so he had to throw himself into it with a powerful leap. But on the other side were helping hands to hold the wardrobe while he clambered out. Felix climbed out, but rubbed his hands together in pain.

"I don't know why they have to carve patterns into the back panel of a wardrobe," he grumbled. "When I jumped in, one of the carvings cut my hand."

They looked in amazement at the inside back panel of the wardrobe. There, where nobody normally looks, the flat surface was covered in regular squares, and in each square was carved a number. There were single- and double-digit numbers side by side, apparently without any system.

"What used to be kept in this wardrobe?" wondered Alma.

Baker shrugged his shoulders. "We don't know."

"All we know is that it's decidedly heavy even when empty," added Farthing.

As the puzzle of the carved numbers didn't seem particularly important, Farthing shut the doors. All that was left was to unhook the chain from the wardrobe, and carry the heavy piece of furniture to its destination: the guardroom. Felix tried for a while to use the tip of one of the swords lying on the ground to open the lock, but to no avail. Then Farthing flung himself at it three times, trying to break the door open with his body-weight. In the end, Bella had a good idea.

"Remember Felix? Once you said you'd seen a film where a detective picked a locked door with a hairclip. You could try with mine."

Wonder of wonders, the little hairclip fitted so neatly into the lock, that Felix managed to open it. They carefully pressed down on the handle and stepped into the room.

X. THE GUARDROOM

The guardroom was completely empty. The sentries must have been patrolling who knew where. Through the arrowslits they had an excellent overview of the countryside, or rather countrysides. For here too, in this highest of positions, each narrow window opened onto a different landscape. The middle of the room was taken up by a sizable table. On it were the remains of a half-eaten snack: a loaf broken in two, the end of a sausage, and a jug with the dregs of some cider. Drifter felt the bread cautiously. It was soft, and even the part where it had been torn was still moist. It could only have been eaten about half an hour ago. Next to the scattered food on the table were wooden squares with a number chiselled into each one. It looked like the pieces of a memory or board game had been left lying around.

The children were amazed to find that there was no stairway or door leading out of the guardroom; the only way to get out was where they had just come in. They couldn't imagine where the guards had gone. They couldn't have left through the door and down the corridor, because of the gaping chasm, and anyway, they would have bumped into each other on the path winding up through the turret. The chasm couldn't have formed after the guards left, because then they would have heard the boom of the collapse. So it was reasonable to assume the guards had left the room in another direction. But which way? They couldn't possibly have vaporized through the arrowslits, and aside from the table and bench there was no furniture in the room that might have concealed a secret passageway or hidden staircase.

Drifter shrugged his shoulders, and pointed at the wardrobe outside.

"Another impossible situation. But let's get that monstrosity in here! Perhaps some change will take place when we have fulfilled the mission exactly."

"I'm beginning to get fed up of this castle," grumbled Felix irritably, but all the same he left the room to help carry in the wardrobe.

The boys and the two old men lugged in with difficulty the wardrobe that they had taken so much trouble to transport there. Baker and Farthing nodded in agreement at the back wall of the room: that would be the place for it. When they finally put down the enormous wardrobe, they all turned expectantly towards the door. They thought perhaps the vanished sentry patrol would appear from nowhere or maybe a herald from Lord Dharma to congratulate the company and accompany them to the master's reception hall. But their hopes, expectations, and wishes were in vain: there was no change whatsoever.

Felix grew angry. "So that was really worth wasting several hours for." And in his rage he gave the door such a shove that it slammed shut.

"Felix, no!" screamed Bella, reaching for the door, but it was too late. A second before her desperate move, the door shut with a resounding thud. Drifter jumped up as well to open the exit quickly, but in vain. The door was shut for good, and couldn't be opened with a hairclip or by any other means. And to make things worse, the walls suddenly shook, and over their heads they heard such a squeaking and clattering that fear gripped their hearts, their mouths ran dry, and their stomachs tightened.

"What's going on?" stammered Baker, lips a-quiver.

Drifter stared at the ceiling, then spoke with a tense, measured voice:

"I'm afraid it's a bit like that scene in Star Wars. The ceiling's coming down. They're going to squash us."

The others could see it too now. With slow creaking, the top of the guardroom was steadily falling, as if a huge pressing machine was bearing it down to the floor.

"Bravo Felix, you've really done it this time!" burst out Alma.

Felix stared in horror at the approaching ceiling. It wasn't moving too fast, but he reckoned even at this speed it would finish them off in five minutes.

"There's bound to be a solution this time too," he said hoarsely. "It's another test."

"But this time it's fatal!" wailed Baker, and with a sob clung on to Farthing.

"Come on, move everything you can!" said Felix. "Perhaps one of the objects is also a lever to stop it!"

In a desperate frenzy, the children grabbed and moved every mobile item in the room. Drifter had the idea of lifting the table and touching the legs onto the floor in various orders, to see if it triggered some hidden mechanism. The two old men hammered on the door, then Farthing suddenly decided to pick up the bench to batter the door down. But even that didn't work: the small bench smashed to pieces.

"Let's not get flustered. Think everything through logically," said Alma trying to calm the panic. "If it's a test, first we have to find the puzzle. We can't be expected to flatten ourselves to squeeze through the arrowslits, and dive down to the ground."

"The only thing that could comprise a puzzle is that board game on the table," frowned Felix. "Let's see if there's any connection between the numbers."

While Baker and Farthing tried to wedge the pieces of the broken bench under the dangerously lowering ceiling, the children ran to the table and pored over the scattered wooden squares. But try as they might, they couldn't find any logical relationship between all the one- and two-digit numbers.

Drifter had an idea. "How about moving the wardrobe to

the middle? Maybe it's huge enough to hold up the ceiling."

"If you ask me it'll break, but let's give it a go!" said Alma.

"Hey, the wardrobe!" yelped Felix, with a jump. "The wardrobe and the numbers!"

Without waiting for an answer he leaped up and tore open the carved wardrobe door. This revealed the strange carvings on the inside of the back panel, that had scratched Felix's finger.

"There are numbers carved here too!" he shouted. "Maybe there's a connection!"

"Look, Felix, one square is missing from the bottom corner!" noticed Bella.

They all looked at the bottom right hand corner, where there really was an empty space for a wooden square.

"Quick, quick, we don't have much time!" Farthing urged them. "The roof's coming down!"

And indeed, the ceiling was already bearing down on the top of the wardrobe. The strong wooden structure cracked, but for the moment held out. Perhaps it would resist the pressure for a few minutes. But the creaking from above made it clear that no obstacle could stop the huge machinery – the only way was to switch the mechanism off.

With eyes aglow, Felix stared at the carved back panel of the wardrobe. He knew that this time he would have to find the solution, because he had put the others in peril. In the back panel the numbers were carved in groups of three, like this:

$$4 - 6 - 5$$
$$3 - 9 - 6$$
$$6 - 10 - 8$$
$$3 - 7 -$$

Drifter stood next to Felix and looked at the numbers too.

"Look! Every row has a 6, except the bottom one!" he said. "Perhaps that's what's missing."

He rushed to the table, grabbed the wooden square with the

number 6 on. The creaking overhead was more and more intense, and the wardrobe let out another resounding crack. It wouldn't be able to withstand the terrible weight for long.

Felix grabbed Drifter's arm: "No, wait, that'd be too simple! Let me think!"

"Hurry up, Felix!" screamed Bella, as a crack opened down the side of the wardrobe, and it gave out a laboured groan signalling it would hold out no more.

"Got it!" said Felix jumping up. "The 5 is missing!"

Alma picked up the square with the number 5 from the table, and put it into the empty space. The square fitted into place with a satisfying click. But it didn't stop the downward motion of the ceiling.

"Get out the way, Alma!" commanded Drifter. "If we don't open the exit, we're done for!"

As Alma flattened herself against the side of the wardrobe, Drifter ran with all his strength at the back panel with the carved numbers. The wardrobe shook from the impact, and behind the back panel there opened a narrow corridor.

"After me, quick!" shouted Drifter, before disappearing through the narrow opening.

Bella and Alma followed him immediately. Felix ushered the terrified old men through, and finally stepped into the tunnel himself. The following second the wardrobe split in two, and the ceiling came crashing down, as if the driving mechanism had suddenly let it fall. Rubble and dust poured down into the tunnel, barricading the exit for good.

"Felix, did you get through?" screamed Alma.

"Yes, I'm fine. We escaped," sighed Felix, and leaned back, exhausted.

"Where are we?" asked Bella in a thin voice.

"A secret corridor, obviously," said Drifter. "This castle really is full of tricks."

"Wait, I've got some light!" called Felix confidently, and fished his smartphone out of his pocket. There was no network coverage or Wi-Fi, but the flashlight still worked. Drifter felt like providing light too, and got out his own phone.

"Listen, Drif, I reckon it's better to use only one light at a time," suggested Felix. "Who knows how long we'll be here. It does no harm to have reserves. We certainly can't charge up."

"Sure," nodded Drifter, "but first let's have a look round!"

In the flickering light of the two phones they saw a rather narrow passageway, leading steeply downwards. One child fitted easily between the cold, damp walls, but in places plump old Baker had to pull his tummy in so as not to get stuck.

"Felix, how did you know the number five would open the passageway?" asked Bella.

"All I knew was that five was missing. In each row, the third number was half the sum of the first two numbers. Four and six is ten, half of that is five. Three and nine are twelve, half of that is six, and so on," explained Felix. "But it's thanks to Drifter that we found the door. I certainly wouldn't have rushed at the wall."

"Let's get moving!" interjected Alma.

"Drifter, are you leading the way?" asked Felix. "Then I'll switch off my flashlight."

They set off. The corridor was dark and dank, the ground uneven, and now and again they bumped their sides on the rough projections from the stone walls, but nevertheless they stumbled on, relieved the mortal danger was over. They all suspected that their adventures were far from being at an end, but they felt sure they had nothing particular to fear until the next obstacle. The light from Drifter's phone showed the way encouragingly.

After half an hour they encountered the first difficulty. The corridor branched out, continuing in three passageways, all identical in height, width, and darkness. The group weighed up the possibilities. Baker and Farthing's knowledge of the place couldn't be relied on, since they knew nothing of the castle's secret passages, and didn't have a clue where they were. Felix got his light out again and the two boys lit up all three entrances thoroughly. At first they saw nothing special. The three corridors seemed exactly the same.

But then Bella noticed that over the arched entrances there seemed to be some kind of shape. Felix stood on tiptoe to dust off the cobwebs and mould that had accumulated on the figures. Now they could see clearly that the relief figures represented chess pieces. Over one passage was a pawn, over the second a king, and over the third a knight.

"Does this mean something?" wondered Drifter.

"I shouldn't think so," dismissed Baker. "The whole castle is full of decorations like this. Lord Dharma spends most of his time playing chess."

An idea popped into Alma's mind.

"Drifter, can you shine the light backwards? Let's see if there's a sign over our passageway too!"

They all turned round and stared up at the arch over the corridor. Felix reached up again to wipe the cobwebs off the stone surface.

"That looks like a castle, which in chess we call a rook!" announced Alma triumphantly. "So these aren't just decorations, but signposts. Obviously, we've come from the direction of the castle turret, or the rook, so the question is, what do the other three figures indicate?"

"Maybe the knight takes us back to the wild horses again!" said Bella longingly.

"To the castle stables, more likely," said Felix, dampening her enthusiasm. He hated unrealistic situations more than anything.

"The pawn might indicate the troops' mess," said Farthing falteringly. "Lord Dharma's troops are stationed in the basement rooms."

"Does he have many soldiers?" asked Bella in alarm.

"Loads. It's not surprising he's always thinking about fighting," said Baker.

"Anyway, if we want to find the master himself, we probably have to choose the passage under the king," said Alma decisively.

"There's no royal road," said Felix with mock seriousness.

"But there is! What makes you say that?" Bella was angry. "The middle way is the king's passage."

"Just joking. The king's passage makes me think of the royal road. There's a saying that there's no royal road to geometry."

"And what does that mean?" asked Bella suspiciously.

"That kings have to study and practise just like anyone else if they want to understand geometry. Just because someone's a king doesn't mean he learns any easier."

"We could say the same about chess. You have to practise loads," nodded Alma.

Drifter said nothing, but thought to himself that not just anybody could have done the skateboard jump. The only way to succeed was to put time and energy into learning. Sure, to the others skateboarding hadn't seemed a very useful pastime, but at the chasm his underrated skill had saved the day. Deep down Drifter was glad he'd had a chance to prove that unfashionable sports had their uses too.

Meanwhile Alma was beginning to feel that the dark corridor leading goodness knows where was more and more depressing, so she urged the others to continue on their way. Finally they reached a consensus to choose the path marked by the king. Drifter went first again, trying to pick out with his torch all the protruding stones and pits, so nobody would trip up while they stumbled forward by the weak, flickering light.

The path went on for so long that the narrow dark passage slowly brought a disagreeable, depressing feeling to all of them. They were tired, hungry, and more than anything, thirsty. Bella would have happily clambered up onto Felix's back, or curled up in a tearful ball on the ground, but she knew that showing her weakness would weaken them all. Alma sensed Bella's spirit was flagging, so she turned round and held her hand. This made the monotonous walking more bearable for the small girl.

Everything comes to an end sooner or later, even this nightmarish winding in the dark. The path suddenly stopped, and a door without a handle or a knocker blocked their way. The boys immediately set about trying to force it, but try as they might the door was as strong as if it were part of the stone wall.

"I can't believe it!" raged Felix. "There's no way I'm going back!"

"It's bound to be another puzzle," sneered Drifter.

"And I'm not solving any puzzles either. I've had enough of this idiotic castle altogether," Felix informed them.

"Watch what you say!" warned Baker. "The castle sees and hears everything. Don't make it angry with you!"

"I'm angry with the castle!" Felix kicked at the door. "Does it think I'm frightened?! Well I'm not. I'm not going to take fright at a couple of stupid puzzles."

Alma looked at him angrily. She was fed up of the walking, guessing, and puzzles too, but she restrained herself. If everyone lost their tempers, there would be utter chaos. They had to overcome themselves to find the way home.

"Cut it out!" she said sternly to Felix.

"No, I won't! I've had enough, get it? I hate this castle."

Felix kicked the door again.

"Control yourself!" Alma told him angrily. "Even Bella isn't shouting, even though she must be exhausted. There's no need for fury anyway. If the castle hears everything, perhaps we can ask it nicely."

"Well write it a letter, like you do to Father Christmas!" retorted Felix indignantly.

"Perhaps we don't need to. I think the simplest thing would be to say what we want. Either it works or it doesn't, but there's no harm in trying."

Alma took a deep breath, turned to the door, and in her politest voice she said:

"Dear door, we'd really like to find Lord Dharma. Please open, and lead us to him!"

For a moment, everyone held their breath. They only breathed a sigh of relief and wonder when, with a subdued click, the thick wooden door swung open before them.

XI. THE BLACK UNIFORM

Drifter was the first to step from the dark corridor into the room. Squinting from the sudden light, he cast a suspicious glance round even the far corners. The room was quiet, so the group followed in one after the other. Drifter, the girls, then Farthing and Baker stepped into the invitingly bright area. But before Felix could enter, the door shut with a deafening slam right in front of him.

"Felix!" Bella cried out her brother's name in despair.

Drifter and Farthing tugged at the door, and Baker clapped his hands to his head in fright. Alma told everyone to move back, and tried once more to ask the door to let Felix through too, but it stayed closed.

"Felix, can you hear me? You should talk to it! You upset it, and it's probably waiting for you to say sorry!" shouted Alma, hoping her voice would carry through the solid walls.

On the other side, Felix had come to the same conclusion himself, though he couldn't hear the others' cries. For a while he fumed quietly, then tried to take deep breaths and calm down, just as his coach had showed him. Finally he pulled himself together, and reluctantly spoke to the door.

"All right, I admit, it wasn't very nice of me. Sorry. Please open, and let me go on with the others!"

Nothing happened, so Felix repeated his request. But the

castle remained silent. It had no intention of accepting this half-hearted apology. Felix grew angry.

"Don't take offence now! I didn't get angry for nothing, the guardroom nearly crushed us to death! And you needn't think I'm going to stand here pleading until kingdom come!"

The surface of the door emitted a strange creak in response, and weird noises came from the doorstep, like thin stone sheets splitting open. Felix directed his phone flashlight down and was staggered to see that the door had started to wall itself up, from bottom to top. One row at a time the door was being replaced by stones.

"No, don't do that, hey! Please, let me through!" pleaded Felix. But the door had disappeared. In its place was a thick, impenetrable stone wall, complete with cobwebs. Not a trace remained of the former entrance.

Felix stood for a while, slapping and pressing the wall, but soon he had to admit the path to the others was cut off. Angry and exasperated, he turned his back on the blocked door, and retraced his steps down the corridor. He hoped that when he got back to the junction he could find another underground corridor that would lead out into the light.

The dark corridor wound on frustratingly for ages. Felix reckoned he should have reached the junction a long time ago, but there was no sign of it. It seemed the castle had redesigned itself again. At first Felix shuffled along sulkily and dismayed, but gradually he gained self-control. Now even he realized that the walls could hear and understand what he said, and what's more they were sensitive. Bad behaviour and impoliteness were immediately punished. He remembered the words of the two old men: you would only find your way through the castle's maze if you followed the true path. Whoever loses confidence or turns back will never find the starting point again.

"I upset the door, and now the castle is punishing me. All right, that's fair, I accept it," muttered Felix to himself. "The castle's playing a home match, it can set the rules. I'm fine with that. So no more bad temper, swearing, or insults, even to the smallest of stones."

Felix stood up, looked round in the dark, and was unable to keep his thoughts to himself, so he continued them out loud.

"Do you hear, Castle? I accept the challenge. I admit you're capable of the impossible. From now on I'll play by the rules and I won't insult you. But I expect fair play from you too. Don't keep me here in the dark. I'm not going to get scared, but time is running out. Give me a chance to prove myself, and to find the others!"

Felix waited in silence. Deep down he hoped that his words would open a door to lead him back to the others, or at least to a corridor, but nothing like that happened. So by the light of his phone, he carried on stumbling through the dark passage.

But he didn't have to struggle for long in the dark. Apparently the castle had considered his request and decided to grant it. After a few minutes he came to a three-way fork in the passage. Felix immediately saw it was a different junction from the one they had passed previously: here the passages branched out at different angles, and this time all three possible directions led down a relatively narrow, low passage. But this time too, over the arches round the entrances Felix could see the outline of a chess piece. He looked carefully at the possibilities.

He remembered that at the previous junction when the whole group was still together, they had arrived through the passage with the rook sign, and after thinking a bit they'd chosen the passage with the king. This time there was no rook and no king, in fact, the passage Felix had emerged from had no sign at all. Felix smiled.

"At least that shows the castle doesn't over-exert itself. This passage won't lead me anywhere, why would it bother giving it a sign. Let me see what my options are."

The other three branches of the junction were emblazoned with a queen, a knight, and a pawn. Felix wondered. He had no wish whatsoever to meet any kind of horses, so he dismissed the knight passage right away. He didn't play chess, but he knew how powerful the queen was. Perhaps alongside Lord Dharma there lived a queen, who was beautiful, kind, and pleased to receive the devotion of visitors.

"More likely that cold, proud woman lives alongside Lord Dharma, somebody like the statue we saw in the staircase before the turret," thought Felix. "I'd do better to mix with common people, peasants from the villages. Though it's possible the passage with the pawn really does lead to the troops' mess. No matter. Among the troops I'm bound to find someone who can help."

After thinking through all the options, he set off down the passage under the pawn. He had to stoop and go carefully, because there was only enough headroom for someone of Bella's height. But instead of getting angry, Felix perked up, because the castle was prepared to make peace. In good cheer, he gave the wall a tap:

"And before I forget: thanks!"

Although the castle was willing to give him another chance to get out, it didn't make things particularly easy. Felix was tired out from stumbling along the passage, which in places was crumbling, and elsewhere was extremely narrow. After a good half an hour he came to the end of the passage, to another wooden door. This time he didn't rush at it or kick it. He spoke to it, asking for its permission to pass through it. With a creak, the door opened, and Felix finally stepped through into the light.

On the other side of the door, the same passage seemed to continue, though a little wider and without cobwebs. There was no sunlight, because the passage had no windows. The light came from the flickering flame of torches fixed to the walls in iron rings. Felix had probably come out of the underground passage deep down, on one of the lower levels. He proceeded cautiously and silently, to find out where the bright passage led. But in vain was he as quiet as the wind, and in spite of him not seeing a soul nearby, somehow someone had noticed him.

Suddenly a door opened, and three armed men appeared before him. All three of them wore black uniforms. Two of them held spears, and the third, who judging by his bold stance must have been an officer, pointed his sword at Felix.

There was no chance to fight or escape. Felix put his hands up and backed towards the wall, while the two spears were lowered to point at his chest. When the boy showed no resistance, the officer replaced his sword in its sheath and started to shout.

"Who said you could go walk-abouts? I said clearly, the new recruits have to wait in the troops' mess! And you come loitering here, without so much as a uniform!"

Felix wanted to explain that he wasn't one of the new recruits, in fact he wasn't even from this world, but the officer nearly had a fit when he saw the boy open his mouth to speak.

"Oh, you want to talk back? If you know what's good for you, hold your tongue! If you dare open your mouth, you'll be put in irons and shoved in the dark cell! That'll teach you some discipline."

With fire in his eyes he turned to the two guards with spears:

"Take him back to the new recruits immediately. There'll be an inspection in one minute, and he'll be in uniform. See to it that he is! Turn right, and run to it!"

The officer watched in anger as Felix and the two guards quickly left. Felix ran ahead, but all the time in his left shoulder blade he could feel one of the guard's spears. The other ran beside him and poked him in the side with the tip of the spear. For a moment Felix thought he could suddenly sprint off, and before his escorts knew it he'd have disappeared round the corner, but then he realized it wasn't a particularly wise plan. Even if they couldn't catch up with him, they could easily get him from behind with a spear, and even if he escaped it would be a matter of minutes before a whole patrol of soldiers was searching for him. It would be better to obey for the moment, and wait for the right moment to escape.

The two guards pushed him into a large but fairly crowded

room. The windows were closed, and the stale air was warm and reeked of human sweat. Felix nearly fainted from the stench of hot bodies. Fortunately even the guards were shocked by the smell of the air, and shouted to the soldiers near the back to open a window. The new recruits looked at the newcomers, some dejectedly, others indifferently. The atmosphere in the room was dominated by gloom.

One of the guards went to the cupboard by the door, got out a black tunic and trousers, and gave them to Felix. The other pushed him in the back with all his might, and bawled at him:

"Line-up in one minute! You don't want to find out what happens to slackers!"

Felix cowered as he made his way through the soldiers preparing for the line-up, heading for the window so as not to be too conspicuous as he pulled on the black uniform. Looking around he had the impression that Lord Dharma recruited soldiers from nearby villages: the room was full of thick-set peasant lads not much older than Felix. Some of them had a touch of down on their chin, and a few of them were fine tall lads, but most of them were short and muscular. Felix, who played centre in basketball, was tall compared to them, so it wasn't surprising that in the passage they'd taken him for a soldier in spite of his age.

Since the uniform was slightly too large, Felix pulled it on easily over his normal clothes. When buttoned up to the neck, the tunic covered his T-shirt completely, and the trousers covered his jeans too, which were very odd in the castle. Felix was ready in no time, and even had a chance to look round to see if there was a mirror in the room. Of course there wasn't, but his eyes met those of a freckled lad with a pointed nose and a piercing gaze sitting next to him. The boy was openly staring at him.

"Why didn't you take off those odd clothes?" he asked curiously.

"Um, I feel the cold," answered Felix evasively.

"You can't escape from here," said the freckled lad. "I've

thought through all the possibilities."

Surprised, Felix looked at the boy's warm brown eyes. He looked back seriously, and stretched out his hand.

"I'm Angelo."

"Hi. My name's Felix."

"I hate war," whispered Angelo, after they'd shaken hands, "and I hate being shut inside. I'm a bird-catcher, and my place is in the forest."

Before Felix could reply, the officer appeared in the door, blew his whistle and started shouting. The soldiers rushed to line up. The officer scrutinized the group of recruits sternly and sneered scornfully, but was obviously short of time, so he didn't make any comments. He gave the order to set off immediately.

"Recruits, follow me! Everyone take one spear and one sword from the armoury, then out to the parade ground. You'll soon be mobilized, so we're going to give you a crash training course! Follow me!"

The soldiers hurried after the officer in silence. Angelo was in line behind Felix, but was unable to stay quiet, and gave a running commentary in a barely audible whisper throughout the journey.

"They used to say that even the walls have ears here. And they're right too! Just watch. Sometimes the officers say where they're going out loud! Otherwise they'd go the wrong way, because the castle doesn't let just anyone go where they want. Apparently the walls move. Watch now!"

The officer leading the troop stopped a moment in front of a junction in the passage, and announced firmly:

"To the armoury!"

It looked like he was repeating the order to the soldiers behind him, but that was silly, because they all knew full well where they were going. Was is possible that the officer was really making it clear to the walls where he wanted to go?

Felix's gaze rested for a moment on a lion's head carved into the wall over the officer's shoulder. Alongside the chess figures the grinning lion was the most common decoration in the castle. Felix had seen one like it in almost every passage and room. Suddenly he recalled what the two old men had said, when the children couldn't believe they'd been in the castle for one hundred and eighty years. They said that Lord Dharma gave them a draught from the water from the fountain with the lion, which stopped them from growing old. Obviously the fountain with the lion contained the water of life which they had to take to Katalina's grandpa! No wonder the lion was held in such respect.

They turned into another passage. Angelo shoved Felix from behind to indicate the officer had said their destination out loud again. Felix saw in surprise that they were going past another lion's head. Could it be that the castle heard words spoken within its walls through the ears on the carved lion? Felix turned back and shared his idea with Angelo, who pondered the idea for a moment, then snapped his fingers in admiration.

"You'd make a brilliant bird-catcher, Felix!"

Seeing that Felix was perplexed, he added:

"We have to be very observant, because everything depends on whether we understand the tiniest of the birds' signals. I'd never thought of this lion thing, but now you mention it, I remember what's happened over the last few days. And you're right. When the officers speak 'to themselves', there's always been a lion's head nearby."

"Then that's the solution!" beamed Felix.

"Don't you believe it," Angelo shook his head. "Do you think that if you said 'I want to go home' the lions would graciously open the main entrance for you? I think they'd take you to the dungeon!"

Felix nodded sadly. This was indeed the most likely case. After all, if someone leaves the right path, the castle confounds them and leads them astray, so they become utterly confused and fall into a trap. It was impossible to simply walk out of the castle. People who hadn't come into the castle of their own accord could probably only leave by permission or through some trickery.

Felix took a deep breath and came to another conclusion. He remembered what the teacher at maths club used to say when they were solving maths puzzles together. "Every puzzle has its internal logic waiting to be discovered." For sure, this castle also had a modus operandi, even if what happened sometimes seemed like pure magic and wizardry. There must be a system, otherwise nobody but Lord Dharma would manage. Sooner or later everyone would get lost, fall into a trap, or die lost and starving. Obviously the lions' heads understood where a traveller wanted to go; all they needed to work out was how to out-think the castle walls.

Meanwhile the troop had arrived at the entrance to the armoury. The store provided them with weapons of varying degrees of rustiness. While the officer handed each soldier one spear and one sword, Felix wondered whether such a continuously changing labyrinth might not have some permanent fixed points.

"A few central halls or passages that never change, and the other walls are transformed in relation to these fixed points. The gnomes said there was a map room somewhere. Why else would anyone need a map or a plan if not to set out the permanent places? After all, if everything is always in motion, it would be impossible to draw a map of the castle."

Felix decided what he would do. There was no chance of escaping from the castle, but if he set about locating the map room properly, perhaps he would reach his destination. Once there, he might come across some clues about where to look for the others, or where he could meet the elusive Lord Dharma, about whom he was getting more and more curious ever since beginning to understand the complex system of the castle.

"Listen, Angelo, I'm going to go somewhere!" he whispered to the freckled bird-catcher. "I have to find my friends. Are you coming?"

"Don't risk it Felix! You can't escape from the castle! I want to escape during the military exercises, outside in the open! I'll hide in the forest so even the owls can't find me!"

"Then we have to part. I've got stuff to do here!" said Felix. "Good luck!"

The boys shook hands, then picked up their weapons to follow the officer's instructions and set off to the parade ground. Felix lagged behind to the end of the line, and when the troops went past a statue he hid behind it. When the recruits had gone, he set off after them, but only as far as the nearest lion's head. He stood up straight, and in a firm, confident voice he said:

"I'm going to the map room."

Tense, he looked around to see if anything would change, but there were no transformations at all. The path of the passageway, the statues, reliefs and carvings all stayed the same, no doors appeared, but something quickened inside him. A strange tingle started at the nape of his neck, a barely perceptible vibration, which suddenly turned into a clearly formed idea, and Felix suddenly felt and knew that he had to go into the next room.

He went up to it, pressed the handle and found himself in a quiet room. Without hesitating he closed the door behind him, and went across the room. There were three doors opposite him: he chose the middle one. Since there was a lion's head on the wall here too, he repeated his destination out loud, and opened the door. A sure instinct guided him through about five rooms. Each one had a different layout and ambience, but undaunted and flying through them, Felix went on to the map room.

In front of the last door, he felt he had arrived. With confidence he opened the door into what he hoped would be the long sought-for map room. He felt such calm and confidence he put all his caution aside. He expected to find maps, scrolls, and a scale model of the castle, which he imagined would be in the middle of the room, to show how the castle walls were laid out. But when he entered the room, he froze for a moment. The walls were indeed covered with shelves, old books and yellowing maps, but instead of the model castle that Felix had imagined, there stood a foreboding-looking man dressed in black, who greeted the shock on the young boy's face with cold disdain.

"Lord Dharma?" stammered Felix, though deep down he knew that the stranger waiting in the map room could not be anyone else.

"I expected you would recognize me," said Lord Dharma in a subdued voice. "After all, you are wearing my uniform, and you'd do anything to be on the winning side. I allowed you to find me because I wish to speak to you."

"I want to speak to you too!" said Felix angrily, straightening up. Suddenly he was flushed with anger over the trials and dangers they had been through over the last few days, and he decided that either by words or by strength, he would persuade the lord of the castle to send him and his friends home.

"You are clever, daring, and courageous, but far too hot-tempered," observed Lord Dharma. "Yet for me to accept you into my service, and to fulfil your wish, you will need to be cool, calm, and collected."

Felix wanted to answer, but Lord Dharma raised his finger, and continued implacably:

"Be silent and listen, for you will have no other opportunity to hear my proposal. I need strong, decisive officers in my army. You would suit very well, so I offer you the chance to join my invincible team. Your friends will perish, but you are worth more than them, so you may have a chance to survive. Come over to my side, and you can save yourself! And to show my goodwill, I will even offer your sister's life. If you join me, I will let her live too."

Felix's eyes flashed with anger, and Lord Dharma began to shake his head.

"There's no need to see it as betrayal. Why should it be? Your parents charged you with your sister, and you would be betraying them if you let her fall. And the only way to protect her and yourself is to follow my orders. There is no need to answer now. First calm down, think it over, weigh things up. You will see that you have no other chance for survival. You will know when I send for you! When you receive my signal, from then on you will follow my orders. If you don't... I hope you understand."

Lord Dharma took two steps back, and vanished into thin air. Felix was numb and confused by what he had heard. He stepped towards the place where the lord of the castle had disappeared, but he was now completely alone. He flexed his fingers and realized in shock that a metal ring had fastened itself to the third finger of his left hand. It was a simple, wide flat ring, which instead of a precious stone had an inscribed lion's head. Felix tried to wrench the ring off his finger, but the strange object was stuck, and it seemed to cut into his flesh and burn. Finally Felix could bear it no longer and gave up struggling. As he let go of the ring, the pain left him, but at the base of his tortured third finger he felt the grip of the ring.

Meanwhile the shelves laden with books and maps hung on the walls had also disappeared, and by the time Felix recovered himself, he was in an undecorated room, and in his ringless right hand he was once more clutching the spear and the sword from the armoury. Having no other choice, he stepped to the door to return to the castle. But in the room behind the map room instead of the furniture he had seen before, he found a line of sacks against the wall, and from behind the wooden partition dividing the room came a desperate shrill cry for help.

XII. The Black King

When Felix's outburst of anger caused the door to turn to stone, the group of friends on the other side fell into despair. Drifter and Farthing started pounding on the wall again, though they knew full well that their efforts were in vain. Bella was inconsolable as tears poured from her eyes, and Alma, with fists clenched in nervousness and worry, fixed her gaze at the wall.

"Why couldn't you say sorry?" she murmured, meaning her words for Felix. "I can't believe you can't talk to people normally!"

"Because he's always angry. He's always arguing with someone," sobbed Bella.

"Don't cry!" Alma gave her a hug. "Felix does have a temper, but he's clever and strong. He's bound to turn back and look for another route. Good job he's got his smartphone, he'll be able to light the way. We'll find each other sooner or later."

Since they couldn't do anything to help Felix, they had no choice but to leave the stone wall and look around the room. They were in a large room, and it struck them all immediately that although there were no windows, it was bright. The light streamed from the ceiling, like when the sun filters through a thin veil of cloud to bathe the countryside in golden light. In the middle of the hall was an enormous chessboard, on which were black and white pieces as large as people. The position looked like the game was coming to an end, because the only pieces left on the chequered board were the black king and rook, and a few white pieces. The other pieces stood higgledy-piggledy on either side of the board.

On the wall opposite they saw eight doors, all identical. Drifter hurried over and tried all of them.

"They're all shut. I thought so," he said with a glum face.

There was no sign of any living being in the room, not even furniture to suggest that someone from the court of Lord Dharma might pass through now and again.

"Oh no, what shall we do? We've got into a trap again," wailed Baker.

"Moaning won't get you anywhere," boomed a voice.

"Lord Dharma! Where are you, Your Majesty?"

"You should know by now, I am everywhere!"

"The chessboard!" Bella pointed at it with wide-open eyes.

And indeed, the head of the king on the chessboard had taken on human features, and the voice was coming from that direction.

"That's the bloke that was behind Alma on chessboard alley! I recognize him!" shouted Drifter. "Watch your step with him! He's the one that brought us here, for sure!"

"Who else could it have been?" the black king sneered at him. "Nobody comes to my realm of their own accord!"

"People at home are worrying about us. We'd like to go back," said Alma, looking him in the eye.

"Who is stopping you?"

"You are. And this castle. And this whole country."

"Oh, come now! You just have to follow the path home."

"What path home?" said Drifter indignantly. "The castle keeps changing, the plan isn't stable. What's more every door we find is shut, and sometimes we're in mortal danger!"

The black king gave such a hearty laugh the sides of the chess piece shook.

"The only true challenge is a fight for life and death. It is in the shadow of death that we can differentiate between light and dark, the worthy and the unworthy."

"What do you want of us?" thundered Drifter.

"Life, and death. Certainty, and submission."

"I bet he wants to play chess!" said Alma. "Everything has been about chess so far."

"Chess is like life. And life imitates chess," said the chess piece enigmatically.

"All right then. I'm up for a game," said Alma determinedly. "But the others can't play chess. Let them go home, at least!"

"What self-conceit," said the king with Dharma's face, pouting his lips mockingly. "Do you imagine you're worth anything without your companions? You overestimate yourself, young lady!"

"Well at least let Felix come back to us!" implored Alma.

"Oh, Felix, that angry hot-head. The raging lion," chuckled the chessman. "It wouldn't do him any harm to learn to control himself a little. And the others! Here's Drifter, the solitary oddball, who won't even talk to his classmates."

"I'm all right without them," the boy shrugged his shoulders defiantly. "It's none of your business, anyway."

"Drifter, Drifter," said the black king, dawdling on the word. "What a peculiar name. Why do they call you that?"

"I chose the name myself," said the boy proudly. "From a game, where a guy called Drifter was always exploring new places."

"Far more likely, he was a vagabond, a vagrant. A rolling stone, who was never truly at home."

"That's my nickname on the net and at school. I don't care what other people think. If you don't belong anywhere, you're free."

"You are not free; you are lonely!" announced Lord Dharma in a razor-sharp voice. "And you know it. But who else is there? Oh, yes, little Bella. A little cry-baby, she'd be better off at home."

"Let her go home then!" retorted Alma.

"All in good time. Have you learned no patience in all these games? I cannot abide hasty children."

"Miss Alma, don't argue with him. It's not the real Lord

Dharma," whispered Farthing under his breath. "Our master is a real person of flesh and blood, not a chess piece. This is another trap!"

The black king laughed malevolently. The rook on the chessboard, and the black figures idling by the edge, all laughed along with him. The children were horrified to see that now Lord Dharma's features were on all the black chess pieces. The chorus of ghostly laughter echoed on the walls of the room, and the mocking chuckle enveloped the group of children, rooting them to the spot.

"I exist in every form!" hissed all the chess pieces with Lord Dharma's face. "I am chess, the struggle, and the destiny."

"Instead, why don't you tell us where the way out is?" Drifter fired a question at the black king, but when he got no answer, he stepped onto the chessboard to grip the taunting chess piece, or perhaps to knock it over. But to his surprise the pieces standing by the edge moved, grabbed their weapons, and pressed him back among his companions.

"You are unfit for a genuine battle!" scoffed the king. "You are unworthy! I fight a hundred battles in a simul, and even as the hundred and first you are unable to challenge me. You are lost, all of you!"

"Lord and master, what will become of us?" asked Farthing, screwing up all his courage. "You said we can return home if we complete the task assigned to us. We took the wardrobe to the guardroom, we solved the problem. Keep your promise, and let us go home!"

"Very well," nodded the chess piece coldly. "You are free. For once in your life you overcame your lack of skill, and laziness. Your reward shall be granted. You may go!"

"But which way?" asked the old men in astonishment.

"That is out of my hands. Find the way yourselves, or find a leader you can follow. I hold you back no longer."

"You cannot do this to us, master!" wailed the two wretches, but Lord Dharma paid no heed to them. His face slowly became lifeless, and the haughty king's features soon gave way to the smooth surface of the chess piece. The features of Lord Dharma gradually disappeared from the other pieces too. Even their mouths had vanished, when a last, enigmatic phrase rang out and echoed:

"I can do all things except one!"

When the last soundwaves had faded away, only faceless chess pieces remained on the board. Even when the children addressed them and prodded them, they stood as if they had only ever been lifeless wood.

The children gazed in bewilderment. Lord Dharma's fearsome words were still ringing in their ears. "You are lost, all of you!" Although it was reassuring the black king and the others had gone back to being chess pieces, and would no longer heap vindictive remarks on them, the experience had cast a gloomy mood over them. The threat had settled on them like a curse, and they shuddered to think of it.

"He's a crazed maniac," was Drifter's conclusion.

"I'd like to know what he meant when he said he could do all things except one," pondered Alma. "We have to find that one exception, to catch him out."

"We knew it!" broke out Baker. "Lord Dharma is evil. He wants us to die."

"I'm not so sure, not sure at all," said Alma furrowing her brow in thought. "If he just wanted us to die he could have destroyed us ages ago."

"Perhaps that is the one thing he cannot do?" said Drifter with a sparkle in his eye.

"It's possible that he cannot kill arbitrarily, for no reason," reflected Alma. "He cannot launch a sly attack while we are extricating ourselves from danger."

"He said we are unworthy opponents," sniffed Bella, who had still not got over being separated from Felix. "I don't even want to oppose him."

"Yes, that was his fixation," added Drifter. "He wants a fight to the death. And a worthy opponent. And he fights a hundred battles in a simul. What a boaster!"

"What is a simul?" asked Bella.

"Simultaneously means at the same time. It comes from Latin. Your brother would be bound to know it," said Drifter, with a little bitterness.

"But in chess it also means that someone plays several games at the same time," added Alma. "There's a load of chessboards, and each one has an opponent. The player goes round and makes one move on each board."

"But that's not fair!" exclaimed Bella "He's outnumbered. All the others are against him."

"Not exactly," explained Alma. "Each board has a fair game, one against one. The opponents all play out their own battle. The simul exhibitor is usually such a good player that he can concentrate on several games. He might lose half the games and win the others. But if he's really good, he might win them all."

"And has Lord Dharma got a load of chessboards and opponents here in the castle?" asked Bella curiously. She liked the idea of simultaneous games, and thought with admiration of the enormous mental capacity necessary for this kind of challenge.

"I don't remember seeing chessboards next to each other, or opponents," Farthing shook his head.

"He's tricked you too! Lord Dharma is wicked and cruel!" Baker burst out again.

But Alma suddenly had an idea. All through the conversation with the chess piece she'd had the creeping sensation that although the black king was neither friendly nor helpful, in some vague and puzzling way he was nonetheless showing a route to the solution and escape. All they had to do was work out the meaning behind his words. He probably wasn't showing off when he used the word 'simul'. For a chess player that was just normal. He must have been thinking about actual simultaneous games. Another thing that was clear was that he wanted combat, a fight. He was looking for an opponent for a final decisive battle.

"Chess is life itself, and life imitates chess," mumbled Alma. "That's what Lord Dharma said, more or less, isn't it?"

Drifter nodded. Lord Dharma seemed to be as fond of making profound-seeming statements as their English teacher at school. Alma, however, thought differently. With gritty determination she turned the words over in her mind, seeking the hidden meaning concealed in the phrases.

"And what if he wasn't talking about a simple game of chess? After all, Katalina said he was always at war."

She looked wondering for a moment at Baker and Farthing.

"And you guys said there weren't many chess boards or opponents in the castle, but the master is always thinking about chess. On the other hand, there are stables, soldiers, and weapons. Perhaps Lord Dharma's battles take place out there, outside the castle. Chess battles to the death on the fields, in the forests, and on the edge of villages."

"Get a grip, Alma, even in a film that'd be exaggerated," said Drifter to calm her, but Alma was in full swing.

"Why, Drifter? Realistic battles with living characters, according to the rules of chess. It doesn't sound that crazy in the world of Lord Dharma. Just think about everything that's happened! The horsemen in the forest, the village preparing for war, and the gnomes here in the castle. And... oh, yes!"

Alma went quite pale when she realized. She felt quite certain she had finally found the key, and understood one of the great mysteries of the castle.

"Listen!" she whispered. "Now I get why we see different landscapes through every window! The castle windows look onto simultaneous battlefields! Lord Dharma fights all his chess battles out there! Each window looks onto a different battlefield. And I reckon he wants the same from us. To fight out there, a fight of life and death."

"That's impossible. I mean, we don't know how to play chess."

"Precisely! That was the first thing I said to him, remember? That I'd be up for a game, but he should let you all go. But his answer was that I was arrogant to think I was worth anything without you."

Then it dawned on Drifter too.

"Right. In a simple game of chess over a table, you really wouldn't need us. But if there's an actual battle, it wouldn't be a bad idea to have us by your side."

"You and then some!" sighed Alma. "In chess an army has sixteen pieces."

"And there are only four of us," nodded Drifter. "Three, actually."

He looked at Bella's swollen eyes, and as her mouth began to curl into a wail, he corrected himself:

"I mean, four. Obviously Felix will join us soon."

"If you will permit," interjected Farthing nervously, "we're here too. Without you we wouldn't have got this far. So we'll stick with you."

The old man looked tellingly at Alma.

"After all, Lord Dharma said we should choose a leader. Let us join your team, Miss Alma! Then there'll be six of us."

"And Katalina's waiting outside. That's seven," added Bella hopefully.

"So now we just have to find the way out, and Felix, get hold of nine other people, weapons, and the like. Simple, really," said Drifter uncertainly.

"And horses," added Bella with a serious look. "You need two horses for chess, don't you?"

"Yes. We'll need horses too," sighed Alma. "And some food and drink, because if we don't eat properly we'll fade away before actually fighting anyone."

"Well, let's say this is really what we have to do," wondered Drifter out loud. "The first thing is still to get out of here. It's all very well there being a battlefield and an enemy army waiting to spill our blood, but what good is it if we're stuck here?"

Baker and Farthing went obediently to the doors and tried to open them once more. But the eight exits stayed firmly shut.

"Let's take a look at the chessboard," said Alma. "So far it was always solving a chess problem that showed us what the next step was."

The pieces stood there immobile as the group gathered round the chessboard. Some of the pieces were taller than the children, so Alma looked around for a stand or a chair she could climb up to get a better view of the position. There was no furniture at all in the room, so Farthing suggested she climb up on his shoulders. From there she finally had a good view of the chessboard.

So far she had noticed only the black king and rook, and hadn't paid much attention to the white pieces. Now she studied their positions too.

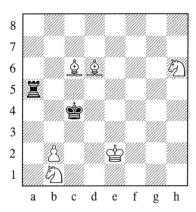

As well as the white king and a pawn, there were two white knights and two white bishops on the board.

"So, can you give mate to the black king?" asked Drifter.

Alma thought for a bit. It was clear that one or even two moves wouldn't be enough for checkmate. Although the black king had little room for manoeuvre, his rook was covering the whole of the fifth rank. It would definitely need to be captured before giving mate.

"Drifter, could you move the pieces as I say?"

"Sure. I just hope they don't want to mow me down again."

Alma issued instructions for the first move.

"The knight on b1 jumps to d2. Check. In response the black

king moves to d4. Then the knight gives check again by moving to b3. The king retreats to c4. Now let's get rid of the rook. Can you capture it with the knight, on a5? Right, it's no longer defending the king, who's in check yet again. He has nowhere to go, except to move back to d4. And that's the end!" burst out Alma. "The other knight deals the final blow: f5, checkmate! We've won!"

The two old men clapped to congratulate her, almost causing Alma to tumble down from Farthing's shoulders. Drifter hummed in admiration.

"Alma, you are so clever!" sighed Bella, and gave her first half-smile since they had entered the room.

Farthing gestured for them to help Alma down from his shoulders. When she was back on the ground the others looked at her questioningly.

"So what happens now? What do we do next?"

Since nobody had any better ideas, Baker tried the eight doors again, but they were still all locked. The chess pieces didn't come to life, and the room was filled with quiet and calm. Alma's brilliant solution seemed not to have changed anything.

"But there must be some solution," mused Alma. "The key must be in our hands, we just have to interpret what we can see. Let's think over what Lord Dharma said. 'Chess is like life, and life imitates chess.'"

Drifter shrugged.

"Okay, let's see if we can apply the chess position to ourselves. I suppose there's the same number of white pieces as there are of us. Or at least there would be if Felix were here."

"And what do you think that means?" Alma raised her eyebrows.

"I don't know. Maybe it's just a coincidence."

"Not necessarily!" Alma's eyes sparkled. "I captured the rook in the penultimate move, that was the only way I could give mate. And just an hour ago we brought down Lord Dharma's bastion. The same thing happened on the chessboard as in real life. We destroyed his system of defence."

"Does that mean you are the knight?" wondered Drifter.

"Maybe we shouldn't take it so literally. I can't actually ride a horse. But there are three of us here now, I mean, three from our original group, and I made three moves with the knight. Felix isn't here, so the fourth move was made with the other knight. So the knights solved the problem."

"What about us?" asked Baker, somewhat indignantly.

"Perhaps you are the two bishops. Reliable and indispensable pieces. In this particular case they didn't move but they provided the cover by standing next to each other. That's fairly true of you too."

"Okay, what about the pawn and the king?" asked Drifter.

"The pawn isn't a noble piece, it's more like a peasant, isn't it?" asked Bella. "Because Katalina is a peasant girl, that's what they said in the village. Maybe she is our pawn. If she is, then we really do have to find her!"

"I can see you miss her," smiled Alma. "Yes, if we really do have to fight, we'll need her too."

"So we're still missing the king."

"We're bound to find him sooner or later. Providing we've interpreted the problem correctly."

They exchanged puzzled glances. It was one thing to solve a chess problem and work out theoretical explanations of who is represented by which piece, but quite another to transfer all that into practice. The solution might appear to be correct, but what good was it if the doors stayed locked? And locked they were. Baker tugged at the handles for the third time, but to no avail. Alma looked at the chessboard again. Could she have given mate in a different way? She certainly couldn't see any other solution. Bella sighed deeply.

"It was so easy at the beginning, when at the entrance to the castle we realized that the initial letters open the door."

"Yes, that was a great idea," nodded Drifter. "Pity there are no letters here."

"Actually, there are," said Alma. "Every square has a letter and a number, and that's how we notate each move, with a letter and a number. Let's go over the moves I made to give checkmate: d2, b3, a5, f5.

"That's crazy!" shouted Drifter. "Those are our initials again! Drifter, Bella, Alma, Felix: d, b, a, f. Plus, it was the other knight that moved to the f square, so that corresponds to Felix."

"Right, let's see if we can open the doors like this!" instructed Alma in excitement. "First I moved to d2, so Drifter, your door is the second one, then I moved to b3, so Bella's is the third, and mine is the fifth."

The children rushed to the doors, turned the handles, and to their astonishment, this time it worked. All of them could open the door Alma had chosen on the basis of the chess moves. The other doors remained shut. They weren't even surprised when they changed places and stood in front of someone else's door to see the door slam shut.

"Well then?" asked Drifter.

"Everyone go through their own door. Hopefully we'll meet up again on the other side, like we did at the entrance."

"What about us?" asked Baker in a whining voice

"Go with Bella, if the castle lets you. And take good care of her if we don't meet up on the other side!"

"Alma, what will happen if we go to different places on the other side?" asked Bella with a sniffle, hugging the taller girl with all her might.

Alma released herself from the embrace, took both of Bella's hands and looked seriously into her eyes.

"The most important thing, Bella, is not to be afraid! It's clear now: we have to fight Lord Dharma, it's the only way to get home. We have to put together our team, and find the battlefield. If we are brave, and keep to the right path, we'll be bound to find it. After all even Lord Dharma wants us to, and so far that's been the point of every test. In other words, there's nothing to be afraid of. Go where your heart leads you. Be brave, and always remember, we'll meet up at the end. Felix, Drifter, you, and I, and hopefully Katalina, we'll fight the great battle once and for all – together!"

At Alma's words the worry vanished from Bella's face. She glanced at her older companions as she stepped determinedly to the open door. Baker and Farthing followed her obediently, like two old guard dogs.

"I see, Alma. I won't be scared. I hope we meet up soon!" Bella waved at them.

"Be careful though!" said Alma as they went. Then she looked questioningly at Drifter, who nodded in reply. There was nothing left to say. When he stepped towards his own door, he remembered Saller's favourite saying.

"Keep your chin up, while you've still got one!" he winked at Alma, then he too stepped into the unknown.

XIII. IN THE LABYRINTH

Drifter was uneasy as he stepped through the second door. Even though since the beginning of their adventure he had been the one who best accepted and understood the odd events and rules of this new world, right now he didn't feel remotely at ease. It was pie in the sky to hope they would meet on the other side of the door. His path led somewhere completely different from the others, and it wasn't at all to his liking that they had had to split up. True, generally he didn't mind being alone, and even at school he usually sat apart. If he could he sat alone on one of the back rows, and didn't even need the others' company in the breaks. He stuck his earphones in his ears, let his matted hair droop over his face, and allowed the others to get on with their lives without him.

It was no coincidence he liked the name Drifter. He enjoyed the independence and the distance that separated him as an outsider from his classmates. He liked being alone and spending his time as he pleased, getting lost in the fantasy world of computer games and letting the adventures carry him this way and that. The only time he felt at home with other people was with his skateboarding friends, though even then Drifter had no desire to speak to them about anything else; practising jumps and stunts provided quite enough human contact.

Now though, he suddenly felt lonely and forlorn. He wasn't

scared, but he had to admit it was a fretful business being alone in this place, which was like an enchanted castle from fairy tales. It would be good to meet up with the others as soon as possible. So far his keen intuition had warned him every time of approaching danger, but now he sensed no ill in the air, so he wasn't particularly worried. Deep down he felt that neither he nor his companions were in immediate mortal danger.

The door led into a completely windowless, deserted, gloomy passage. After a few metres the passage branched out. Drifter set off first in one direction, then the other, but he found that both passages soon led to another crossroads that also forked out. There was no sign or pattern to help in orientation, and Drifter soon realized he had walked into a labyrinth. He tried to get back to his starting point, to mark at least the position of the door, but it was no use: he couldn't find it. In other words, he was already lost in the maze, or more likely, the door had simply disappeared after he had walked through it.

Ideas raced through Drifter's mind. He remembered from history lessons the legend of Ariadne, the daughter of the king of Crete, who gave a golden thread to her sweetheart Theseus, so he could find his way out of the labyrinth after he had killed the bloodthirsty Minotaur, a monster with the head of a bull.

"I hope there's no wild brute at the middle of this maze," thought Drifter, and swallowed hard to get rid of the sudden lump in his throat. "Actually I could do with a ball of string, so at least I can find my way back to the starting point," he thought, but then, crestfallen, tossed the idea aside. Since the door had disappeared, there was no point talking about a starting point. Why would he want to go back there anyway?

Then he remembered a computer game where after losing several lives he ended up in a system of continually forking passages. The graphic artist who designed the game must have had a gruesome sense of humour, because he had filled the labyrinth with spiders, rats, and human skeletons. Drifter was glad that here in the castle he didn't have to face any such horrors. At least not yet.

"But it would be reassuring to think I had a few lives left," he muttered to himself. "Blow it. I'll just have to make do and look after the one I've got."

But which way should he go? Every fibre in his body cried out against just wandering blindly at random in the completely identical passages, and leaving his fate to chance. Then he had an idea. If he touched the right hand wall with his right hand while he walked, and kept it on the wall all the time, sooner or later he would walk his way round the whole labyrinth. After all, unless the system was infinite, in the end you could walk all through it. Of course it was time-consuming, because he had to go round every single corner, but at least he could avoid going back to the same place without realizing it. Just to be on the safe side, he put a paper tissue on the floor so that he'd notice if he did come back that way. Then he set off.

He went resolutely on his way, keeping his right hand on the wall all the time. He felt that hours had passed, when he remembered he could check the time on his phone. He was shocked when he saw he'd only been wandering in the labyrinth for forty minutes.

An idea flashed to him: "Perhaps if I'd set off in a different direction, I'd already be out of the maze," but he dismissed the thought. It was utterly pointless to let such insoluble and uncertain questions bother him.

"What happened to the others?" he wondered.

He reckoned that Bella was relatively safe alongside Baker and Farthing. Alma was fairly sharp and clever; she'd probably be able to look after herself. Drifter caught himself thinking admiringly of her stamina, determination and commitment. What's more, she could communicate with everyone! She protected Bella, and chatted happily with the village folk, the two old men, and even Felix. The words of the chess piece with Lord Dharma's face suddenly struck him. "You're lonely, not independent!" He shook his head despairingly: actually there was much truth in this. The price he paid for always being an outsider was loneliness, and not belonging to anyone.

Felix, on the other hand, had oodles of friends. Even though he looked down on people, even though he was sometimes quick to get angry and intolerable, he was the centre of attention surrounded by friends, girls as well as boys. He was the one that Katalina first spoke to, and at school even the girls from Year 7 spoke to him. At this point in his train of thought, Drifter involuntarily jerked his shoulders. He, for one, wasn't jealous of Felix's popularity. He didn't need his friendship either. He was quite happy to be spared Felix's stinging comments. But all the same, it would be good to know what had happened to him. Although he'd been pretty unfriendly all the time, you had to admit, he had behaved bravely all along, even in the greatest danger.

Drifter shuddered slightly. It was one thing to risk your life, be chased by monsters, solve impossible problems, or wander through a labyrinth in a computer game, but completely different in real life, where something was really at stake with every move.

At this point in his train of thoughts, he heard a strange scuffling noise nearby, like a mixture of birds cheeping and rustling their wings. Astounded, Drifter stared towards where the sounds were coming from. The sound of birdsong inside an endless, deserted labyrinth seemed totally unbelievable. He was about to lose contact with the wall to go and look for the bird, when he realized that this could be a trap, another trick by the master of the castle, to distract him from his path and render his efforts so far. So he took out his last paper tissue, tore it up, and rolled it into small pellets, so he could mark his way with the little white balls. If he couldn't find the bird, at least he could continue the path from where he had let go of the wall.

"If it worked for Hansel and Gretel, it'll work for me" he thought smugly.

The precaution turned out to be unnecessary. He soon found the source of the song: after turning a few corners he reached a

hall where he saw a strange bird in a cage hanging from the wall. In size and shape it best resembled a blackbird, but it was white all over, and its tail-feathers seemed to have been borrowed from a small white peacock. Drifter rubbed his eyes. He felt as though he had stepped into a dream. Slowly and carefully, he walked towards the bird. The little creature greeted him, hopping cheerfully in its cage. Drifter looked inside, and noted that the floor was clean, and the bird seemed to have enough fresh water and food. It was short of nothing. He examined the cage more carefully, and saw that it had no door, as if the bird inside had been condemned to lifelong imprisonment.

Drifter felt a strong urge to help the poor animal, so he tried to unhook the cage from the wall. Then he had his next surprise: the cage was fixed to the stone wall, and he couldn't move it at all. The bird, which seemed to have understood his intention, began to sing. Drifter had often felt that animals wanted to convey messages to him, and what's more, on this strange day he had had several encounters with strangely behaving birds. He grasped the new situation at once. He looked expectantly at the bird and listened to its "message". He heard only the usual birdsong, but he felt that the small white songbird was encouraging him to continue his journey alone.

When he looked around to see which way to go, he saw three identical doors. He could have sworn that when he entered the hall, they hadn't been there. Drifter moved hesitantly towards the doors, although he was convinced he'd find all three of them locked. All the greater was his surprise, then, when he reached the wall and the three doors opened one by one, as if they had been struck by a magic wand. He looked into each of the openings, and was more uncertain than ever.

One led into a vast plain, where there were neither trees nor bushes, only a sizeable windmill nearby. On the other side of the second door a crystal-clear mountain stream was babbling away, with a narrow plank stretching over it. Through the third doorway he saw a field of sunflowers, guarded by a scarecrow with a menacing grin. Drifter had no idea which door to take. All three landscapes seemed friendly enough. But the others were still here in the castle! Having no other source of help, he looked expectantly back at the bird.

The little songster immediately began to sing. Drifter listened attentively. He felt certain that if he heard the same song in a dream, he'd understand every word. But now all he could rely on were his hunches and intuitions.

"Please help me find the others!" he asked, and then he shut his eyes and continued to listen.

The bird sang loud and clear, and suddenly Drifter felt that he had to go through the door on the left, towards the windmill. He closed his eyes, shook himself, said thank you to the snow-white songster, and stepped resolutely over the doorstep of the second exit. The door immediately slammed shut behind him, and judging from the bangs he heard from the right, the other two doors had also closed. Drifter set off resolutely. Now he had made the decision, there was no point hesitating.

He went straight to the windmill. He knocked on the door, but when there was no reply he decided to try and enter unbidden. Perhaps the miller couldn't hear him for the noise of the mill wheels. But before he turned the handle, Drifter stopped and thought. His internal radar, which so far had been at rest, now warned him of a new danger.

"Perhaps I didn't choose the right door after all," he wondered. "I don't even know whether the bird was on my side or not."

But no. While he was listening to the birdsong he had been sure the little songster wanted the best for him. And he could have sworn the song told him of the far left hand door. But perhaps the bird's message had been to avoid that very door, because there was some mortal danger ahead? Drifter shrugged. He was familiar enough with the castle by now to know that there was no point going back to the bird to rethink what he had done. Whatever was waiting for him in this creaking, rattling building, he had to face it.

"Alma would probably say this is just like chess," he thought. "Once you've made a move, you can't retract it. My only chance is to explore this mill and find out what I'm supposed to do."

He took a deep breath and opened the door. At first he didn't understand where he was. All he saw was a poorly lit room with large sacks stacked round the walls. On the left, in the gloom, he could make out the figure of a motionless standing man. Drifter thought the man must be the miller, so he made a polite greeting, and took a step forwards. The door closed behind him with a firm click. Drifter spoke to the man again; he obviously wasn't the chatty type. He still gave no answer, and even his stiff body didn't turn in Drifter's direction.

Only when Drifter had moved right up close did he realize that the figure was not the miller. It was a statue, wearing strange clothes and spectacles, and it was most out of place alongside the sacks of flour against the wall. Drifter looked round again. This time he noticed that the floor of the mill was paved with large black and white flagstones. He pulled a face.

"Surprise, surprise, another chessboard. Trust me to think of that!"

But since there was no sign of chess pieces or a chess problem, he slowly left to explore the inside of the mill. He took a few steps on the chequered stones when he heard a rustling sound behind him on the right. Drifter turned round, hoping that he had found the miller at last. But in horror he saw that a soldier in uniform was approaching him, brandishing an enormous broadsword. Drifter immediately began to back away, but when he turned to run, his feet seemed glued to the spot. More armed men in black uniforms appeared on the other side too. First there were only three of them, but then a fourth stepped from behind the sacks, and he was wearing the royal crest: now all four of them stood before him threateningly, holding swords and spears.

He was shaking, his mouth was dry and his heart was beating so hard he could hardly breathe. He knew the five men in black had come to take his life, and alone and unarmed he stood no chance against them. He tried to say something to them, but his shaking, uncertain voice got no reply. The four figures next to the wall took a step forward, and one of them raised his sword to strike. Drifter instinctively shouted for help, although he knew that nobody could hear him in the deserted plain.

And just to make things worse, the next moment a door opened, one that Drifter hadn't noticed before. In the door appeared another soldier in black.

"Now I've really had it," flashed through Drifter's mind, but then he had a strange feeling.

The last figure to come in was somehow familiar. It was Felix! But how did he get that black uniform, and where did he get the weapons? Had he joined the enemy?

"Felix, help!" shouted Drifter.

Felix halted. Until then, he had gone through the castle thinking that sooner or later he would find the map room, and there he could work out how to find the others. Now he was thrown into the midst of the fray, and had to save Drifter, who should have been somewhere entirely different, and this thoroughly confused him.

He immediately saw that the odds were stacked against his classmate, in fact even the two of them together would be too weak. If he stepped in, he too would probably be killed or seriously wounded. The door he was looking through was still open. Beyond it all was calm and peaceful. He had just a second to decide whether or not to risk his life to save Drifter. Felix did not hesitate. With fiery determination he rushed through the door.

He could see that Drifter was practically paralysed with fright and helplessness, and the soldier closest to him was about to deal a fatal blow. Felix rushed straight toward the attacker, but on the way tossed his spear to his terrified classmate.

"Use this to keep the others away!" he shouted.

The soldier preparing to strike Drifter followed the spear with his eyes, and this broke his concentration for a split-second. This was enough for Felix to charge at him and immobilize him with two enormous blows. The attacker lay on the ground without the faintest resistance. The soldier in the corner with the royal crest was the first to realize what had happened. He took a step toward Felix, but Drifter raised his spear in his direction. The crested enemy stopped dead. Then, as Felix started towards him like an angry wild beast, he instinctively backed into the corner.

The next moment two things happened. The attacker on the far right, who so far had watched bewildered while a private in black attacked an officer of his own team, now came round, and he too began to attack. He must have been one of the cross-bow platoon, because he had arrows and a crossbow with him. He took the bow down from his shoulder to aim it at Felix.

Meanwhile behind Drifter the door through which he had entered the mill suddenly opened again. The sunlight outside, and the quiet, peaceful deserted field beckoned invitingly. Drifter had the chance to run out pell-mell, leaving Felix and the other fighters to their fate. He would just have had time to get out before his enemies realized what had happened. But Drifter had no intention of leaving Felix. Instead he shouted with all his might:

"Felix, behind you!"

Felix turned round immediately, and took three strides towards the archer. Before he could release the arrow in the bow, Felix dealt him a blow, and with his sword gave him such a bash on the head that he fell with a gasp. Meanwhile Drifter used his spear to hold the crested soldier at bay, otherwise he would have rushed to help his mate. But at the same time the soldier behind Drifter was at work. Until now he had watched the battle in bewilderment, but now he brandished his broadsword and prepared to attack. Felix did not wait for the large, muscular man to charge at them. He bent down, picked up the crossbow and arrow lying on the ground, and shot at the attacker. He struck him in the arm. Crying out in pain, the soldier dropped the broadsword, and ran in a cowardly fashion through the open door. The two remaining soldiers quickly weighed things up and decided it was risky to continue the battle against the two enraged boys, so they too ran off.

Drifter and Felix were left alone. Panting for breath, they stared at each other and the two soldiers lying on the ground. It was difficult to say if they had just passed out or actually died from the enormous blows Felix had dealt them. Drifter examined them one at a time. He managed to find a pulse in both of them, but they lay unconscious on the stone. The boys had thousands of questions, but they both knew it would be dangerous to stay any longer in the mill. They looked at each other, and unusually, they were in total agreement.

"Let's clear out of here!" suggested Drifter.

"We can talk it over outside," nodded Felix, as he rubbed his ring finger in pain. The lionhead ring was excruciatingly tight again.

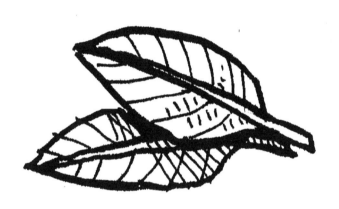

XIV. The Forest of Shadows

When they stepped through the doorway, Bella and the two old men came to a welcoming, sunny passage. There was no sign of Drifter or Alma, but the castle seemed so inviting that they didn't think this unknown area could be dangerous.

"Shall I close the door?" asked Farthing helpfully.

"Yes, sure. We have to go forwards, not backwards." Bella looked at him seriously.

"At last, somewhere cosy," sighed Baker in relief. "Nothing to be scared of!"

Farthing agreed, and he gently closed the door behind them. The next moment, he was fumbling in terror for the door handle, but he was too late. As soon as the door closed, there was a blinding flash of lightning in the passage. The flash of light was followed by complete darkness and a tremendous clap of thunder. Then it got lighter again, but shaken as they were, this just filled them with renewed horror. For in the growing light they could make out the shapes of dense bushes, trees with low-hanging boughs, branches and twigs, and a network of vines. The wall and the door were gone, and in place of the radiant passageway there was a gloomy, uninviting forest.

The two old men were scared to death, and stood shaking next to Bella. It wasn't quite clear whether they wanted to protect her, or if they expected her to soften their terror. But after the sudden change nothing else terrible happened: no people, animals, or other monsters came out of the undergrowth, so the three of them calmed down a little.

"Where do you think we are?" asked Bella.

The ghostly light of the forest and the unnerving silence prompted her to speak in a whisper.

"I've never been here," whispered Baker in a choked voice. "I just hope it's not the Forest of Shadows."

"Oh Baker, don't even say its name, because it will come to life!" said Farthing in horror.

"What is the Forest of Shadows? What do you know about it?" said Bella turning to Farthing.

"Oh, Miss Bella, don't you say it either! That place is the most terrible and most dangerous in the whole world. It is inhabited by frightening monsters. Even the sight of them is unbearable."

"In the castle the word is that nobody gets through the forest alive," said Baker interrupting. "The evil demons and wicked monsters snuff out your life like you would blow out a birthday candle."

"They say that whoever looks at one of the forest's demons becomes a demon himself, and lives on in the forest," added Farthing.

"Let's get out! Let's get out of here!" wailed Baker, and hearing his own words he started trembling with fear.

Bella grew angry as she watched the two old men work themselves into a right old state. It made her furious to see them whining and fearful. She would have liked to take the two of them and give them a good shaking for giving in to fear so easily. Then she remembered that Felix always got angry if things didn't go the way he wanted them to, and at times like that he could be really rude.

"So we seem to have something in common," she thought, then something occurred to her to make her chuckle to herself. "Felix would probably be really irritated if I told him that."

After that, she calmed down. The first unexpected clap of

thunder and the changing landscape had given her a mortal fright too, but now she had pulled herself together. But that's exactly what Alma said! Lord Dharma was putting them to the test, to see if they could find each other and the way out. Most likely, they had arrived in such a frightening place so that they could prove how brave they were.

"This is like in a fairytale," thought Bella resolutely. "The youngest boy never takes fright, and never turns back, but he always helps everyone, and even to the wicked witches he says 'God bless, miss.' Then at the end he always defeats the dragon and wins the princess's hand. I'm not the youngest boy, I'm the youngest girl. But I'll show everyone what I can do."

Bella looked hard at the two old men, who were shuffling nervously, chewing their nails, and shaking with fear.

"Just now you said that nobody had ever survived being in the woods, but you've never been here. Then you said that the creatures here change into wicked demons. Have you ever seen a wicked demon? Because my mum says there's no such thing," announced Bella firmly.

"I haven't seen one yet," admitted Farthing, "but they said that if a demon from the shadow-world looks at you..."

"Oh, get a grip!" interrupted Bella. "That's just hearsay, gossip, to give you something to be scared of! You have to accept that we're going to carry on our journey here. At least I am, whether you come or not! Look, the path leads that way."

Bella's determination stunned the two old men into silence. They exchanged a glance over the little girl's head, shrugged their shoulders, blinked and dutifully set out after Bella, who had already bravely started on the path. She looked neither right nor left, because the quivering of the branches in the dense forest, and the play of the shadows in the gloom really were frightening. Determined though she was, she needed great strength and courage not to turn back. Even more so when the path led through even denser undergrowth, and instead of the rustling and brushing of leaves, they heard scurrying sounds, and the crack of branches breaking under far-off footsteps.

Then from behind one of the trees a tall, slender shadow appeared, much taller than either of the old men, and it darted across the path. Now even Bella's feet stuck fast to the ground. She was scared not so much by the size of the shadow, but that however hard she looked she couldn't see the size of the body that cast it. It really was as if a ghost had flitted before her eyes. Then the forest suddenly came alive. In every direction shadows with sharp pointed ears and long arms appeared, coming closer and closer to the startled threesome.

Baker and Farthing were shaking so hard they almost forgot to breathe. Even Bella felt cold fear slowly choke her body and soul. At the last minute, though, she managed to overcome this feeling. Although she was easily scared, she still retained a child's sure intuition and keen observational skills. She suddenly noticed that something very odd was happening around them. Frightening it may be, but it was so peculiar, it demanded an explanation.

Felix sometimes told her ghost stories and frightening tales, so she knew that ghosts and demons had no physical body. But the enormous shadows here had scurrying footsteps, the leaves and twigs crackled beneath them, so they had real bodies and weight. In fact, they probably had small, feather-weight bodies, because the noise they made was hardly more than that of a squirrel.

Bella peered into the undergrowth to see if she could catch a glimpse of one of the bodies producing the terrible shadows, but Baker and Farthing lost their nerve completely. Their legs were unable to help them escape, but flapping their hands around they sought protection against the monsters. Almost at once they bent over to pick up stones from the ground and throw them into the dark.

"Stop it! Don't hurt them!" shouted Bella. "They might not be wicked!"

But the two terrified tradesmen couldn't be stopped. In a fit

of panic, they flung every branch and stone they could lay their hands on into the dark. Suddenly from the undergrowth they heard a pained whimper, followed by a distressed muttering and a thin yelping sound. Bella could stand it no longer, and grabbed Farthing with both hands.

"Stop it! You'll hit them!"

The little girl's outburst finally had the desired effect, and the old men let their arms drop by their sides. After a moment's silence Bella's timid voice sounded:

"Who is there? Come out! You needn't be scared of us!"

This was met by a flurry of rustling, but the shadows dared not come out any more.

"Don't be scared!" continued Bella. "And please, show yourselves, so that we needn't be scared either!"

The rustling grew louder, then a terrifying black shadow stepped out of the undergrowth. Bella held Farthing's hand, which instinctively rose in the air, aiming for the dark shape. There was a quiet rustle from the forest floor, and Bella carefully stepped forward and crouched down. She could hardly believe her eyes when she saw that the terrifying three-metre shadow belonged to a small common rabbit. The rabbit sniffed continuously at Bella's outstretched hand, and finally touched her with his wet nose.

"So was that terrifying shadow you, then?" said Bella, stroking the rabbit's silky ears.

The rabbit replied with comprehensible words.

"The guardians of the Forest of Shadows are harmless beings. We have never hurt anyone. Yet people approach us fearfully, casting stones and cursing us, sometimes trying to destroy us with fire and sword, or running from us screaming, but nobody ever had the courage to ask who we are and what we are doing."

"Well, who are you, and what are you doing?" asked Bella warmly.

"Beyond the Shadows everyone finds the place they are looking for, where they can be truly themselves. But first they must wrestle with their inner demons, fears, superstitions, and prejudices. Those who cannot, or dare not, see what we are truly like, can never penetrate through the forest."

"Do you frighten everyone at the command of Lord Dharma?" asked Bella curiously.

"The guardians of the Forest of Shadows are the subjects of his lordship. For many hundreds of years Lord Dharma has presided over the law, so it is he we serve. But it was not always thus, and will not remain so for ever. The order of life here is that the victorious rulers succeed one another at the helm of the kingdom. You are a brave child with a pure heart, so you may get through the Forest of Shadows."

"Where does the path lead?"

"Where you wish, or where you most need to go."

"I'd like to find my brother and my companions," said Bella. "But then we have to fight Lord Dharma, otherwise he won't set us free. For that we need to find helpers, weapons, and horses. I don't know how I can help the older ones with this, but I'd like us all to get home in the end."

The rabbit thought for a moment, then nodded his ears in agreement.

"Very well, continue your way. Beyond the Forest of Shadows you will find where you have to go."

"Tell me one thing!" asked Bella. "Explain how a small creature like you can cast such a big shadow!"

The rabbit gibbered in satisfaction.

"I do so like children! You are interested in all sorts of things. Only he can know the world who remains forever curious."

"Well then?" asked Bella with mounting excitement.

"We have an ointment. It's a simple charm, any sorceress can mix it. All we do is rub it into the base of our ears, and the shadows grow larger."

"Wow, I'd like to try that!" gasped Bella.

She imagined what fun it would be to invite her friends over, and prance round the garden with an enormous shadow, or to give Felix a fright one evening before going to bed.

"The shadow cream is not for your world. But I will give you a small jar, in case you need it while you are roaming through our world."

Then from the folds in his coat the rabbit pulled out a tiny jar, gave it to Bella, and with a hop and a jump disappeared into the ferns. When Bella straightened up, the Forest of Shadows had changed. The undergrowth opened up for the travellers, the impenetrable bushes changed to shrubs, the dark sombre trees now had branches with bright green foliage, and the dark gloom was dispersed. The sun shone in the sky, radiating warmth, and almost immediately beads of sweat formed on Farthing's brow.

There was no trace now of small animals or thick forest, and even the castle which had held them all captive had vanished. Beyond the shrubs was a vast grassy plateau, specked with a few distant clusters of trees. The sweet fragrance of the wild flowers in the field beckoned to the three travellers. Bella examined the little jar the rabbit had given her, then popped it into her pocket, and smiled at the two men.

"Off we go then!"

Baker and Farthing were brimming over with thanks for Bella's cleverness and courage. Now, heartened and encouraged, they continued the journey. When they emerged from the trees they stopped to survey the wide meadow. There was no sign of any man-made building, and the only figure they could make out in the distance seemed to be a scarecrow. Bella looked about, perplexed. The rabbit had promised they would arrive where they needed to, but this large field offered no clues. She couldn't imagine what business they might have there, in this uninhabited countryside, or who they might meet. Then she remembered that in the story of The Wizard of Oz, one of Dorothy's companions had been a scarecrow.

"I don't think I'll meet a scarecrow, a lion, or a tin man, but maybe this is some kind of sign," she thought, and set off determinedly toward the figure in the distance. "Anyway, what on earth is he protecting on this meadow? There's no grapevine and no crops to scare the birds away from. Come to think of it, there aren't even any birds."

Bella's curiosity grew as she walked towards the strange figure, who had his back to the three travellers. The two old men followed Bella like faithful dogs. As they drew near the figure, they noticed he was wearing rags and his arms were spread out. Farthing noticed that a bit further on was a garden surrounded by a poorly made makeshift fence. As far as they could see, inside the fenced-off area the grass grew just as everywhere else on the meadow. It wasn't really a garden, just an empty fold with no animals. In place of a straw hat the scarecrow wore an angular helmet, and seemed to be guarding the fold.

The figure stood motionless in the distance, with his back towards the threesome from the forest. But when Bella and the others came close to him, he suddenly turned round. This surprised them so much, they were rooted to the ground. The scarecrow looked at the three of them as if he were seeing an unearthly vision, and couldn't decide whether to be frightened or just surprised. For Baker, Farthing, and even Bella, their hearts missed a beat when the figure they assumed to be a dummy suddenly turned to them. Bella breathed deeply to calm her racing heart, and remembered that in fairytales, after the first shock the first thing to do was to offer a polite greeting to people we meet. So she spoke to the scruffy man.

"Hello, Mister Stranger. We are peaceful travellers, and we come in friendship!"

The helmeted scarecrow gaped in wonder at the small girl's tinkling voice. His features softened, and clumsily and reservedly, he approached them.

"Well now, do my eyes see right, or is the light playing tricks on me? Can it really be that a little girl-child and two mature fellows have come to pay me a visit?"

"It's not a trick of the light!" Bella assured him. "My name's Bella, and these are my friends, Baker and Farthing. We're looking for our companions. Have you seen two boys and a girl this way? They're a bit bigger than me but in the same kind of clothes," added Bella, when she noticed the look of bewilderment as the scarecrow eyed her jeans and patterned T-shirt.

"I haven't seen a living person this way for many years," croaked the scarecrow in a voice so hoarse it sounded as though he really hadn't spoken to anyone for years. "I am a prisoner in this realm, and I cannot escape until I get my horse back."

"What kind of horse?" asked Bella with a sparkle in her eye.

The strange figure took another step towards Bella, and looked intently into her eyes, as if to decide whether he could trust her with the secret. His blue eyes were surrounded by deep wrinkles, his tousled grey hair poked out from under his helmet, and his straggling pointed beard dangled sorrily on his protruding chin. His eyebrows shot up, the furrows on his brow deepened, he took a deep breath, and began to explain.

"My name is Don Espolín, I am a knight errant, and a chess aficionado. One fine day a man dressed in black stood before me on the road, and invited me to a game. I accepted the challenge, for more than anything, I like to play chess. I tied my horse, Tempest, but I was too lazy to unharness him. I was interested only in the game, and the dark-clothed opponent with the peculiar look. The game started out well, but then I made an error, and my opponent gained a great advantage. In the sultry heat we sipped wine from Malaga, and, perhaps somewhat inebriated, my thoughts drifted elsewhere for a moment. When I came round, there was no sign of the chessboard, nor the opponent set to win, nor the familiar landscape. I woke up next to a village I had never seen, and that is when my trials began. Tempest, my horse, had broken free, and was galloping away towards a distant castle. The village folk set me on the right road, and said the lord of the castle, one Lord Dharma, would surely put me up for one night and send me on my way. I got into the fortified building, and there I found the dark lord of the castle. I could hardly believe my eyes when I recognized him as the man I had played my last game of chess with. Outraged, I demanded an explanation, but he laughed at me. He said he would help me to get home if I found my horse and accepted the challenge of another game. But how would I find Tempest? On that he was completely silent."

"I started to roam about the castle, I looked into about a hundred rooms, when finally behind one of the doors I heard whinnying. I stepped in, and a herd of horses galloped towards me. At the back of the herd was Tempest, with saddle upturned, and harness awry. I tried to stop him, but he didn't notice. His eyes seemed to flash bolts of lightning, and his body was practically foaming with sweat. When I stepped towards him the door behind me closed, and ever since I have been on this meadow. It has been years. I've grown familiar with the ways of the horses, but I cannot harness Tempest. The herd gallop this way every afternoon, round the wood they come, and away they dash. Tempest doesn't recognize me, or pretends not to. Fair enough, I wasn't a good master. Sometimes I treated him badly. And now I am stuck here for ever without him."

"Did you build this fold?" Bella pointed to the ramshackle fence.

"Yes, it took me years to collect and strip the trees that had fallen over in the forest. I bound them together with vines and wedges, using no tools. I hoped that once I had driven Tempest in there, perhaps I'd be able to win him over to me again. But horses are wily beasts, they're always a step ahead of me. If I stand in front of them, they go round me, and before I know it they've galloped away. I can't harness my unbridled horse alone."

"Perhaps if we helped you, you might manage," suggested Bella. "If several of us stand in the way of the herd, perhaps we'd manage to separate a few horses. Does Tempest have his own place in the herd?"

"Yes, he always gallops at the back, next to a grey mare. They seem to have become good pals."

"When will they next come this way?" asked Bella excitedly.

Don Espolín looked up at the sky to work out what time it was from the position of the sun.

"In a good hour's time," he said finally.

"Then we've still got time!" Bella stood up straight. "Baker and Farthing, you'll help, won't you? We have to chop some branches to help drive Tempest into the fold. And we need a young tree to block the exit once the horse is inside. Come on, let's get to work!"

Baker and Farthing dutifully set off to the closest group of trees, but they heard clearly as Don Espolín expressed his thanks to Bella in a quavering voice.

"My dear young lady, surely you have been sent by heaven to help me! Allow me to be your grateful knight-protector forevermore!"

XV. THE WHITE QUEEN

Alma stepped through her own door with an anxious heart. She wasn't happy about leaving the others, and was genuinely concerned about Bella. Fair enough, with Baker and Farthing she wouldn't feel so lost, and the two older men would certainly protect her from all dangers, but the knowledge that she had had to leave this small girl alone in the hostile castle, in this strange world, was decidedly worrying. Felix and Drifter were fairly independent and had enough nous to avoid trouble, but a child of her age wouldn't necessarily notice all the dangers, or might unwittingly ignore a sign.

"I must trust Bella," thought Alma, "and I have to trust her companions to help her. Bella promised she wouldn't be scared. And if she isn't scared, I mustn't be either. I have to trust that soon we will find each other, and together we'll fight our way out of this situation. Actually, I have to trust myself most of all, otherwise I won't be able to combat Lord Dharma. If I let him deter me, I won't believe that I can defeat him."

In spite of being so determined, she could feel her stomach tighten as she thought of all the uncertainties. It wasn't easy to believe that a hopeless situation would resolve itself. And it was even more difficult to believe that a handful of children would be capable of defeating a well-equipped, cunning, powerful opponent on unfamiliar territory, in an alien world, without any help.

Alma took a deep breath and screwed up her courage. Ever since starting to play chess, many times she had had to pit her strength and skills against better trained, older opponents. And she came out victorious: the skill won through countless practice sessions, the courage and confidence that she was able to win, had so far usually helped her to find the right solution. From time to time of course it happened that she lost a game, but mostly she was able to conquer her fear, and find the path to victory in most situations.

Lord Dharma said that chess is like life, and life imitates chess. In real life she would never be able to overcome a strong grown man, but playing by the rules of chess, a small girl could indeed overpower an adult. If the lord of the castle wanted to fight, so be it. They would just have to be careful not to break the rules of chess, because if the field of play became a real battlefield, they would be done for.

"The most important thing, then, is to find my companions, weapons, and the place where we can fight out the chess war for real. Since the others don't know how to play, I'll have to command the battle," thought Alma to herself. "I'll be the commander of our forces, one of the players in the game. But I won't be moving chess pieces; I'll be commanding real live fighters."

A shiver went up her spine. It was difficult to imagine shouting orders to Felix, or commanding Drifter where to go and what to do.

"And what if they don't follow my orders?" she wondered. "Felix has such a temper. And Drifter is a law unto himself. Some of my moves might seem madness to them. Will they still do what I ask? They won't have any choice. If they don't trust me, all is lost."

She powered forward determinedly. The passage was bleak and desolate, and her footsteps echoed clearly on the stone walls. No doors or windows led off the corridor, there was no fork in the passage. It seemed as though the route forward had been mapped out for her in advance. Alma plodded on resolutely, like a commander of troops. Now and again she was niggled by the thought that in the echoing passage she wouldn't hear if a shady figure started to follow her, and the thought gave her goosepimples. But this was just the prompting of fear, which was continually in the back of her mind. Alma decided she wasn't going to let it get the better of her. The more she was tormented by the idea someone might be following her, the more firmly she looked ahead, and resolutely refused to look behind her. On she went, unflinchingly.

After a while she simply wasn't scared any more. She had been wrestling with the anxiety for so long she felt she didn't care about it any more. The goosepimples disappeared from her arms and back, and her heart was no longer pounding. That was when she noticed the door. There it was at the end of the passage, painted plain brilliant white. Alma stepped forwards calmly. She knew she had to go through it, and she also knew that inside another test awaited her. But she wasn't scared or worried. She didn't even wonder what kind of challenge she would have to face. She simply focussed on being able to make the right decision at the right moment.

She didn't even stop as she drew close to the door. She felt sure that this time it wouldn't be locked. She pressed the handle, and the door opened silently before her. Alma found herself in a bright, shining, snow-white room. The windows were hung with net curtains, through which shone the beams of the afternoon sun, shedding a warm light over the room's simple furniture: a bed covered with white brocade, a huge mirror, and a small table on which there was a carefully made chessboard, with pieces of ethereal delicacy.

Alma shut the door behind her without thinking. She knew she wouldn't escape from here. Whatever was in here, she would face it. But for the moment, there was nothing. The room was empty, though it gave the feeling of a place the cleaners had left just a moment ago, after changing the bedding and finishing dusting the furniture. In the opposite wall was another brilliant white door, with an ornamental frame.

Alma walked around, examining everything thoroughly. First she went to the opposite door, to check whether that was open too. She wasn't remotely surprised to find it locked. She knew for sure that she wasn't going to leave the white room yet. She stopped for a moment in front of the bed to stroke the invitingly soft bedspread. She glanced in the mirror, but instead of her own reflection she was much more interested in what challenge this white room held. She went on, and settled down next to the small table.

On the chessboard the pieces were in an interesting position.

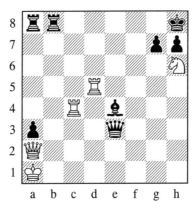

Alma instinctively began to think how she could solve the problem. Although Black had an advantage of three pawns, she hoped she'd be able to give mate with White. But it seemed far from simple. Alma immersed herself completely in solving the problem, the cogs of her brain whirred away, and her face went red from concentration. Finally, she found the solution. It was a pickle of a problem. In order for her to defeat Black, who already had a numerical advantage, White had to sacrifice almost all its pieces.

Alma played the game out, mobilizing her pieces one by one against the enemy, who steadily cut them down. First she moved the rook from c4 to c8, as bait for the opponent's rook. He captured it immediately. Then she moved the rook on d5 to d8, to face the firing squad. Black took this piece too with his rook. Alma now pushed the white queen across to g8, next to the black king. Check. Black had no choice but to take the white queen, who had come too close to the fire. This could not be done by the king, but the rook on d8 dealt the blow. The white queen was removed from the board, but this way the black rook on g8 prevented the king from moving at all. Now the time had come for the white knight! One jump to f7, and the battle was over. Checkmate. And Alma knew that this particular kind of victory was called smothered mate.

After this mental exertion, she sighed and leaned backwards. It hadn't been an easy game. Still nothing happened, so she suddenly felt like looking at herself in the mirror. There hadn't been a chance at Katalina's house, and even combing her hair had been perfunctory, running her fingers through her tousled locks. Now, she stood before the mirror, relinquishing with mixed feelings the vanity of teenage girls. Obviously she wouldn't be at her best, and would probably look awful in clothes she'd been wearing for two days, unkempt, but somewhere within she was tickled by curiosity and the hope that she would see herself as beautiful.

It was a strange feeling to look in the mirror. It was as if, on the shiny, polished surface, an invisible curtain had been drawn between her real self and her reflection: the Alma in the mirror seemed faint and mysterious. In fact, she looked a little taller and older, more like an adult woman, than Alma really was. Alma looked at her reflection and screwed up her eyes. This was a strange mirror. It gave you the feeling it was slowly transforming your whole being. It looked as if her hair were getting longer, and her clothes... Amazing! On her chest there grew armour decorated with silver scrollwork, and her curls slid obediently beneath a veil, which was fixed to her forehead by a silver crown. She became taller and slender in build, and her snow-white clothes seemed to enclothe a regal figure; her waist was encircled by a diamond-encrusted belt from which hung a dagger in an ornamented sheath.

In a few minutes, her reflection had changed from an ordinary girl from the city into a beautiful armed woman. Alma rubbed her eyes. The resplendent white queen in the mirror looked her straight in the eye. Although she too rubbed her eyes, her movements were noble and graceful.

"This isn't me," mumbled Alma doubtfully.

"It's not you, and yet you see yourself," said the mirror queen with a cold gaze. She continued to bear Alma's features. "You will command the troops, if you take up the challenge. You shall be the white queen in battle, do not delude yourself!"

"We're not on the battlefield yet," retorted Alma stubbornly, who was less and less enamoured of her reflection.

"You are not on the battlefield yet, but now is when you must decide if you will be able to engage in combat, to fight, and if necessary, to sacrifice your army for ultimate victory."

"Any chess piece can be sacrificed for the sake of checkmate!"

"For sure, for sure," chuckled the white queen mockingly. "But don't forget, my angel, that chess is like life. Are you prepared to sacrifice your companions, if the situation so dictates? And how do you feel about sacrificing the queen? As you well know, at times, that is what is required."

Alma's gaze fell to the chessboard. Next to the board stood the two rooks and the queen, which she had been forced to sacrifice in solving the problem. They had all, metaphorically, been felled on the battlefield, and there were no survivors but the white king and the last knight, which had finally decided the outcome of the battle.

"Will you also be capable of this in reality? Can you do the same thing, if the rook is one of your classmates, or the little girl who so loves horses? Are you strong enough and determined enough for this?" asked the queen in the mirror. Alma felt an ice-cold shiver run right through her at the sound of the

razor-sharp voice.

She pursed her lips and looked angrily into the mirror. She could not allow herself to be put off by subterfuge and plotting! The white queen wanted to break her resolve, to plant the seeds of fear and doubt in her heart, but she girded herself against this. An anxious player was not capable of victory. Alma tried to pull herself together and order her thoughts.

"We must set down the rules of the battle, so that whoever enters into combat knows what they are taking on. But if sacrifices are necessary for victory, then I will make them. Even sacrificing the queen!" she said determinedly.

Upon these words the image of the queen in the mirror slowly faded, and once more she was looking at the familiar Alma in jeans. She collapsed onto the bed with a relieved sigh, but immediately jumped up again, because something hard was poking into her side. She reached down to touch it, and cried out in shock. The uncomfortable spike was the handle of a dagger, which hung at her side from a belt encrusted with diamonds. The weapon of the queen in the mirror was now hanging from the real Alma's waist.

The white door opposite, which had so far been locked, now suddenly opened. A man dressed in black clothes with a black hat and a stern face stepped in. Alma recognized him immediately. In the previous room, where she had had to part from the others, this was the face on the black chess pieces!

"Lord Dharma!" she exclaimed, startled, but then gained control of herself. "So we meet at last!"

"Well, I see you have accepted the challenge," replied Lord Dharma, and cast a pointed glare at the dagger hanging from Alma's belt. "You are not scared of battle, and you do not fear losses. Excellent. I am beginning to believe you might be a worthy opponent for me."

"Actually, I would prefer to do battle with you on the chessboard! I don't want to put my friends in danger."

"You came into my world together, so you must prove

yourselves together. These are the rules."

"And when the battle is over, can we go home?"

"That depends on whether you stand your ground. But one thing I promise! If you defeat me, I shall grant your wish, whatever it may be."

"Even that all four of us can go home?"

"I shall grant any wish," said Lord Dharma seriously. "But only one. And I have another condition. If you win, and I keep my word, you too shall grant my wish."

"I don't quite understand," said Alma shaking her head. "You said that if I win, it is your decision whether or not we can go home, in other words we will still be at your mercy. How can you ask me to grant you anything? I have no power in this world."

Lord Dharma frowned for a while before speaking.

"You will understand this too, when the time comes."

"Very well," nodded Alma, then suddenly she thought of something that made her blush like a beetroot. "I hope you're not going to ask me to marry you or anything like that!"

Lord Dharma made no reply, but looked at the small blond girl. Finally he said:

"Don't forget, you are still very far from victory! You cannot stand against me in combat without a complete army and equipment. Go then! For the battle begins tomorrow at dawn. If you are there, we shall measure our forces. But if you do not appear on the battlefield with your team, you shall never see home again!"

"Where can I find my companions?" asked Alma somewhat alarmed.

"Where you seek them," came the enigmatic answer.

"At least tell me where the battlefield is!"

"A good commander finds where to mobilize the troops."

"I see. I have to work everything out myself," nodded Alma. "I have just one question. Is there really a lion fountain in the middle of the castle, from which the water of life runs? A friend's grandpa is in great need of it. Please, give us one glass of it!"

Lord Dharma's face darkened.

"Only those chosen by me can drink of the water from the lion fountain."

"Katalina's grandpa is dying!" said Alma in a choked voice. "Please give him some! You must help him!"

"Do not tell me what to do!" snapped Lord Dharma. "And yet, if you defeat me in battle, you may ask me for the water of life as a reward. For you know, I promised I would grant a request. Just one!"

With that, Lord Dharma turned on his heels and left. The white door slammed behind him. Alma collapsed on the bed, buried her face in her hands, and thought. She tried to think what to do next. Where to go, which way? How would she find the others before dawn, and how would she find other helpers?

Whatever happened, she had to try. She stood up, and made towards the door through which Lord Dharma had left. But before she got to it, the door opened once again, though this time it was not the lord of the castle she saw. Two figures in black entered. One was squat and plump, the other lanky and bony. At first Alma didn't recognize the two fools they had met in the forest. Before, the two friends had been dressed in blue and red, and their current black clothes made them look far more grave and solemn. They bowed together before Alma, then the taller one began to speak.

"Greetings to the white commander! We have brought to you a gift from our lord and commander. Please accept it, your ladyship!"

The squat figure stepped forward and set a black box on the ground before Alma. This object, decorated with embellishments and carvings, was encased by strong iron bands. There was no padlock, but on the top was a hole for a sizeable key. Before Alma could look to see what was inside, the lanky figure stepped forward to present her with a chess set in a small box. The chess board was painted on either side of the container, which had to be unfolded so that the game could begin. The chess pieces were inside – Alma had heard them rattling as she took the gift. She had a similar chessboard at home too, which she had got from her grandparents when she was in kindergarten.

"In the box you will find everything you need for the battle tomorrow," said the lanky figure after bowing again.

"You won't need the chess board, it's just a present," added the portly man.

"But there's a message to go with it!" said the taller fool, raising his long, crooked finger. "Lord Dharma sends this to remind you that in the realm of chess, the key to success is always in your hands."

All of a sudden Alma didn't know how to respond, but the two men obviously didn't expect a reply. They bowed once more, and before Alma could say a word, they left. She would have liked to go after them, to see if she could get some guidance or help, but the door closed, and Alma could not open it.

Since there was nothing else to do, she began to inspect the box, but she was disappointed to find that the lid was locked shut, and Lord Dharma's messengers had given no key. Just to be sure, she opened the chess set, but there too she found no key to the box, only sixteen white chess pieces, and the same number of black ones. Alma sighed deeply. For the moment the gift was of little use. She searched the white room high and low for the key to the lock, looking in every nook and cranny, and in all the pleats in the bedclothes, but to no avail: she could not work out how to open the box which allegedly held equipment necessary for the battle. She even thought of picking the lock with the dagger hanging from her waist, but all her attempts met with failure.

"If the worst comes to the worst, I'll have to look for a saw to cut the wood open," thought Alma defiantly, and she decided that she would set off to look for her companions with the box under her arm, and keep her eyes peeled in case she found some instrument to open the trunk on the way.

But the door remained closed, and she couldn't manage to

open the other exit either. Alma plopped down on the white bed with another sigh. It seemed as though she would have to work out how to open the box here and now.

XVI. The Reunion

Getting out of the windmill was far from a simple business. Drifter and Felix tried and tugged at the two doors through which they had entered, but they wouldn't budge. After the black soldiers had run off, both exits had slammed so firmly they couldn't be coaxed open with words or prised open with brute force, but there was no other way to get out of the room. The boys looked at one another, nonplussed. Finally Felix pointed to the back corner:

"There's nothing here but these sacks, this daft statue and that cupboard. Let's have a look to see if we can find some keys or some kind of clue."

When they opened the cupboard, out fell a chessboard. Strangely, one of the white pieces was fixed to it. Perhaps someone had deliberately glued it there, or nailed it, because the board and the piece were made of wood.

"Rats. If we're supposed to play chess, we'll be stuck here for ever," scowled Drifter. "I can't play at all. I only just know the moves."

"I'm no good either. Anyway, there's nothing else here," said Felix pouting. "Even the pieces are missing."

Apart from the piece stuck to the board, which seemed to be a king, there were two white and five black pieces in the cupboard.

"Huh, these aren't much good!" grumbled Felix with a flick of the wrist. "Let's have a look around to see if we can find a secret door behind the sacks!"

They looked and searched for a good ten minutes, heaving all the bags of flour around with all their might, but they found no secret exit. All they found was another stone statue, lying on its side behind the sacks, covered in flour, dust, and cobwebs. It seemed that apart from the two closed doors, there was apparently no way of leaving the place. Felix got so angry that he gave one of the doors a mighty kick.

"Don't!" warned Drifter. "Remember how sensitive it is!"

Felix nodded. He had to acknowledge Drifter was right: he had lost control of himself again.

"Hey, let's do what Alma suggested!" said Drifter after thinking. "She said we have to analyse what happened so we can identify our strong and weak points."

"Working out what we are good or bad at isn't going to make the door open," protested Felix, but Drifter persisted.

"Then let's at least talk over what happened in the fight, just in case we come across something that helps. Maybe we saw something out of the corner of our eye on the wall, but now we don't remember."

"You watch too many adventure films, mate," said Felix scathingly. All the same, he watched with interest as Drifter set the chessboard in front of him and stood the figures next to each other at the edge of the board.

"Let's say this board is the room, after all the flagstones are chequered," began Drifter. "The piece stuck to the board could be that statue in the corner."

He picked up one of the white pieces – a bishop.

"This is me, and I came from this direction. First I went over to the statue, then when I went on, I noticed the guy brandishing the broadsword."

Drifter placed the white bishop somewhere in the middle of the board, then took a black piece and put that on the board too. Then he tried placing the other four pieces on the other side of the chessboard, distancing them from each other and the wall more or less how it had happened in reality. Felix developed a taste for the game too, and picked up the last white piece, a finely carved rook.

"I must be the white rook! Good job my black uniform confused the attackers for a bit. Now let's see where I came in from!" he said excitedly. "I came into the mill about here, then struck down the first guy right away."

"Wait, first let's put you in the initial position!" said Drifter. "Look, you must have been standing about here when you tossed the spear to me!"

The boys looked proudly at the chess pieces they had positioned. What luck that the number of pieces was the same as the number of participants in the battle.

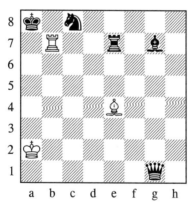

This way it was easy to recall what had happened. They played out how Felix's rook had taken the rook on e7 (or the soldier brandishing the sword), then went back to the king for a moment (the soldier with the royal crest), whom Drifter held in check with the spear, and then ran on to disarm the bishop on g7 (the archer). Finally he struck down the queen on g1, who was the solder with the broadsword.

"As I see it, we didn't manage to give checkmate," Felix said, shaking his head. "Although we are definitely winning. Thanks for not letting the officer with the crown rush after me. He was so brawny he would have flattened me easily."

"I kept him in check with my spear," said Drifter proudly, because looking at the chessboard, his standing there helpless and terrified now seemed a key manoeuvre. "But I should be thanking you. If you hadn't intervened, I might not be alive now."

"Anyway, we survived," muttered Felix. "But what now?"

"Come with me, I shall show you the way out!" said a deep, croaky voice behind them.

The two lads jumped up in terror. At first they thought one of the opponents, whom they had carelessly forgotten to tie up, had come to. But the two soldiers were still lying unconscious on the stone. Incredible though it seemed, the stone statue with glasses had become a man of flesh and blood, and addressed the boys in a deep, other-worldly voice.

"Who are you? How did you get here?" asked Felix suspiciously, as he stepped forward and picked up his sword, which was still lying on the ground. "Don't take a step further, until you answer!"

"I am Thomas Cosinus, mathematician and amateur chess player. Many, many years I have been waiting, as a statue, for the spell to be broken, to become a man once more."

"What spell changed you into stone?" Felix was shocked. "Did Lord Dharma do it?"

"Of course, who else?" said Cosinus spreading his arms in resignation. "Though I was also to blame. I might say that I deserved my punishment."

Seeing the boys didn't quite understand, he began to explain. He told how many years ago a strange miracle had happened when he was with his old friend and chess partner, Ferdinand Vector. They had been playing a particularly exciting game of chess under a pergola, when a storm suddenly blew up, and they found themselves in this strange and hostile world. After they had roamed for miles, some villagers gave them directions and suggested they go to seek Lord Dharma in the castle.

After the castle gate opened for them, they searched for the lord of the castle in vain. From time to time they had a chance to play chess, and strange well-wishers even provided them with food and drink, but one day a terrible thing happened. While roaming around they came to a mill, and they were attacked in much the same way as Drifter and Felix. But both of them were so terrified that they ran for safety, not thinking about what fate awaited the other. They just wanted to save their own skin. But then Lord Dharma appeared, with anger flashing from his black countenance, and with a flick of the wrist he turned both of them into statues. He lay a curse on them, saying they could only return to human form if someone else succeeded where they had failed, and was willing to sacrifice himself for his partner, instead of deserting him.

"If only I knew where my dear friend had got to!" sighed Thomas Cosinus.

"He's lying there behind the sacks!" realized Drifter.

They hurried over to where they had found the overturned statue, pulled the sacks of flour from around him, and helped the shaking, haggard Ferdinand Vector get up, after awakening from a sleep of several decades.

"My dear friend, forgive me!" groaned Ferdinand, and embraced Thomas Cosinus with a shaking arm.

"Forgive me too for my cowardice, Ferdinand!" mumbled the mathematician in a choked voice.

Now it was the boys' turn to explain how they had got into the tight corner, and how frustrated they were at not being able to find the way out. Ferdinand Vector was still a little weary, and hardly understood what they were saying. But the sparkle returned to his eye when he spotted the chessboard on the floor.

"Were you playing?" he asked with interest.

"No, we were just playing out on the board how we overcame the opposition."

"Show me too!" implored the old scientist, who had obviously not yet grasped the fact that the spell was broken, and now he was a captive in a prison with a few others, who were all looking for a way out.

"Well, as we have nothing better to do..." agreed Drifter, and they played out the moves on the chessboard once more. Ferdinand Vector and Thomas Cosinus watched with sheer fascination. Felix was still staring at the locked doors, and he was thinking out loud.

"There's something here I don't get, even less so than the other puzzles. How did I get into this mill? As far as I knew I hadn't even left the castle. But here we are in the middle of a field."

"And why a mill in particular? It might as well have been a barn, a stable, or a church," said Drifter, looking up from the chessboard.

"I'll tell you why!" announced Ferdinand Vector unexpectedly. "You've just shown us! The battle you fought, that broke the spell over us, could only have been fought in a windmill. In chess, windmill is when two pieces, usually a rook and bishop, take many of the opponent's pieces. One of them, in this case Drifter, keeps the king in check, while Felix took out the opponents one by one. It was an exemplary battle, a brave struggle. A perfect windmill."

"All right then. But then we don't need the windmill now, do we?" asked Felix.

The others hummed and nodded. For sure, there was little reason for them to be there. They weren't going to start milling flour. Although so far they hadn't met the miller or seen a mill wheel, and even the deafening grinding noise typical of windmills was completely absent. The whole building seemed to be merely a prop, the scenery for the battle they had just fought.

"Do you hear, windmill? We don't need you any more! Let us out!" Felix straightened up.

His commanding voice rang with determination. To the others' greatest surprise, the wall opposite suddenly creaked, and slid to one side like a sliding door. The exit to the outside world was open. The two elderly men and the boys set out cautiously into the radiant sunny meadow. It seemed the way was open, so one after the other they stepped out into the sunshine. When all four of them were taking deep breaths of fresh air, Drifter gave Felix a pat of admiration on the shoulder.

"You might tell us how you did it!"

"I've been learning castle-speak. We understand each other now," grinned Felix.

XVII. TEMPEST AND STELLA

Baker and Farthing, the two old tradesmen, looked at the saplings in the small group of trees with hawk-like eyes. Next to them stood Bella and Don Espolín, the Spanish knight who had lost both his horse and his hope. They had to collect branches to drive Tempest, Don Espolín's escaped horse, into the fold. He would soon be arriving with the herd. The morose-looking knight had been wandering the countryside for many years, and he knew exactly which trees had been damaged by the last storm, so they soon managed to equip themselves with long sticks, and branches with wilting foliage.

They were concentrating so hard on searching and selecting branches they didn't notice the four figures approach them from the other side of the copse. The approaching men didn't notice Don Espolín and the others either, and the two groups heeded one another only at the last moment. The knight nearly fell over in shock when he saw the four of them draw near: one of the young men must have been a soldier of Lord Dharma's because he was wearing the black uniform of the castle guard, the other boy was wearing loosely hanging clothes and a ridiculous cap that looked as though the visor of a helmet had been pushed up to his forehead. The clothes and appearance of the two older men were strange, reminiscent of a far-off time. His initial astonishment caused him to recoil. But his amazement only turned to pure incomprehension when Bella, who noticed the approaching figures, shouted out in joy, and threw herself into the arms of the young man in black.

"Felix!"

At the unexpected delight, Felix too completely forgot about the distance he usually kept with his sister, and hugged her with gladness and wonder.

"Hey, how did you get here?"

The two groups quickly gave accounts of what had happened to them, listening to the others' stories with either astonishment or alarm.

"Do you have any news about Alma?" asked Drifter eventually, blushing slightly.

Bella shook her head, Baker sighed deeply, and Farthing spread out his hands. It would have been nice for all of them to be together again. The moment's silence was broken by the excited voice of Don Espolín.

"I think the horses will soon be here. Please, my friends, let's not waste time. Help me drive my horse into the fold."

Fortunately there were plenty of twigs and switches for driving the horses, so there were enough for the new arrivals too. Felix, Drifter, Thomas Cosinus and Vector Ferdinand took up their rustling branches and joined the chain. Don Espolín explained the plan. They had to stand in the path of the galloping herd, so the horses would be forced to go round them. Then they would approach the animals at the rear of the herd, and if possible try to separate Tempest from the others. It was possible his ever-present companion, the grey mare, would rush to help him, but more probably they would manage to drive Tempest into the fold alone. Once he was inside, Don Espolín would close the exit with the tree trunk placed there ready. Then all they needed to do was to harness Tempest, but the knight had no worries there.

"The main thing is to drive Tempest into the fold."

"And how do we recognize him? Is the tackle on him?" asked Drifter.

"He lost it about a year ago," said Don Espolín with a wave of his hand. "I found the saddle, the bridle and the bit in the grass, and I keep them in my hut. You'll recognize Tempest: he's a handsome bay horse with a proud bearing."

"I don't know much about horses. What does bay mean?" asked Felix.

"The colour," said Bella.

"Oh, I'm sick of puzzles. Can't you just say, white, brown, or black?"

"There is no such thing as a white or brown horse!" said Don Espolín, drawing himself up dignifiedly. "A white one is called grey, a brown one is called chestnut, as long as it has no black tail and mane. Because a horse with chestnut short hair and a black mane is called bay."

"Wonderful," Felix smiled sarcastically. "And red grapes are black because they're not white."

Don Espolín's eyes flashed with anger, but then they heard the rumbling of the galloping herd of horses in the distance.

"Quickly, into a line! Everyone to their positions!" shouted the knight, and he immediately forgot Felix's cheekiness.

"Be careful now, very careful!"

The herd of hundreds of horses swept across the plain like locusts. Felix was panic-stricken. What if these angry, snorting horses ran right through them all? He was most worried that they might crush Bella. The same thought flashed into Bella's mind too: the horses might not see them. She knew that horses are instinctively careful not to step on people, but if the person in question is so small that they're hardly visible over the waist-high grass, an accident could happen. The herd drew closer, and Bella suddenly had a good idea. She had just enough time to reach into her pocket to fish out the shadow cream from the Forest of Shadows, and quickly applied a little ointment behind her ears. Then she held the two leafy branches the knight had given her, and began waving them around.

The thundering horses noticed the people waving sticks,

and swerved to avoid the danger. But even though the knight and his company rushed to block off the horses from the other direction, with their waving branches they were not frightening enough to force the herd to change direction completely. Then something astonishing happened. An enormous shadow, taller than a tree, towered over Bella. The shadow of the branches in her hands also grew, and the leaves rustling at the end of the twigs cast huge black shadows. Compared to the horses, Bella's shadow was like a sea-hawk compared to new-born lambs. It was as if an enormous bird of prey had swept down from the sky to seize a small horse to munch on.

The horses whinnied in terror and swerved to avoid it. There was great confusion in the herd, the stallions rallied and turned, and several of them collided. There was no accident, but the horses were in utter turmoil. Then Don Espolín and his team brandishing branches rushed forward. In the general confusion, they managed to separate Tempest from the others. Only his faithful companion, the grey mare, stayed with him. She stuck so fast by Tempest that she had no choice in her fright but to follow the same path as Don Espolín's bay horse. In a few minutes, the two horses were galloping round and round in the fold.

After they had managed to enclose Tempest and the mare, the knight and his helpers threw the branches down, and the herd of horses galloped away. The ground rumbled as they ran into the distance. Don Espolín, Felix, and the others who had come with him stared round-eyed at Bella's enormous black shadow.

"Bella, are you all right?" asked Felix, in the voice you might use to address a dragon. He wasn't sure his little sister hadn't been possessed by some terrible demon.

Bella laughed. Although they'd given an outline of their adventures, they hadn't had time to talk about the rabbit's gift. Now Bella got out the pot and showed it to the others.

"I don't know how long the effect will last, but perhaps you should get used to me being the biggest and the scariest, for a while at least," chuckled the little girl.

"I would like to thank you all for your courageous assistance!" said Don Espolín in a croaky voice. "If you are interested, you can watch how I mount my trusty steed."

"Will you saddle him?" asked Bella.

"First I'll harness him, and mount him bareback. It won't do him any harm to learn who's the boss!" said the knight sternly. "Watch!"

The group of friends stood round the fold to watch the determined Spanish knight jump up on to his long-lost horse's back. But it soon became clear that the feat wasn't going to be that simple. Although Tempest and the grey mare had calmed down now, and were no longer galloping madly round, as soon as the knight stepped into the fold both of them started to run off in abject terror. Don Espolín coaxed the horse softly, but then he lost his patience and began to shout, calling for a whip and lasso, and finally, seeing that things were hopeless, he dejectedly climbed out of the wooden enclosure.

"I might have to starve them. But that will take time, because there's grass a-plenty growing in the fold. I'll have to throw a rope round Tempest's neck, then if you help, we'll tether him, hobble him, until he's broken in again. It'll be tough, but I can't give him the silk glove treatment, with that disobedient temper. I have to break his will!"

Bella frowned as she listened to Don Espolín, slowly shook her head, and when the excited knight had finished explaining his plans, she piped up:

"What makes you think you can harm your horse? What you're talking about is torture! It's no wonder that Tempest doesn't want to obey you. Why would he take your orders if you just torment him? You tether him, hobble him, thrash him, and would even starve him!"

"But Miss Bella, he won't obey me otherwise! If I don't use a whip to show my will, he won't learn respect."

"But you're so wrong!" said Bella, and went red as a beetroot with excitement. "Horses are our friends. If you approach them carefully, they'll choose you as a companion of their own accord, and will follow you everywhere of their own free will."

"Dear Miss Bella, I admire your goodness and courage, but you are living in a fantasy world. There's no horse in the world who of his own free will would choose to serve man over freedom! My horse is wild, wilful, and stubborn. If I don't break him in, he will stay that way for ever!"

"Let's make a bet! Give me half an hour, and Tempest will be as tame as a new-born lamb," said Bella, standing up proudly.

"Impossible!" Don Espolín shook his head irritably.

"I said, let's make a bet! If I lose, afterwards I'll help you break him in. But if I win, then you and Tempest join our team, you look for Alma with us, and you fight with us against Lord Dharma!"

"Very well, it's a bet," the knight proffered his enormous hand. "Though even after meeting you, I promised to be your faithful knight. But if you manage to tame Tempest too, I will go into the foulest of battles for your sake."

"Bella, don't!" interrupted Felix. "It's one thing to trot around the riding school with reins, good equipment and a teacher, and quite another to go into a fold with two wild horses. You're tiny, they'll flatten you in no time!"

Bella laughed, and made scary faces, lifting her hands.

"Don't forget Felix, for the moment I'm a fearsome black shadow! Anyway, I know what to do. Kata, an instructor at the riding school, can tame even the wildest horses. I learned what to do from her."

"Sure you did! Tell us what you've got in mind. If it doesn't seem too dangerous, perhaps I'll let you try," mumbled Felix.

Bella started to explain. The others were amazed to hear how self-confident the little girl was. She spoke of horses and their habits like someone who really understands these four-hundred-kilo animals. Bella explained that horses always follow a leader. Once they accept him, they follow only him. The leader of a herd is called the alpha, and the whole herd runs, goes to water, and rests, when the alpha feels like it. They follow him of their own accord, out of love, because they want to belong to him.

"When I go into the fold, first I'll be mild and friendly. I'll let the two horses watch me, and be reassured that I won't hurt them. I won't look into their eyes, because they perceive that as aggression, and I'll move very carefully, so as not to alarm them. I'll get them to feel they can be my friends, they can belong to me, if they'd like. If they choose me as their leader, or alpha, they can expect calm and security. Afterwards I'll show them what it's like if they don't belong to me. I'll be aggressive with my eyes and movements, I'll chase them off, all the time looking right into their eyes, and I'll concentrate on making them scared of me."

"Bella, this is tripe!" interrupted Felix.

"It isn't, not at all. Kata has shown me loads of times at riding school. It's called connecting. Kata learned this method in America, from a real horse whisperer, who persuades the horses with gentle gestures, thoughts, and words."

"Do continue, Miss Bella, I find this most fascinating," said Don Espolín.

Bella explained that if wild horses sense danger, they can run up to a mile before calming down again. So she would also have to drive the horses for a good while, getting them to gallop away, because only then would they perceive that a genuine danger had threatened them. When they were both tired out, she'd let them slow down. She wouldn't drive them, or scare them with movements or looks. When they were totally calm, Bella would leave to them the decision of whether they would like to connect with her, and accept her as the alpha.

Felix clasped at his head, saying he hadn't heard such claptrap for ages. Even Don Espolín just hummed, but Drifter really liked Bella's plan.

"I know how sensitive animals can be. I think this method could really work."

"Nothing bad will happen to me," said Bella looking at Felix.

"The cream's effect is wearing off now. I don't look like a giant, but I'm still pretty big. I suppose I must look as big as Dad right now. So the horses certainly won't trample me. In fact they'll be wary of me. If the connecting doesn't work, I'll climb out of the pen, and we can go back to Don Espolín's method right away."

"All right, try it then! But if anything happens, I'll wring your neck. I mean it!" vowed Felix.

Bella didn't reply. Slowly and deliberately, she stepped towards the pen. In her heart and soul, she was already focussing all her concentration on the horses, observing their movements, and the posture of their heads. It was clear that Tempest was the leader of the two, so he would have to be tamed first. When she got to the pen, she called to the horses with a calm, quiet voice, calling Tempest by name. Then slowly and carefully she climbed into the pen. The others lined up outside the fence, some of them excited, others worried, to see how this little girl would manage this enormous task.

The horses looked at Bella with suspicion and alarm, but as she made no sudden movements and didn't look into their eyes, their fear slowly dissipated. Distrustfully, but curiously, they started to circle round her. Bella carefully held out a hand so the horses could smell it. She knew that if she tried to grab one of them now, both of them would run off immediately, and she'd never catch them again. But she took her time, and followed what her riding instructor had shown her, step by step.

When she felt the moment had come, she changed her behaviour. She pulled herself up to her full height, held out her arms, stamped with her feet, and glared daggers into Tempest's eyes. The bay horse distanced himself in terror, and as Bella stepped after him with another swing of the arms, Tempest began to gallop. With the grey mare on his tail, he began to circle round the pen galloping hell for leather. Bella's shadow arms herded the two galloping animals for several minutes. Then the girl stepped forward, and her arms no longer waved towards Tempest's shoulder, but were directed at his nose. Tempest felt that the path to freedom had been cut off, so he turned round and continued his gallop in the opposite direction. The grey was constantly on his tail, and standing at the centre of the horses' circular gallop, Bella began to reel with dizziness.

When she sensed the horses had galloped enough in both directions, she lowered her arms, and no longer threatened them with her eyes or movements. Her posture too was no longer aggressive. Confidently but with a light step, she went to the centre of the pen, no longer even looking at the horses. They reduced their wild gallop to a canter, then to a trot. Gradually they slowed down until they were simply pacing next to the fencing, with one eye always on Bella, when they finally stopped. Then the little girl slowly turned her back on them. The effects of the cream had completely worn off now, and Bella seemed no bigger than she really was, but she had achieved the desired effect on the horses. She didn't look at them, and acted as though she didn't care what they did. After a little deliberation, the two animals made wary steps towards Bella, always ready to make a dash. Tempest nudged her shoulder with his nose.

Bella slowly turned towards them, but was very careful not to look into their eyes. Looking over their ears, she prudently raised her hands, and stroked first Tempest, then the grey mare. The two horses sniffed the little girl, and waited slightly hesitantly for what would come next. Bella mumbled a couple of friendly-sounding words, then turned her back on them again, and set off towards the fence. Tempest followed her closely, and the mare followed behind Tempest. Bella stopped for a moment, and the two horses froze as well. Now Bella started walking again, and curved round to the other side of the pen. The horses stuck close behind her. Bella stopped. When the horses stopped still, she turned to them and stroked them again. She was bursting with happiness and pride. She would have loved to hop up onto the back of the mare and race round the meadow on her, but also felt that every bone in her body was tired from the highly focussed concentration.

Then she looked at the men on the other side of the fencing. Seven pairs of amazed eyes were staring at her. Even Felix's face glowed with admiration. None of them dared say a word, for fear of frightening the horses.

"If you get something to use as a halter, we could try mounting them," said Bella calmly. "Don Espolín, you're sure to manage now. And I can have the grey, can't I?"

"Why, most certainly, Miss Bella. What an amazing young lady!" enthused Don Espolín, as he rushed to his hut to get Tempest's trappings. The grey mare, as if she sensed that Bella would be her rider, stepped close, and began nuzzling the little girl. Bella's hand ran over the mare's forehead, then her mane and neck.

"Now we belong together, my dearest," she whispered devoutly. "I'll give you a name, so everyone shall know who your owner is!"

Bella pondered for a moment, then came up with the solution.

"Your name will be Stella! Grandma always said this name means star. Bella and Stella, that sounds good. What do you think?"

The horse raised its head and neighed into the air. Bella smiled. She understood: Stella agreed.

XVIII. The White Army

Alma scoured every corner of the snow-white room once more, hoping to find a white door, or the key to the black box from Lord Dharma, but to no avail. And yet the fools had said quite clearly that she would need the contents of the box for the battle.

"Yes, the tall one said that, and last time he always told the truth," ruminated Alma. "So somehow I must open this box."

She thought back to what else the messenger had said. He said that Lord Dharma had sent the chessboard as a memento. The mini chess set was a reminder that a chess player always holds the key to success.

"Brilliant. I knew that anyway," fumed Alma, then she remembered the words of the short messenger. The podgy one had always lied when they met in the woods, and he said the gift of the chess set was of no importance.

"But that was a lie! So it must be really important for some reason!" realized Alma. Cursing her own stupidity, she quickly tipped out the contents.

Thirty-two wooden pieces tumbled out higgledy-piggledy on the bed. Now the box was empty, Alma noticed that letters and numbers were engraved faintly on the bottom of the box. She peered and managed to spell out the long inscription. This is what was written:

W: a7, Kh6

B: a2, b2, c2, Nd2, Qa3, b3, Rc3, d3,
Ka4, Bb4, Bc4, Ra5, b5, c5, a6

A chess position! And quite a strange one at that, because White only has two pieces on the board, while Black has fifteen, although all fifteen of them are huddled together. Alma placed the pieces carefully on the board. When she saw the black pieces all in a cluster, she smiled.

"It's just like a black box, with the most valuable thing, the king, inside, so that nobody can touch him, and all around is an unbreakable protective layer. But let's see if I can break it after all."

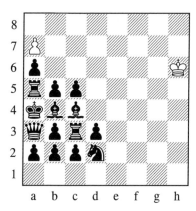

It was obvious she had to move to a8, because afterwards the pawn would be able to return to the board as another piece. But what piece should it become?

"The queen and the other officers won't be much use here. Only the knight will be able to jump over the protective wall," thought Alma. "If I put the knight on a8, then whatever move Black makes, in the next move I'll put him in checkmate on b6. Yes, the knight seems to be the key!"

She took the finely-carved knight and looked at the workmanship on the horse's mane. The detail on the piece was so fine, the locks of hair on the mane would even have fitted into a keyhole.

"How daft I am! Lord Dharma even told me! Chess gives me the key to the situation!" said Alma, clapping her palm to her forehead. Then she sprang up and placed the white knight head downward into the keyhole on the black box.

The knight fitted perfectly into the lock, and when Alma turned it carefully, the top of the box opened with a small click. She looked excitedly at the contents of the box. The first thing to catch her eye was an off-white carved horn, which might have come from a bull. Next to it was a pull-out telescope, and a strangely shaped funnel, the like of which Alma had never seen. She had no idea what it might be for, but she didn't let that bother her. She continued to explore the box.

At the bottom she found a large bunch of keys and a roll of parchment. She hurriedly unrolled the scroll, hoping to find a message or instructions on it. Although the lines running across the scroll seemed at first to be a puzzle in a children's picture book, after pondering over it a while Alma realized that she was holding a quickly sketched map of the castle. All was clear now. The map would lead her out of the castle, or at least she would get to a place where it was worth looking for her companions. The bunch of keys would probably open the doors she found on the way.

All she had to do was take the box, the small chess set, and continue her journey using the map. One of the keys on the bunch did indeed open the white door, and Alma set off to find the others, almost running with excitement. Sometimes her path was blocked by a locked door, or a gate with a padlock, but one of the keys always opened up the way before her. Alma sped forward, completely oblivious to time. She couldn't have said if she had been in the labyrinth for ten minutes or two hours, when after passing through a door she stopped dead. The castle had come to an end. The last door opened onto a clearing at the edge of a forest, and she could continue her journey either through the trees, or on a meadow stretching into the distance. Alma had been longing for fresh air, so she didn't think for long about whether or not to leave the castle. It was possible the others had made it through the castle walls, and were now looking for each other out in the open air. But just to be on the safe side, she thought about retracing her steps. Next to the door she noticed a stone larger than a brick. She pulled it in front of the doorstep, so the door couldn't shut completely. Who knew, perhaps it would be useful to be able to get back into the castle.

After she had wedged the door open, she went forwards. First she took a look at the trees in the forest, then she turned towards the far-stretching meadow. Which way should she go? Suddenly she had an idea. Although the others weren't expecting a call, perhaps it was worth blowing the horn she had found in the box. Alma took the fine, curved instrument, put it to her lips, took a deep breath, and blew into it. She expected a raucous, cawing sound, but actually the tone was a long, deep, doleful wail. Although the sound was strong enough to set the air around her throbbing, it wasn't painful or ear-splitting. Alma couldn't resist blowing into it again.

Then she stopped, and waited. She tried to bend her ears to hear the most distant of sounds. When she heard the far-off rattle of a cart, she set off in the direction of the sound, with a satisfied smile on her face. To stay safe, she flitted from tree to tree, but in her soul so great was the pleasure she felt in breathing fresh air, such was the hope of seeing the others again, that she couldn't believe she was in danger. And how right she was. Soon, peeking out from behind a gnarled tree trunk, she saw a cart pulled by a tired horse, with Katalina and Jack in the driving seat. Alma sprang out from the trees. Katalina was so surprised to see her that she almost fell off the seat of the cart. But her joy was all the greater when she saw who was responsible for the shock.

The girls quickly told each other all that had happened over the last day. Alma climbed up to Katalina's grandpa, who was gasping for breath, and told him that Lord Dharma really did possess the water of life. So far he hadn't given her any, but if they managed to win the battle tomorrow, he would be prepared to give some to the old man. Grandma's and Katalina's eyes lit up at the news, and both immediately promised they would follow Alma faithfully in the next day's fight.

"You can count on me too!" called Jack, puffing out his chest.

Katalina rewarded him with a kind smile, but Alma squeezed the peasant boy's hand tightly.

"We just have to find the others!" she sighed.

At that moment the horse pacing at the front of the cart began sniffing at the air excitedly. First it just snorted and panted, but then with a mighty whinny signalled some unusual and joyful feeling. Through the trees in the distance, a prolonged vigorous whinnying came in answer, and then the neighing of a third horse. There was no time to hide or take cover, and the excited snickering of the horses drew them nearer. Alma hid behind a tree again, so that if the others were attacked, she would be able to surprise the enemy by jumping out of hiding. But there was no need to fight against anyone.

Through the trees there came quite a throng. At the fore Don Espolín rode on the back of his bay horse, next to him was Bella, radiant with happiness, proudly sitting astride Stella. Behind the horses came all the others: Felix and Drifter, Baker and old Farthing, and the two mathematicians who had been freed from the statue spell, Thomas Cosinus and Vector Ferdinand. The initial shock and wonder was followed by overjoyed hugs and catching up on what had happened to the others. Everyone summarized their own trials, and the new friends who had only recently joined the group introduced themselves. Felix was the only one who didn't share all the details of his adventures with the others. He preferred not to speak of his meeting with Lord Dharma, so after telling the story of his escape he jumped straight to how, in the middle of his roaming, he had heard Drifter's cry for help. As he spoke, he couldn't help thrusting his hands into his pockets, so the others wouldn't notice the insidious ring, which found its way onto his finger against his will.

Only Alma noticed that he lost the thread of his story for a moment, but she didn't think it was particularly important. She was already thinking about the battle at dawn tomorrow, and she was glad to see the two horses grazing. An hour beforehand she had had no idea where she would find horses for the knights in the battle.

After everyone else had told their story, it was Alma's turn. She recounted the conversation with Lord Dharma, and she showed them the dagger and the objects from the box. She passed round the bone horn, which everyone examined thoroughly, and they all said that the distant sound had been so familiar and inviting that they knew immediately they had to follow it. Baker recognized the strangely-shaped funnel too. Lord Dharma had a similar one, not made of bone, but of ebony. During battles, he used it to shout commands to his troops. The form of the funnel was designed so that all those wearing the same uniform should hear what their leader says.

Felix pulled a face.

"Well that's not much use. If we are the white team, we won't hear what Alma says, because everyone has different coloured clothes. Although in this black uniform I might hear the enemy's battle plan."

Since Baker didn't know what to say to this, they fell silent for a while. Felix clutched his finger, because he felt the lion ring was squeezing his finger again. Alma felt it was time to hold a review of the troops. If she didn't count Grandpa lying in the cart, and Grandma nursing him, who obviously couldn't take part in battle, there were eleven of them altogether. Don Espolín, Drifter and Felix had weapons, because after the soldiers defeated in the mill had left them lying around, they had gathered up everything they could. This way the two mathematicians had a sword and a spear too. Jack said he needed no other weapon than the garden fork they kept in the back of the cart, but Baker, Farthing, and the three girls had no object that could be used in battle.

"With eleven we still have a significant disadvantage against the enemy's sixteen units, but the outlook isn't hopeless," said Alma, summing up. "But we have to eat a hearty breakfast before dawn, and it wouldn't hurt to have a few more weapons. I saw food and weapons in the castle. The question is, can we risk going back?"

The group was divided on this. Thomas Cosinus thought the most important thing was to get more weapons, so it was worth venturing into the castle. Felix agreed, saying that if there were lion heads on the wall on the way, they'd almost certainly find their way back. Alma fingered the bunch of keys from the black box, which had opened every door, and pondered the idea. Drifter was dead set against the idea of going back into the unpredictable, hostile building. Bella too preferred to stay in the forest, although mainly because she didn't want to leave Stella alone.

Grandpa had fallen asleep in the cart, so Grandma joined the discussion.

"I've brought a couple of baskets of food," she remembered, and when the group had got over their surprise, she gave everyone a piece of bread, some sausage and some cheese. Famished with hunger, they descended on the tasty food like wolves. For the next few minutes nobody breathed a word, until every last crumb had been licked up.

"Another problem is where are we going to spend the night," said Don Espolín, after shaking the breadcrumbs out of his straggly beard. "We can tie the horses to a tree, but Miss Bella and the others need rest and sleep. We must find a sheltered place."

"We're bound to find an empty room in the castle. There might even be beds in it," said chubby Baker dreamily.

"The more I think about it, the more I feel it's wiser to stay out of the castle," said Alma slowly and thoughtfully. "In this chess world, everything happens differently to back home, but one thing is the same: something that's happened can't be undone.

Now we've all managed to get out of the castle, but if we go back we might fall into another trap. We might not get another chance. I think it's better to shut the door I wedged open, and we shouldn't go back to a place we were so vulnerable in."

"But we could at least go and get the weapons," argued Felix. "We could form a chain, with one person next to every door and fork in the passage. That would guarantee the way out."

"If you accept me as commander in tomorrow's battle, then you must accept what I ask now in the preparations!" said Alma, looking at him seriously. "I don't want to risk the safety of our team, I don't want us to split up. The cart and the horses can't enter the castle, so we won't go either."

Apart from Felix, everyone agreed. He would have liked to press his own plan a bit more, because he felt the risk of going into battle with no weapons was much greater, but he resigned himself to the situation. If anyone was a good team player, it was Felix. In basketball he had learned that individual plans usually only work if the team has agreed and prepared the ground for them in advance.

So he nodded: "Right you are, skipper. So where now?"

Alma looked at the others questioningly, and Don Espolín remembered something.

"I know a deserted barn on the edge of the forest. I don't know what they used it for. It's too large for keeping hay, and too far from the castle to keep carts and other vehicles in. As far as I know it's been locked up for years, and never used. If we picked the lock, we could shelter in there for the night."

This idea appealed to everyone, and they got up to find the barn before darkness fell. The knight knew the lie of the land quite well, so they soon found the ramshackle two-storey wooden building, shut with a padlock. Alma's keys wouldn't open the lock, but Drifter gave it such a blow with the handle of his spear that it clattered to the ground. Thomas Cosinus and Vector Ferdinand happily opened up the double wooden doors for everyone.

They left the cart and the horses in front of the entrance, and went to investigate the accommodation. They got their smartphones out again, and used the torch app to examine the dark spaces inside. The musty air smelt of rotten wood and dust, and in the torchlight they saw strange, angular, tall wooden contraptions.

"What are these? High seats for hunting?" said Drifter peering in the gloom.

Inside the building was a series of two-storey structures with a crow's nest at the top. They did look very much like high seats, but at the bottom were wooden wheels, and long arms extended from the sides.

"I know! These are siege machines!" said Vector Ferdinand, clapping his hand to his forehead. In his previous world he had a passion for studying unusual machines. "At the end of the arm is a container a bit like a ladle, and in it you can put stones or other ammunition, and with a swing of the arm, it can be shot for miles. The people operating it are protected by the wooden parapet. The wheels are so you can move it close to the building under siege."

"We had something similar in our history books," nodded Felix. "They used this kind of thing in the Middle Ages."

"We've seen this kind of thing used in one of the wars!" remembered Farthing.

"Who would have thought they hide them here?" said Baker, shaking his head.

"We could have a look to see if they still work!" said Felix with a sparkle in his eye. "We could even deploy them tomorrow."

After they had checked that the barn was otherwise empty, they walked around the four siege machines, thoroughly examining whether the wheels and the catapulting arms were intact, the state of the planks, the floor of the lookout and the parapets. They decided that two of the four contraptions were so rotten and shaky that they couldn't even move them without risking their lives, but the other two machines were stable, strong, and operational. They agreed that at the very break of day they would gather some large stones from the woods round about, and if necessary they would use the siege machines in tomorrow's battle.

Meanwhile they tethered the horses, and towed the cart with Grandpa into the barn, to protect the old man from the cold at night and the morning dew. They set up sleeping berths at the back of the granary, and sent Bella to bed immediately. The others agreed to stand guard in pairs, and that they would rotate every two hours. The first two guards, Baker and Jack, took up their positions, but the others didn't go to bed. The excitement of the day, and the joy of meeting up again, kept them awake, so they settled down comfortably and started chatting quietly.

Half an hour later they began to notice strange sounds. On the other side of the barn, where there was a small closed window in the wall, they heard rustling and scraping.

"It sounds like someone is trying to open the window," whispered Alma to Drifter next to her.

He nodded in agreement, then silently prodded Felix's arm. Felix got up and went quietly to the window, so that if strangers should come through it he could hit them immediately. Drifter, Thomas Cosinus and Jack were right behind him. The others huddled behind the closed door, so that if someone came through it, they could deal him a blow.

A loud creak signalled that the window had been forced open. The group hiding in the barn held their breath, so they all heard the whispering outside clearly. Several men were discussing what to do.

"Wherever we hide in the woods, they're bound to find us. Hundreds of them are combing the area."

"They are searching the villages too. There's nowhere for us to hide."

"That's why I say to climb in here," reasoned a third, whose voice seemed slightly familiar to Felix. "It's the enemy's warehouse, and it's locked from the outside. None of the patrols would look for us here."

Felix's blood froze for a moment. Perhaps these were robbers or forest bandits, and they were going to climb through the window.

"But how will we know when to come out?" asked the first voice, outside.

"I'll hear it in the birdsong," said the familiar voice again. "If they sing peacefully, then we can relax, the patrols will have returned to the castle."

Felix, who was hiding under the window, realized that this must be Angelo, the bird-catcher, whom he had met in the company of new recruits in the castle. Angelo had been planning to escape because he had no desire to fight on the side of Lord Dharma. It seemed he'd invited a few other recruits to escape with him, and now they were hiding from the soldiers on their trail.

With a gentle motion Felix signalled to the others that he knew who one of the voices belonged to, and that they were probably not dangerous. Meanwhile Angelo and his companions had agreed to hide in the barn, so one by one they climbed in. By the time all four were inside, Felix, Drifter, Jack and Thomas Cosinus were ready to jump on them. But there was no fight, because Felix addressed Angelo quietly. At first, the four escapees were scared out of their wits, but they couldn't pull out their weapons because Felix's group confiscated them. Felix quickly explained who he was and why he and his friends were there.

Angelo could hardly believe his ears when he learned that he and his fellow deserters hadn't fallen into the hands of their pursuers, but could really spend the night in a safe place. It transpired that the four deserters had got into an impossible situation. After their escape Lord Dharma had issued orders that they should be captured dead or alive. Their homes were under constant watch by guards, so they couldn't go back to their families or villages; but in the forest patrols were always looking for them. They weren't safe even in Angelo's famous forest hideouts.

Meanwhile Jack recognized one of the other lads: it was none other than Steve from the next village. He and Steve had often watched over the flock together, on the hillside between the two villages. The lads hugged one another. Jack enthusiastically explained that now they had the chance to rise up against Lord Dharma, and perhaps, if Alma was clever, they would defeat him for good. The deserters thought it over, and admitted that as long as Lord Dharma was in power, their lives would be that of outlaws or runaways, because they would never be able to go home; they would be condemned to forever evading the military and the severe punishment for escaping.

"Although I can't stand any kind of war," said Angelo, "if I do have to fight, I'd rather fight for freedom against a tyrant, than on the tyrant's side."

"I agree! If I have to take up arms, then I revolt against the despot!" added Steve.

Their other two companions, Nando and Fredo, shared their sentiment, so the four deserters quickly decided to join the white army, and fight for freedom beside Alma. And to give credibility to their words, there and then in the depths of the dark barn, they swore loyalty until death to Alma.

XIX. THE BATTLE BEGINS

The rest of the night was uneventful. Exhausted from all the excitement and ordeals, they soon fell asleep. Some of them slept a calm, deep sleep, others tossed and turned. The guards changed every other hour. The first pale strip of dawn light was just beginning to glow in the eastern sky when Alma woke up. She knew it was still early, and she could rest another half an hour, but she wasn't sleepy any more. She was used to not being able to sleep much before important chess competitions. In fact she actually liked these periods of early morning wakefulness, when she could think with a clear head about the contest ahead of her.

Before important tournaments chess players usually find out all they can about their opponents. They look over their previous games and analyse them, trying to find their strengths and weaknesses, and to detect what situations they feel uncomfortable in. Based on that, they build up their strategy, and think through what opening moves or defences it would be good to use. Thorough knowledge of the opponent can be a great advantage during a game.

Two days ago Lord Dharma had been standing behind Alma in the park. Who knew, perhaps he had also watched over her earlier games, and he had probably had the opportunity to become acquainted with her playing style and prepare for the battle. Alma, on the other hand, knew nothing about her future opponent. She had no idea if he was an aggressive player or a more deliberate one, who played for safety. She didn't know his favourite gambits or combinations of moves. This time, she had only her own mind and intuitions to guide her. The rules of chess dictate that White always starts, so Alma took it for granted that she would have to make the first move.

Alma favoured an aggressive style of play, and sometimes bulldozed her opponents in a seemingly reckless manner. This tactic could become very dangerous, because one false move, or a little slack in the momentum of the attack, was enough for the opponent to exploit the weakness of the defence. After all, someone who continually initiates attacks doesn't have time to waste on defence. But if the initial pace remains unbroken, and she makes no mistakes in the attack, then no opponent can withstand her. What is more, her daring moves often surprise the other player, and in chess surprise is one of the most important weapons.

Alma screwed up her courage. She wasn't going to let Lord Dharma dictate the pace of the game. She would do everything to keep the initiative, to attack rather than play defensively.

"I will not let him castle," she decided. "I'll delay him as long as possible. If I'm brave enough, he won't be able to hide the king in time!"

That reminded her of the next difficulty. Chess requires sixteen pieces, but counting the willing, determined youngsters and middle-aged adults, they were only fifteen. With Grandpa ailing and Grandma nursing him, she could hardly draft them into the army! But she couldn't confront Lord Dharma with fewer fighters.

"I'll have to ask Grandma to take up a position with the cart," thought Alma. "And I'll try to keep them out of danger's way."

That problem was solved, then. But Alma was tormented by other doubts. She knew that Lord Dharma's battles were fought on real locations, but she had no idea how she would see these places. She could imagine that a copse, a meadow, a farmhouse or a pasture might each represent a square on the chessboard, but how could she get an overview of everything, and track the moves, while she herself was standing in the place of one of the chess pieces. What was more, at the beginning of the battle the enemy fighters would be very distant. Who knew what haystacks, stables, or barns Lord Dharma's soldiers might be hiding in? How would Alma find out about the enemy moves?

Then she thought of the telescope. Clearly, Lord Dharma had not put it into the black box by chance. Perhaps she could use it to see the battle from a different viewpoint. Alma wanted to check whether her hunch was right, so quietly she got up, took the telescope out of the box, and crept silently to the door. The others didn't hear her moving, and the only ones to move their heads were Drifter and Don Espolín, who were on guard. Alma signalled to them that all was well, then opened the barn door slightly and stepped into the cold dawn air.

It took her a moment to get her bearings in the dawn twilight, then she realized that the map changed constantly not only inside the castle, but here too, in the surrounding countryside. In place of the forest and the far-stretching meadow was a landscape with far more divisions and movement, containing groves, piles of stones, arable land, orchards, and stables. Not far away on the left the silhouette of a windmill towered in the half-light, and she could hear the babbling of a brook in front of her.

First Alma looked at the landscape with the naked eye, squinting a little because in the dawn twilight she could only just make out the contours of the more distant details. Then she raised the telescope to her eyes, and nearly cried out in surprise. Seen through the disc of glass, the landscape was divided into sixty-four sharply divided units. It was perfectly clear which meadow, pen, or pond was a black or white square. Alma thought she could even see the algebraic notation for the squares. Yes, right in front of her lay a round meadow: that was square d1, the starting position for the white queen. To her right was a series of haystacks, this was e1, where the king would stand. To her left was an enormous windmill, and further back was an animals' fold. Obviously one of the bishops would start from the windmill, and one of the knights from the fold. The telescope was able to see through walls too, and the area behind the windmill was just as crystal clear as if the massive building hadn't been there.

Now everything was clear. Using the telescope she would know which landmark represented which square on the chessboard, and it would be easy to direct her fighters. Not being able to see the game from above, as she would have done on a chessboard, was not going to be a problem. Like every truly good player, Alma could play blindfold chess. She didn't find it difficult to follow the entire game in her head, and didn't need a chessboard to keep an overview of what was happening. All she needed was to see the location of the squares, and the telescope solved that problem.

"This will be like a half-blindfold game," thought Alma to herself. "I've never done that before. I can see what's happening, but at the same time, I can't. One thing's for sure: my chances are no worse than the enemy's. He's bound to have a telescope too, so he'll be playing half-blindfold against me."

Alma took stock of the terrain. She noticed that there was only one bridge leading over the brook for those on foot. Those on horseback might be able to ride through the water, but the current was too fast for the others to safely wade on foot or swim across. But the bridge was too narrow for the cart to be pulled across, so Grandpa and Grandma certainly couldn't be sent that way.

"I'll ask them to be the king!" thought Alma in a flash. "They'll be safe for a while among the haystacks, then if necessary, I'll try to castle. They could hide in the windmill on the queenside."

Meanwhile the lowering sky grew lighter, and Alma suddenly felt she had little time left, and she had to wake the others immediately so could start to get ready. She hurried back into the barn, and threw open the double doors to let some fresh air and a little light into the dark space. The guards were standing up, and soon the whole company woke up, stretching and rubbing their eyes. They were glad to hear there was a stream nearby, because everyone wanted to wash and drink some fresh water.

Another helping of food appeared from Grandma's basket. Although with seventeen of them they couldn't all eat their fill, they were happy to have a little something in their stomach before the great battle. As Katalina and Bella returned from the brook, they brought heaps of strawberries in the peasant girl's apron, so the frugal breakfast was rounded off with a dessert.

After eating the boys and men heaved the two operational siege machines out of the barn. It wasn't easy to shift them, but Alma's view was they could serve in place of rooks. Nearby, they found stones the right size to use as projectiles, so in the reddish-orange light of the rising sun they tested the two contraptions. Everyone aimed and fired, and they all experimented manoeuvring the gigantic machines. One of the best aims was Vector Ferdinand, who had already studied machines like this in his old life. The other good shot turned out to be Drifter. Don Espolín, the knight, couldn't resist asking: how was it that a rather lanky boy with droopy hair had such a good feel for directing the catapult arm. Drifter shrugged. In computer games you had to aim in the same way, and he had a lot of practice.

"Would you take one of the siege machines to serve as a rook?" asked Alma.

Drifter nodded. Perhaps he would be of more use to the others shooting stones from the siege machine, than in close combat. Vector Ferdinand volunteered to take the other contraption. Now all that remained was to give the others their roles and weapons, and to line up for battle.

Obviously, the two horse riders should take the role of the two knights. Alma sent Don Espolín to the large horse-fold, which was in square b1; Bella she sent to g1, to a clearing dotted with small bushes. Next she had to decide on the bishops. She needed fighters who were able to move quickly and in a coordinated fashion, who were indefatigable, and would not shrink back from combat. Baker and Farthing couldn't be asked to do this: the two old men were shaky and lacked energy, and had little strength for fighting. For this task, Alma asked Felix and Thomas Cosinus, who was still muscular. The others would be pawns, and would be sorely needed both for attack and defence.

Looking in the telescope Alma noticed that mobilization had begun on the other side too. The enemy troops and fighters were lining up in the locations opposite them. The four deserters had enough weapons to share with the girls, so all they needed to do now was occupy their designated places. Don Espolín suggested they all stand round to swear allegiance to their commander, or as the Spanish knight enthusiastically put it, to Queen Alma.

Felix stepped back a little. Suddenly he felt the black ring squeezing into his finger. Somehow this feeling was different to before. He realized that the time had come for a final decision. The dark lord was calling him to join the army on the other side, and let his friends down. He looked at their determined faces, his gaze resting for a second on Alma's excited, rosy face, and finally came to rest on Bella, with her shining eyes, whose tiny form was almost lost among the adults. Now was the time to grab his sister and escape, if he didn't want them both to end up dead on the battlefield. The black ring dug more keenly into his flesh, like a knife, but Felix had decided. Ignoring the pain, he pulled the ring, and with all his might he twisted it off his finger. His rock-solid determination broke the metal's resistance, and the ring from Lord Dharma splintered into smithereens. Felix's vision went dark for a moment with the pulsating pain in his finger and his head.

"I swear that I will take part in this battle, to the last drop of my blood, and will faithfully follow Queen Alma's orders!" proclaimed Don Espolín.

The others repeated the words of the oath after him. A second later Felix joined the others in swearing allegiance. After the last word was uttered, something very strange happened. Alma already knew this feeling, but even so, the experience was thrilling. The whole group underwent a transfiguration like the one Alma had experienced the previous day in the white room with the mirror. Their figures became more slender and vigorous, like true warriors; the youngsters' bodies gained stature and musculature, the older men recovered their former strength. Bella was transfigured from a small, fragile girl into a slender maiden, and looked like a young woman in her teens. Their rough-and-tumble clothes were transformed too: snow-white ornamented armour, breastplates, arm bracers and shinguards glided over their forms, helmets appeared on their heads, at their sides hung sharp-edged swords, and in their hands they now gripped sparkling shields. Even the horses were resplendent in snow-white harnesses studded with silver. Grandpa was breathing more easily now, and they were all relieved that he would survive until the end of the battle.

"Wow! Now I can believe we'll hear the white megaphone! Honestly guys, I'm getting really excited about going into battle!" said Felix with relief, basking in triumph, while looking admiringly at the silver-ornamented armour that followed the contour of his muscles.

Drifter brushed his hair out of his face, and took a furtive look at Alma. Her slender form in beautiful armour really did give the impression of a queen – a young, combative, feisty queen preparing for the decisive battle at the head of her army. Never had Drifter desired victory so strongly, and he suddenly felt a desire to prove his skill and courage, and also he could feel keenly how important the team was, the community he belonged to.

Alma surveyed the determined team, whose members had just this minute promised to follow her orders without question.

"I will not disappoint you!" she announced determinedly, then she asked everyone to take up their assigned positions. Katalina, a pawn, stood on the hillock in front of Bella, so she could be as close as possible to her friend. Jack, with his sword drawn and his eyes flashing, occupied the square next to Katalina. When everyone was in their place, the position was as follows:

NANDO (Pawn)	FREDO (Pawn)	STEVE (Pawn)	ANGELO (Pawn)	BAKER (Pawn)	JACK (Pawn)	KATALINA (Pawn)	FARTHING (Pawn)
DRIFTER (Rook)	DON ESPOLÍN (Knight)	FELIX (Bishop)	ALMA (Queen)	GRANDPA (King)	THOMAS COSINUS (Bishop)	BELLA (Knight)	VECTOR FERDINAND (Rook)
A	B	C	D	E	F	G	H

Scanning the enemy positions with her telescope, Alma ascertained that Lord Dharma's soldiers had lined up, and what's more, there was considerable military might on the other side, not just a motley band of fifteen occasional fighters and two old people. The squares of the pawns were occupied by a whole corps, and the knights were represented by an entire division of cavalry. How on earth Bella or one of the boys would confront twenty-five mounted, armed fighters didn't bear thinking about. In the places of the black king and queen were two curtained, six-horse carriages, painted black. Alma couldn't be certain which one was occupied by her arch-enemy, Lord Dharma. In the place of the bishops she recognized two old acquaintances, now dressed in black: the two fools, one who told the truth, and the other who lied.

In the distance a battle horn sounded, and Alma knew the time had come to make the first move. The battle had begun. She planned a forthright attack on the kingside, so she raised the megaphone to her lips and spoke in a confident, calm voice:

"Baker! Please occupy the bower next to the farmstead: e4."

Baker shuddered, slightly embarrassed, then he pulled himself up to his full height, pointed his arrow in front of him, and walked stiffly over to the vine bower. Lord Dharma's voice didn't carry as far as the white army, but they could see one of the infantry formations move forward to a pond surrounded

by reeds. Alma identified it using her telescope: c5. In response to her e4 he had moved to c5: in other words Lord Dharma had chosen what was known as the Sicilian Defence. Alma knew all the variations of this opening, so she was on safe ground so far. She didn't have to think long about how to respond: it was clear she would have to push forward with the knight. At Alma's command Bella jumped forward beside Katalina, and occupied the kitchen garden behind the farmstead. She tried to hold back her horse so as not to damage the vegetable patch too much, but still, Stella trod all over the rows of lettuce and turnips.

Meanwhile Lord Dharma's infantry unit had gone on the attack. Alma knew that she would have to sacrifice one of her soldiers in order to stop them.

"Angelo, get ready to fight! You have to stand in their way on the pasture!"

The bird-catcher nodded resolutely, drew his sword, and blew into the bird-catcher's pipe that hung round his neck. At the sound of the cooing came an answer from the woods: with a rustling of wings and chirping a whole flock of snow-white birds flew to the battlefield. Drifter, who was watching from the lookout on the siege machine, was shocked to see the lead bird was the peacock-tailed blackbird, which determinedly led his companions to Angelo's defence.

But the feathered host entered the battle in vain at the call of the pipe, because behind the enemy position a flock of crows rose into the air, and cawing loudly they turned on Angelo's defence.

While the infantry rushed at the terrified bird-catcher and forced him to his knees with their weapons, the crows threw themselves at the white birds wheeling over Angelo's head. The next moment a blinding light flashed over the pasture, and Angelo and the birds had vanished. Bella, who was standing nearby, cried out

in terror, then quickly clapped her hand over her mouth and scanned the surroundings in case she should see Angelo's figure in the distance. But the first victim's body was nowhere to be seen on the battlefield. Beneath the infantry's feet the trampled grass was covered with black and white feathers.

Alma, who was also watching with concern what happened to her soldier, scanned the landscape with her telescope, until on the other side of the trench at the edge of the battlefield, where the captured pieces are normally placed, she saw Angelo. Turned to stone, he stood at the edge of the trench. A shiver went down Alma's spine, because from this distance it was impossible to make out whether the captured player was still alive or whether he had been turned permanently to stone.

"Anyway, I must concentrate on nothing but the game!" she said, screwing her resolve. She focussed her attention on the battlefield.

"Come on Bella, let's take revenge for Angelo!" she roared.

Bella's eyes had the flash of battle. She dug her boots into Stella's flanks, and with her sword drawn she jumped onto the feather-strewn pasture. In alarm the fifteen sturdy men jumped out of the way of the horse. Bella swung her shining

weapon, and with another flash of light she and her horse were left alone in the pasture. The defeated infantry division were on the edge of the trench on the other side, frozen stone statues, close together. From the back row a formation of black horsemen stormed forward, and Alma thought the time had come to take a more aggressive tack, and deploy her army for attack. She wanted Lord Dharma to be preoccupied with defence, for him not to have the time or the opportunity to move his officers

forward, to castle, or to set a trap for the white team, a raggle-taggle bunch. For this, Alma had to open up the path for her own officers, and at the same time begin the deployment.

First, she sent one of her bishops forward, Felix, but then she decided on an even faster thrust forward. Meanwhile the black army had begun to shower the white team's positions with flaming arrows. They weren't aiming at the players; the arrows whistled blindly through the air, but after them haystacks

caught fire, and the air was filled with the smell of acrid smoke. Two flaming arrows fell onto the planks of the bridge over the stream, and the dry wooden railings caught some of the sparks. Alma knew that the attack could only continue if she sent someone across the bridge, even if that meant opening up the

area behind the pawns, and making it impossible for her to castle on that side.

"Katalina! Cross the bridge before it catches fire: g4!" she shouted. Katalina pulled her long skirt up to her knees, and whizzed over the smoking bridge as if she'd been shot out of a cannon. A few seconds after taking up her position on

the other side of the bridge, the planks creaked and fell away. The burning wood sizzled and threw up grey smoke as it sank under the water. Meanwhile Lord Dharma continued to push the infantry units, his pawns, forward, but then a terrible thing happened.

The hills in the distance were covered by a black shadow, and from the craggy peaks a monstrous figure rose into the air. Its breath was like a fire-brand, and its two enormous wings caused a whirlwind. It approached the battlefield swiftly, blackening the sky, covering the earth in shadow, and instilling cold terror in the hearts of mortals.

"The dragon!" shouted Katalina, and terrified, she sank to her knees in the waist-high grass.

The white army shuddered as they stared at the sky. None of them had expected to have to battle with supernatural powers. But Alma's team was not alone in their fear; even fighters in the black army were scared to death as they observed the approaching danger.

XX. The White Flag

In a few minutes, the huge dragon had reached the battlefield. As it drew near the sky darkened, the air was filled with a revolting smell, and the mere sight of the greenish-yellow flames emerging from its nostrils brought a cold sweat to the soldiers' trembling bodies. Everyone waited motionless for the beast to blast the whole region with a single breath of fire. But for the moment, the dragon made no attack, and restricted itself to wheeling over the battlefield with ominous roars, and while it clicked its tremendous claws, it shed a shower of sparks on the land. Trees creaked as they swayed in the wind created by the flapping wings, but the beast wheeled in the air as if giving careful consideration to who should be its first victim.

Suddenly Alma saw clearly. There was no need to be afraid of the dragon – it was nothing but scare tactics! There is a position in chess called the Dragon, which usually forms after the black pawn moves to g6, and every chess player knows this represents great danger to the opponent. But the position on the board was not a real Dragon! Obviously, this beast had been brought to life because Lord Dharma had directed one of his infantry divisions to g6. The dragon's appearance surpassed any of the

horrors they had so far seen, but Alma's coach had told her the origin of the name 'dragon'. She knew that in this position the layout of the pawns was similar to the dragon constellation in the night sky. The beast had been brought to life by a momentary position on the board, so it couldn't threaten their lives – that would be quite against the rules. Lord Dharma was probably hoping he could surprise and terrify his opponents with this.

"If anyone gives a surprise it'll be me!" said Alma, stamping her foot stubbornly, and she forced herself not to look at the awful monster a moment longer.

"Just ignore it, it won't hurt you! Concentrate on the battle!" she shouted into the megaphone. Then she ordered Katalina to continue the advance, and threaten the enemy horsemen. The peasant girl rose up from the ground shaking with fear, but Alma's confident voice filled her with strength, so carefully, holding her weapon before her, and all the while sneaking glances at the sky, she proceeded into the enemy position.

Meanwhile Bella decided to do something daring. She remembered the shadow ointment that had helped her to break the two wildly galloping horses. Perhaps an enormous shadow would be able to scare off this terrible dragon? She quickly got out the ointment, spread it on her forehead, and then rubbed the rest behind Stella's ears. By the time Katalina had occupied her new position, the shadow of Bella and Stella was flickering ghoulishly far above the treetops. The sight threw the enemy soldiers into utter confusion, and the dragon turned against the unexpected enemy with an ear-splitting screech. Now it was breathing real fire from its nose, scorching the air around Stella, who was rearing up on her hind legs and neighing wildly.

"Bella, no!" shouted Alma in horror, but it was too late.

In the background battle horns sounded, and an infantry formation came into motion at the same moment as the dragon came down on the shadow horse and rider. The attack came with a blinding flash of light, then suddenly a total hush descended on the battlefield. When Alma's eyes were clear of the golden rings the flash had caused, and she could finally see again, she saw that Bella's place had been occupied by a team of Lord Dharma's foot-soldiers, the dragon had vanished, and Bella and Stella stood frozen at the edge of the trench as an enormous equestrian statue.

"That's cheating! The dragon doesn't count!" shouted Alma, beside herself with rage, but her enemy turned a deaf ear.

Bella couldn't be brought back to the battlefield now. Felix's vision had returned now too, and a searing cry went up from him when he realized Bella had fallen victim to the beast. He felt like tearing off his armour and rushing to embrace his petrified sister. "It's my fault, they killed her because of me!" He was wracked with desperation and guilt. Then he remembered that Lord Dharma might well carry out his threat, and after Bella, the dark lord would destroy him too. Felix pulled himself together, took some deep breaths to calm his fury, and defiantly and resolutely looked toward his distant enemy.

"I swore allegiance to Alma, that I would stick by her even though it may cost me my life!" he muttered sternly to himself.

Apparently Alma sensed Felix's inner turmoil, and looked at him with sympathy. The others, however, breathed a sigh of relief, because at first all they noticed was that the threatening dragon was gone from the sky, and the black stormclouds were already beginning to disperse. Jack looked at Alma with wild, flashing eyes.

"Let me smash them to bits!" he pleaded, pointing to the infantry occupying the place Bella had been.

"No, you can't go!" Alma shook her head. "We're not cheating. You can't strike legally from there! Baker will mete out revenge!"

Alma and Jack watched with satisfaction as the old tradesman launched into the enemy with his sword drawn.

They couldn't enjoy the vengeance for long, because Alma noticed that the haystacks that had escaped the flaming arrows were now catching fire from the sparks that had flown off the dragon's claws, and the two horses harnessed to the cart between the haystacks began to whinny in fright. Alma saw that the situation was becoming intolerable for Grandpa and Grandma. She needed to castle as soon as possible, to get the two old folk to a sheltered place. She had

already irrevocably opened the short side when Katalina went over the bridge, but on the long side she couldn't castle, because as queen she herself stood between Drifter – the rook – and the king – the two old folk.

Although Lord Dharma was meanwhile advancing another infantry formation, endangering both Don Espolín and Felix, rather than saving her officers, Alma went forward herself, right as far as the kitchen garden, where at the beginning of the battle Stella's hooves had trampled on the vegetable patch. This way the path for castling was clear. In the next move Alma sent Katalina's grandparents to a safe place. The castling on the long side was complete: the two old folk were sheltered in the windmill, while Drifter – the rook – occupied the meadow where

Alma focussed her eyes in determination. She was prepared to sacrifice anything to prevent her opponent castling in the same way.

Her satisfied gaze swept over the battlefield. Although at first sight her position seemed worse, because during the fray with the dragon she had lost Bella, (or in other words she had sacrificed a knight for a pawn, and she had lost pawns too) she felt firmly that the battle was going according to plan. For several moves Katalina had been threatening Lord Dharma's cavalry formation. She could have attacked the horsemen a while ago, but Alma felt that to threaten was more important than to strike. If her opponent did not know when the inevitable blow would come, his nerves would get frazzled, tension would wear him down, and later he would be more likely to make an error. Moreover Lord Dharma hadn't been able to deploy his officers, because their commander had been occupied with defence and moving the pawns. For sure, the advance of a black pawn formation to the pasture on d4 threatened both Felix and Don Espolín, but at least her opponent was occupied with that rather than with castling.

Alma thoughtfully looked at Felix's heroic figure and the elderly knight astride Tempest. Both were in mortal danger: in the next move the infantry opposite them could massacre either of them, and Alma could only save one of them. She was well aware that at this point she could allow nothing to influence her but military strategy. On an

open diagonal the bishop was the more useful fighter, plus she could surprise her opponent once more with another attacking move. So she ordered Felix to retreat for a short while from the field under threat. Don Espolín saw that Alma was going to sacrifice him, but he made no objection. Raising his sword he saluted her, then bravely looked the enemy right in the eye, and awaited the fatal attack. The division of footsoldiers were quick to surround him, and yanked the old warrior off his horse in no time. After the knight had disappeared from the battlefield, Alma signalled to Felix to avenge his death. With a flash in his eyes and a wild war-cry erupting from his throat, Felix threw himself at the enemy.

Though Alma's losses were mounting (by now she had lost both knights, while her opponent had sacrificed only pawns), she felt increasingly convinced things were going well. Her whole being was buzzing with the excitement of attack, and she knew that soon she could put the enemy in a very tight corner. She had always enjoyed pinning her opponents' pieces. This meant adopting a position so the other player could not move his pieces, because an apparently harmless move could open the way for a full-scale attack.

Through her telescope Alma watched whether Lord Dharma would manage to castle. Actually he had no need to; in that position perhaps he would be better off making another move. But since the

beginning of the battle the dark lord had been preparing to move his king to a safe place, and was irritated at having had to keep postponing this move because of Alma's attacks. Now he was glad of the unexpected opportunity, and exploited the situation to carry out his plan. Perhaps he insisted on this bad move because he had been planning it for so long. Alma's eyes sparkled. Because of the castling, the king's carriage was stuck in the corner, and had little room for manoeuvre, so if she managed to get near it, Alma could put a lot of pressure on him.

Until now the black cavalry had been threatening, but now the time had come to release Katalina on them. The peasant girl threw herself with relish into the fray among the horsemen, paying no heed to the movement of Lord Dharma's queen's carriage as it rolled down the hill where it had been stationed, and forcing her to her knees

with a flash of light. Jack cried out when he saw that Katalina had collapsed in the grass, but Alma paid no attention. She fixed her eyes on the black king, hiding in the protection afforded by the castling. The moment was approaching to launch an all-out attack on him. Now she herself moved one square on, to find a convenient viewpoint between the vines, then in the next move she ordered Jack to come alongside her. The peasant

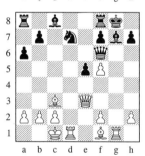

boy stared hopefully at the infantry formation stationed in the arbour opposite Alma.

"Please, let me fight them, at least! I'd like to avenge Katalina! If I destroy them, they'll no longer stand in the way of the attack!"

"Lie in wait, Jack, but don't leave your place," said Alma sternly. "We're going to pin them. You won't attack, but they can't harm you either, because if they attack you, it would open up the field for Felix. And they certainly wouldn't risk that. You'll have to put up with not moving for a while!"

Jack nodded obediently, though deep down he would have liked to hack the enemy to pieces. But he knew he couldn't act as he pleased, because at the beginning of the battle he had sworn obedience to the queen, Alma.

Meanwhile the black queen's carriage took an unexpected turn and moved over to the far side of the battlefield, to square b6. There it turned to face Alma, who stood all alone among the vines. The curtain in the window of the carriage lifted, and a man with stern, harsh features and dark eyes leaned out from behind the black velvet. Alma immediately recognized Lord Dharma, whom she had met in the white room on the afternoon before the battle. The mighty lord furrowed his brow and stared, and even had the cheek to raise the telescope to his eye, using it to scrutinize Alma.

The path between the two commanders was clear, so in the next move Alma could have attacked her arch-enemy. But as an experienced player she also knew that Lord Dharma would take revenge for the capture, and his well-equipped cavalry was waiting to strike in the background. If Alma attacked the black queen, that would be her ruination, because in the next moment she would become a victim. It wouldn't be the first time: when the queens destroy each other in chess this is known as a queen exchange. But Alma was certain that if she undertook this, afterwards she would still be able to direct the fight from next to the battlefield. Even without her, the combat would continue, though she wouldn't be able to take an active part in it. So she was not afraid of exchanging queens, but she wanted to act prudently.

Meanwhile, Drifter, who was stuck in the siege machine,

saw the danger that threatened Alma, and started shouting desperately.

"Don't go near him, Alma, it's a trap! They'll wipe you out!"

"Calm down," she signalled and tried to think through the possible steps. But Drifter was not to be silenced. So far he hadn't really taken part in combat. The only time he had to move was when the grandparents took refuge in the windmill, and through the castling he had moved to the other side of the old folk. Since then, he had been observing the others' fighting from a safe vantage point, and was increasingly worried about the way the enemy was picking off victims. The danger that awaited Alma was too much for him to bear, and as he saw Lord Dharma's eyes scrutinizing her, he was gripped by fear just as at home, in Sycamore Park, and again he felt he had to protect Alma from this man. He would happily have moved the siege machine to stand between Lord Dharma and Alma, to prevent any attack. He started moving, hoping that Alma would need him, and that she would ask him to help.

Alma was still thinking, with her back to Drifter: she didn't even turn towards him.

"Let me block the attack!" he shouted finally, incapable of bottling up his anxiety. "Or send me up to the same rank, so he can attack me!"

Alma finally turned to him, and looked at him with a cunning twinkle in her eye.

"Don't worry, Drif, I'm not going to stop fighting him! I have a better idea, and you'll be able to help me. We'll try and give mate to the king!"

"At last!" sighed Drifter with relief. "This idling about was driving me crazy!"

Alma span round and turned her back on the dark lord watching from the carriage, then cut across the vegetable patch to the bank of the stream. Here she was facing Lord Dharma's bishop, the only piece defending the route to the king. Lord Dharma responded by pulling closed the pitch-black curtain of the carriage, as his driver whipped the horses, and he too cut through to the other side, to defend his bishop in person.

"Come on, Drifter!" roared Alma. "Now for the attack! Advance to square d6, and aim for the black carriage. Don't be afraid, he won't attack, because if he leaves the bishop undefended, I'll put the king in checkmate right away!"

"I'm not afraid!" shouted Drifter enthusiastically, and set off to carry out Alma's order. While the huge wooden

contraption squeaked and creaked its way to d6, Drifter's heart started to beat faster. His every fibre was throbbing with the thirst for battle, his heart was in his mouth, his palms were damp with excitement, but the last shred of fear had left him, and he was driven by a desire for victory, and to help Alma.

Lord Dharma recognized the danger awaiting him, and he knew that if he did nothing to defend himself, then in the next move the stone projectiles flying from the siege machine's catapult would destroy the queen's carriage. Because he himself couldn't attack, and he couldn't leave the bishop unprotected, he could only hope that he could block the path of the enraged Drifter with another fighter. So he deployed an infantry formation which was stationed nearby.

With this he won temporary respite from the threat posed by Drifter, but later this move would prove to be problematic. The infantry formation restricted his own movement too, and prevented the carriage going back. But that appeared not to worry him; for the moment he seemed to be pleased having deflected the immediate danger.

But Alma couldn't be stopped now. She commanded Thomas Cosinus, the white bishop, to hunt down the opponent with Felix over the next few moves. Although the mathematician and Felix had only recently met, they worked well together to carry out Alma's orders. With their combined strength, a few moves were enough to block off the black king's last escape route, to bait Lord Dharma's rook then force it to flee, and from time to time to pin down the opponent's pieces. The battle moved to the black end of the field, and Drifter and the two bishops circled round the enemy threateningly.

Lord Dharma's carriage was stranded aimlessly between the two bishops. Perched on the upholstered seat, the commander grew more and more agitated by the minute and with each move. He drew the curtain again, the better to see events on the battlefield. Now that her opponent's face appeared again in the window, Alma also raised her telescope to observe him closely. Through the lens it seemed that Lord Dharma's previous confidence had vanished, his face looked uncertain, and he was unable to disguise his agitation. Alma was pleased to note that although Lord Dharma had a material advantage over her, because she had lost more fighters than her opponent (valuable ones too), in spite of this her spatial and positional advantage was much greater.

White's soldiers were distributed throughout the battlefield, the black king and officers were constantly under threat; the dark lord had neither time nor opportunity to attack, because all his strength was devoted to deflecting Alma's continual aggressive manoeuvres. A few moves later Lord Dharma's rook turned on Thomas Cosinus, and the catapult operators placed huge rocks in the arm of the machine, but Alma already had a solution. She ordered the mathematician

to move one square away, to get some glowing embers from the smouldering ruins of the burnt-out barn nearby. Using these he set fire to his arrows, posing a threat to both the wooden siege machine and to the nearby infantry.

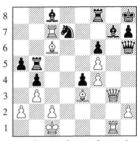

"That's what I like. A real fork, when I attack two enemy pieces at the same time!" Alma thought with a smile. Since Thomas Cosinus was no longer in firing range of the black rook, indeed, now it was him threatening the siege machine with his flaming arrows, Lord Dharma decided to utilize his rook somewhere else. With the ammunition at the ready, he aimed at Baker, who was lolling around in the distance, then after the rocks had struck the unsuspecting old man, the siege machine triumphantly occupied the empty place. Black's rook had escaped, then, and even taken a victim, but Thomas Cosinus still had an

opponent, and he turned his bow and arrows to Black's cavalry.

"Wait, Thomas, don't shoot!" Alma stalled him.

"Don't you worry about me, miss!" he shouted back confidently. "I see how the ground lies. Lots of us will fall now! If I destroy the cavalry, the enemy bishop will take me, but then he will be struck by Drifter. So in the end it will be for our good!"

"I've got a better idea!" answered Alma. "Don't worry, there'll still be a fight, but meanwhile we will lure Black's other rook into play, the one protecting the king! Get ready, Drifter!"

"What's the plan?" asked Drifter through the arrow slits of the siege machine.

Alma fell quiet for a moment. It wasn't easy to tell him what she planned, that she was going to use him as a bait to provoke the enemy rook into moving. Finally, she composed herself. She knew she couldn't make allowances for anyone. All that mattered was victory, whatever the price. She could not afford to be squeamish about making sacrifices.

"You will strike the enemy bishop," she said, "but then, I'm afraid you will be hit."

Drifter looked around, and grasped the situation.

"Black's rook will leave the king alone to come after me! Because once he has taken me and occupied my place, afterwards it'll be easier for you to get even with him."

Alma nodded.

"Don't worry about me! Everything will be fine!" shouted Drifter enthusiastically. Then he aimed at the bishop (one of the fools) standing nearby.

"Don't waste your energy!" shouted the podgy man. "You can't strike me with a catapult!"

"Liar!" hollered Drifter triumphantly, and released the first round of rocks. He didn't want to waste time, in case chatting weakened his resolve. His aim was accurate, the bishop was flattened, and after the blinding flash, Drifter's siege machine rolled over to the empty square. The enemy rook idling on the back rank immediately went into attack, with ammunition whistling through the air at the skateboarder, and hitting the siege machine square on. Another flash of light, and Alma felt a pang of sorrow at having to lose another friend.

But now Thomas Cosinus could shoot his flaming arrows into the cavalry, and once he had occupied his new position, he had to prepare for the next attack. From his new position he was forking the enemy rooks, in other words, threatening both siege machines. Which one would Lord Dharma want to save? The one that had struck down Drifter, or the one that had eliminated Baker? Alma looked on with harsh resolve. She knew that she would have her revenge, and the endgame was approaching. After some thought, Lord Dharma decided to remove from the threat of flaming arrows the rook that had crushed Drifter, so the mathematician shot his arrows at the other siege machine. The wooden contraption quickly caught fire, and when the entire structure was engulfed in flame, there came another lightning-like flash. But the other rook had already

started a counter-attack, and soon Thomas Cosinus too stood as a stone figure at the edge of the battlefield.

She had few officers now, but in front of the patiently waiting Ferdinand Vector, operating the remaining siege machine, the path was open. Now Alma commanded him out to the open file. Lord Dharma could launch no counter-attack, because the way was blocked in front of his carriage, and the rook that had left the back rank was now too far from the king to provide

the necessary defence. The commander made a last, hesitant move, but when Alma launched her attack, Lord Dharma could see that his position was hopeless. Although in terms of losses so far, the two teams stood neck-and-neck, Alma's position seemed impregnable, while on the black side the only option was to flee.

After vacillating a moment, Lord Dharma took his horn and blew into it. At the sound, countless uniformed figures advanced – not to provide reinforcements for the fazed army, but to wave a white flag before Alma. She took a deep breath, cast a gaze over the whole battlefield, and finally put down her weapon. At that point Lord Dharma's carriage moved too, coming straight towards Alma. The black door opened, and the haggard, exhausted man, who for days had been trying to bait and trap the children, descended the steps. At last, the two opponents stood face to face. Alma stared hard into his dark eyes. Lord Dharma took a step forward, and put out his hand to the blond queen.

"I admit my defeat. Victory is yours, Queen Alma!"

XXI. The Dominion

Alma graciously accepted the handshake that acknowledged her victory. Inside she was beside herself with delight, and would happily have danced for joy. But now the battle was over, she suddenly felt exhausted, and wanted to rest, and be reunited with her friends.

"So can we go home now?" she asked hopefully.

"If that is your wish, you may," Lord Dharma nodded gravely. "I shall open the way that leads back to your world."

Alma gave a sigh of relief. Nothing else mattered: they had come to the end of the journey, there would be no more traps or dangers, and the way home would be open. As she looked around with a newfound sense of release, she saw that the remaining members of her team were gradually making their way towards her. They were all tired and hesitant, but their eyes shone with the pride and joy of victory. Alma waved at them with both arms to encourage them to come closer. There were not many of them. Of the officers there remained only Felix and Ferdinand Vector, the pawns on the queenside who were the three deserting soldiers, Fredo, Nando, and Steve, then Jack and old Farthing, who was panting from exhaustion, even though all through the battle he hadn't had to so much as leave his post next to the forest. Then with a creak the mill door swung open, and out came the horse and cart, with Grandma standing on the driver's box, pale and terrified.

"Good sire, have mercy on us! Help us!" she said to Lord Dharma, when the cart halted next to the black carriage with a jolt. "My husband's near to death, and if he doesn't get medicine soon, he'll pass away here in the cart!"

Jack immediately ran to the cart to see him, but Alma turned to Lord Dharma.

"I too request you to give some of the water of life to Grandpa!"

Lord Dharma's face showed no sign of sympathy or understanding.

"I do not open the lion fountain for my subjects. But you, Miss Alma, since you have defeated me, you may have some of the water, and you shall decide whether to keep it for yourself or to give it to the old man. But if I grant this wish, then I have no further obligations to you. I cannot then send you home."

Alma gulped. She felt that she'd been tricked again, and that this situation was even more hopeless than previous ones. How could she deny the old folks' request? She couldn't let Grandpa die before her eyes when she had the chance to cure him. But neither could she allow the group to become trapped in Lord Dharma's world of chess for ever. She glanced at Felix. If she asked for the water from the lion fountain, that would chain her friends here too, in this strange realm. Felix must have been thinking the same thing, because his fist was clenched, and he was looking at Lord Dharma with a flushed face and a flash of fury in his eyes.

Grandpa's condition was deteriorating by the minute. Summoning the last of his strength, he tried to lever himself up to speak, but he was unable to breathe a word. With a wheezing chest he collapsed back onto the soft sheepskin. Alma couldn't stand it any longer.

"I'd like the water of life, but quickly!" she shouted.

To her surprise Lord Dharma nodded good-humouredly, then reached to his belt and unhooked a small flask hanging from his waist, decorated by a golden lion's head.

"I always keep one draught at hand," he said simply, while offering the flask to Alma.

She immediately climbed up onto the cart, unscrewed the cap of the flask, and carefully, so as not to lose a drop of the valuable liquid, began to pour it into the mouth of the unconscious old man. The others gathered around, and watched in amazement as the old man gradually gathered strength. First his arms and legs, which were drooping uselessly, began to twitch, then a flicker of life came to his eyes, the wrinkles of torment smoothed out, and he sat up. He gulped down the last drop on his own without any help. Then he took Alma's hands in his own, and gazed with gratitude at her.

"Thank you, miss. You've given me a new lease of life. I feel rejuvenated!"

Now it was Grandma's turn to hug Alma, then overcome with emotion she put her arms round Grandpa's neck. She was only just beginning to grasp that the miraculous had happened, right at the last moment. They had saved her husband from the jaws of death. The others too stood amazed around the cart, forgetting for a moment the battle they had just fought, their petrified companions, and Lord Dharma, who stood back and watched the scene with interest.

Alma was the first to remember where they were, and squeezed Grandpa's sinewy hand once more, then climbed off the cart and went to Felix.

"You do see that I had no choice, don't you?"

Felix nodded in silence.

"When the others have been changed back to life, I promise, we'll find the way to get home. We don't know how to get to the secret gateway, but we're bound to find it sooner or later. If necessary, I'll play another game against Lord Dharma, on a chessboard, or completely blindfold, and I'll make him let us go home."

"Don't worry, we're behind you, whatever happens!" said Felix, straightening his back.

Now Alma went up to Lord Dharma.

"The battle is over. It's time for our friends captured during the battle to come back to life," she said.

Lord Dharma shook his head.

"I am sorry, my ladyship. It is not within my powers to change them back."

"What?" Alma was flabbergasted. "What will happen to them then?"

"In my humble opinion, they will look splendid in your palace. It is still rather bare, and one or two good statues would brighten it up. The enormous statue of the little girl on the horse is particularly fetching."

Alma was so furious she didn't notice Lord Dharma's strange choice of words. The fact that he had said your palace, and he had called her his ladyship, had escaped her. All she could focus on was that he was once more being unjust to her and her friends.

"You've been cheating, leading us on a wild goose chase, lying all the time!" she shouted, tears welling up in her eyes. "You cannot do this to us! Wicked and cruel, that's what you are! A mean crook!"

With eyes ablaze, Felix clenched his fist and stepped forward.

"Calm your anger, my ladyship!" said Lord Dharma perfectly cool, paying no attention to Felix's threatening gestures. "You see, you think that in all of my actions I was merely toying with you. You accuse me of lying throughout, and of wanting to destroy you. You think me a fraud, evil and cruel, but you should know that beyond the squares of the chessboard, nothing in the world is simply black and white. What seems black on the surface may look quite different inside."

"What am I supposed to think of someone who traps four children in an alien world, sets deadly traps for us, lets towers collapse on top of us, sends armed soldiers to fight us, and even cheats during the game? Don't try and tell me the dragon was in the rules! He destroyed Bella!"

"That was a despicable, ruthless move!" hissed Felix, with

hatred.

"You are both in error. So carried away are you, that you yourselves take things as they seem, but appearances are misleading. The dragon was brought to life by the position in the game of chess; I did not set it against you!"

"But it attacked Bella!"

"Because the little girl opposed it. The dragon has never attacked anyone without reason. It did indeed almost kill Miss Bella, I only just managed to save her!"

"What?" Alma was taken aback. Lord Dharma's claim that he had saved Bella from the dragon outdid any of his previous lies.

"As soon as I noticed the dragon preparing to attack, I sent an infantry formation to combat Miss Bella. My pawns eliminated her according to the rules, and she was moved to the edge of the battlefield. Before it could ignite the reckless girl and her horse, the dragon vanished. You too saw the flash that signals a strike in the battle."

Alma fell silent for a moment. After the flash of light Bella's place had indeed been occupied by Lord Dharma's footsoldiers, while she and Stella had appeared as a stone statue by the trench, with the captured players. And the dragon had disappeared too. But that didn't change the fact that Drifter, Bella, and the others were stone statues. And Lord Dharma had always been against them, craftily planning to snatch away their lives.

"You exaggerate." The dark lord shook his head, as if he could read Alma's mind. "I had to put you to the test. I had to ascertain whether you would be worthy opponents. If I had not laid traps for you, I would never have known whether you were brave, clever, or resourceful enough. I had to know whether the bonds between you were strong enough, whether you would be able to make sacrifices for one another, whether you have enough stamina."

Felix stood there speechless. Could it be that Bella's loss had not actually been caused by his resistance, and that Lord Dharma was not governed by revenge? Could his attempt to lure Felix to his side have been just another trial to prove his faithfulness?

"Our lives were at stake, more than once! In the turret we could have fallen to our deaths! The guardroom nearly fell in on us!" said Alma reproachfully.

"And your soldiers nearly did away with us in the windmill!" added Felix.

"None of the tasks you had was impossible," sneered Lord Dharma. "The path to freedom was always open. Each time I gave you the chance to prove yourselves. I always left you a glimmer of hope, even in the most difficult of trials."

"But now that we've won, you are ruining us anyway!" spluttered Alma. "If you're not really as evil as you've made yourself out to be, why not change our friends back?"

"Because it is no longer in my power," said Lord Dharma, with an enigmatic smile. "Only the all-powerful ruler of the dominion has the power to turn a stone statue into a human being, or vice versa, to condemn a figure of flesh and blood to permanent immobility."

"But that's you! In the room with eight doors, you said that you are chess itself, and war, and destiny. The one and only commander in the world of chess. Who can do anything, except for one thing!" raged Alma.

"Yeah, actually, except for what, exactly?" Felix was curious. "Changing the statues back?"

"No," Lord Dharma shook his head. "The omnipotent ruler of the dominion of chess must keep only one law: a worthy opponent may be defeated only in a fair and honourable game of chess. He cannot kill by ambush, he can destroy only by fighting by the rules."

Alma was about to protest, but Lord Dharma raised his finger.

"Since you always had the chance to escape from my traps, I did not break the rule. I knew that if you were worthy opponents, if you were clever, observant, and inventive enough to find the solutions to the puzzles, if you did not shrink back when threatened, and kept in sight your overall goals, if you firmly resisted temptation and remained true to your friends, then you would disentangle yourselves from every snare, and you would not perish, even when in mortal danger."

He cast a telling glance at Felix.

"I was always convinced that you would prove to be faithful, resilient, and worthy of victory."

"Well, thank you very much," threw in Felix sarcastically.

"And so why can't you change the others back, if you can do everything else?" asked Alma suspiciously.

"Oh, my ladyship, I didn't think you were so slow on the uptake," Lord Dharma shook his head. "I cannot bring your friends to life because I am no longer the omnipotent ruler of the dominion of chess. Your defeating me in chess was just the penultimate trial. In order to become the fully-fledged ruler, you had to prove that you are able to place your subjects' interests over your own. That another human life is more important to you than your own contentment. You were invested with my power when you asked for the flask with the water of life, instead of the way out of this world."

"Does that mean I can bring the others to life?" Alma asked in shock. For the moment she wasn't bothered about all the red tape involved in being a monarch; she just wanted to see her petrified friends move again.

"All it takes is a word from you!" nodded Lord Dharma.

Alma turned to the figures lined up by the trench, and shouted out:

"Live and breathe, as you lived and breathed before!"

Those standing near her gave a murmur of wonder when the stone figures of all the victims of the battle, the white and black fighters seemed to slowly melt back into life. Their faces bloomed, their muscles rippled, and their previously stony locks of hair now fluttered in the early summer breeze.

"Bella," shouted Felix, beside himself, and roaring triumphantly he rushed to his sister. Even Alma, oblivious to everything else, ran to the trench to hug Katalina, Drifter, Baker, and the others, as they awoke dazed from their ordeal, having braved death without complaint or fear.

Lord Dharma looked in thoughtful silence at the faces beaming with joy, the reunion of brother and sister, the tears of gladness Katalina shed for her grandparents, Jack's sparkling eyes, which remained constantly fixed upon the little peasant girl. He noted the men's firm handshakes of comradeship, their faces flushed with victory, and the sheepish but tender embrace with which Drifter momentarily squeezed Alma.

When they finished greeting one another, and heard the explanation of the events of the last few days, Alma led them back to Lord Dharma, who was still standing by the black carriage. She looked determinedly at his dark eyes.

"Lord Dharma, I have thought about this. I do not wish to be ruler of your country. Dharmia is not my home. I have never had the desire or the need to lord it over others. I wish to live in my own world, with my family, and my friends. I'd like to carry on school back at home, studying, and playing chess, just like before."

Lord Dharma's face darkened.

"I am afraid, my ladyship, you have no choice in the matter. Ruling is not just a right; it is also a duty. The power is vested in you, whether you like it or not. From now on, your commands will be fulfilled. If you go back to your world and leave the dominion alone, everything will decay, and eventually perish. Those who live here need someone to look after them. The world of chess cannot be allowed to disappear without a trace!"

"I think the village folk would be a lot happier without a ruler," interrupted Drifter. "Don't kid me that people like paying taxes, going to war, and trembling with fear of soldiers. Just ask the villagers whether they'd be happier living on their own, whether they'd mind working the land as they pleased, with nobody to boss them around."

"Things are not at all that simple!" snapped Lord Dharma, then restraining himself, he continued more mildly. "Of course the villagers would be happy not to pay taxes and fight wars, but somebody has to defend the unity of the dominion. Dharmia is not my own country; it is the vast and eternal realm of chess itself, where all knowledge of the game of chess is preserved, where new strategies are born, where we collect and examine new ideas and solutions, where from ancient times, since the dawn of chess, every single battle has been chronicled."

"But Dharmia isn't for me," Alma shook her head as tears welled up in her eyes. "I couldn't live the rest of my life here."

"For one thing, I chose the name Dharmia. You don't have to keep the same name," said Lord Dharma.

"Almia sounds a bit daft," chuckled Bella.

Everyone laughed apart from Lord Dharma, who solemnly continued his train of thought.

"I no longer remember the original name. The previous ruler also gave his own name to the dominion. When I defeated him, I too wanted to fashion things to my own liking. I renamed it Dharmia, and tried to organize things so my power was incontestable. I was terrified of being ousted from the throne myself. I tried to avoid all encounters with potential contenders for the throne. I built a strong defence system, and organized my own army, and while I drank each day from the water of life, year by year I eschewed any confrontation with new chess players who could vanquish me."

"In other words, you were a coward and a fraud. You abused the power entrusted to you," concluded Felix with contempt.

Lord Dharma nodded.

"At first it was indeed so. I was overcome by the boundless power, by the countless treasures at my disposal, the possibilities, servants, the army, eternal life. It took me centuries to understand that this in itself is meaningless. Chess is made truly combative through the life-and-death struggle. In chess, just as in life, a real battle is the only one worth fighting. Real goals, real combat, real feelings and passions, genuine experiences, these are what make a full life. When I understood this, I too changed. Since then I have constantly sought out chessmasters, knowledgeable, focussed players, so I might find a worthy successor, to whom I can leave this dominion. A reign of over five centuries is more than enough, even if I haven't aged a day."

"And will you age too now?" chirped Bella, curiously.

"If Miss Alma allows me, then yes, I shall," nodded Lord Dharma. "My ladyship, do you recall our conversation in the white room? I requested that if you defeat me, you too should grant me one wish."

"And what is your wish?" Alma raised her eyebrows.

"I ask you to permit me to leave. I would like to return to the real world, to live out my days as a retired chessmaster, to slowly grow old, and quietly die. You have it in your power to turn me into a statue, as I did with my predecessor, and he did with his; or you can, with a single word, strike me down dead, but I would like to live still a while, modestly and quietly, analysing games of chess in a provincial town."

Alma nodded.

"I don't want to take revenge on anyone."

They fell quiet for a while. Alma broke the silence.

"Lord Dharma, do you think it would be possible for me to rule in Chesslandia while being at home as well? I mean, could I live at home with my family, but now and again come back here to attend to business in the dominion, and find a worthy opponent?"

"Naturally," Lord Dharma nodded in relief. "Since you have acquired boundless power, you can do anything. And you do not necessarily have to pit yourself against the chosen opponents in Dharmia. Sorry, I mean Chesslandia. If you wish, you may fight your battles in the real world, over a chessboard. You may organize international tournaments, you can play on a computer, or however you please. But you must not forget about your dominion. As long as you rule, you must attend to affairs of the realm, you must safeguard the chess codex, you must watch the great players, so that when the right time comes, you may pass on the monarch's sceptre."

"What is the chess codex?" asked Alma with a sparkle in her eye.

"Let us return to the castle. I think everyone would benefit from a substantial lunch," suggested Lord Dharma. "Over lunch I shall tell you many things. Then I shall present to you the castle, the codex, and everything you need to know and see as true ruler."

Alma nodded, and she and her friends, who were indeed hungry and exhausted, set off for the castle. This time, the enormous wooden gate stood wide open to allow them to enter.

XXII. Endgame

In the castle the victors of the battle were greeted with refreshing drinks and trays of tasty nibbles. Then everyone was taken to their own personal room with a bathtub of hot water, so they could spruce up and rest while lunch was being prepared. On the beds were comfortable new tailor-made clothes, so the tired fighters could lay aside their soiled, creased, torn rags.

They didn't have to wait long for lunch. In less than half an hour the bells rang summoning the guests to the dining hall. Lord Dharma immediately greeted Alma, proffering his hand to lead her to the head of the table. She immediately noticed how the lord of the castle had changed. His face was warmer and friendlier, and he had changed his old pitch-black costume: only his trousers were black now, but instead of the dark smock he was now wearing a charcoal frock-coat, a brilliant white shirt and a claret silk tie.

At first conversation faltered somewhat, because everyone was preoccupied with the banquet. Over the last few days they had had the occasional snack, but now they were ravenous from the excitement of battle, and they all felt as if they hadn't eaten a thing for days. Only after the starter and the soup did their huge appetites subside a little, when the roast meat, pâtés and sauces arrived, and finally they felt sufficiently at ease to begin to chat freely.

Lord Dharma was happy to answer all their questions. He didn't gloss over his own errors and earlier wicked ways: he admitted that to begin with he had revelled in exercising his omnipotence, and terrorizing his subjects into fighting wars, and even changing the opponents he considered unworthy into stone. When he said that, Ferdinand Vector and Thomas Cosinus exchanged an angry glance.

"Forgive me, kind sirs!" Lord Dharma looked at the two mathematicians, who he had turned into statues.

They nodded sombrely, and Thomas Cosinus mumbled that they owed one another an apology too, for not standing up for each other. After all, it was their cowardice that had prompted Lord Dharma's anger, so they had all done something wrong.

Alma looked intently at Lord Dharma.

"All the people who over the years you have in anger changed into stone or taken captive, I will change back and set free."

"As you wish, my lady!" said Lord Dharma, bowing his head.

After the dessert Lord Dharma escorted his guests around the castle. He showed them the halls, and his most precious treasure, a collection of three thousand chessboards. Enormous showcases displayed chessboards and unusual pieces from every corner of the world. There were pieces made from ebony and ivory, carved in breathtaking delicacy; there were angular figures incised in pale and dark grey pebbles, reminiscent of surly masks; and there were graceful forms of artistic worth made of shellfish and snails' shells. Some of the boards were ornamented with precious stones; others were small and made of slabs of wood joined like a parquet; there was even a collapsible chessboard sewn together from shiny fabrics, and the pieces were tiny dolls dressed in silk. Bella's favourite was an ancient Indian set, in which each piece was an elephant. Don Espolín's eye was caught by an expertly carved wooden set painted in bright colours: the pieces showed painstaking craftsmanship and represented people, in the clothes of a king, lords-in-waiting, and generals, while the knights were realistic statues of horses.

"And which set is your favourite, my ladyship?" Lord Dharma asked, turning to Alma.

With a tranquil smile Alma indicated a white chess set, in which both players had identical pieces made of polished alabaster. Only very good players could use this, ones who were able to retain the entire game in their head while they looked at the pieces, because thirty-two white pieces moved on the monochrome squares incised on the white board.

At the end of the tour came the chess codex, which they examined inside a library stacked full of leather-bound tomes. The ornamental codex was almost as large as a person, and it took two strong servants to get it down from the shelf. The yellowing pages were inscribed with illuminated letters and colour illustrations showing old maharajas and chess players of ancient times, then came more recent masters, games and descriptions, tournaments, struggles, and renowned solutions. Lord Dharma explained that the codex was the greatest treasure in Chesslandia, a repository of chess knowledge, and whoever owned it was the trustee of the power of chess.

"I kept a separate book about you, my ladyship." Lord Dharma turned to Alma and took a small black book out of the pocket of his coat. "Little did you know that I made notes on your every game. In the Book of Alma you can find everything."

Alma was a bit embarrassed, but she took the book to see what was inside. And there they were: the best games she had played in tournaments, the important moves that had turned the tide in other games. Here and there Lord Dharma had made notes beside the notation of the game, and on the last page she found the games played in Sycamore Park. She looked at the notes incredulously, staring first at the book, then at Lord Dharma, then she shook her head, because she had never imagined anything like this. Lord Dharma smiled faintly.

"Accept this trifle as a gift from me," he said.

Alma smiled with gratitude at the former ruler, and quickly pocketed the little black book. Then they returned to the dining hall. Servants brought cakes and drinks, and everyone knew that it was time to say farewell and prepare to go back home.

"How good it will be to get back," sighed Bella happily. "But what will happen to Stella? Can I take her with me?"

"Where do you think you're going to put a horse? In the attic?" asked Felix, scandalized.

"It would be wiser to leave her here," said Alma earnestly. "But I promise that you can come with me anytime to Chesslandia, and you can ride her to your heart's content."

"And I'll look after her when you're not here, miss!" said Don Espolín obligingly. "Because, with your permission, Queen Alma, I would like to stay in your country. Many hundreds of years have passed since I left home, and although, thanks to Lord Dharma's command, time has made no mark on me in Dharmia, if I return I will find neither my family nor my house. I would like to live the rest of my life in Chesslandia."

"We had come to the same conclusion," nodded Thomas Cosinus and Ferdinand Vector. "We have no home now in the old world. Everything changed while we were waiting to be freed from the captivity of the stone statues. We can't put down roots in our old homes any more. Science has changed too. It would be better for us to live here, in this dominion. Perhaps we can start new families too, before we die."

"I think you've made the right decision," announced Alma after thinking it over. "Naturally, you can choose a comfortable apartment here in the castle, but if you prefer to settle in a village, I'll arrange for someone to help you. We can build you houses, workshops, studies, or you can farm the land, if you prefer."

"I'd like to learn beekeeping," sighed Ferdinand Vector.

"Then move to Fianchetto!" exclaimed Grandpa, beaming. "I'm getting too old and slow. Even though the water of life has cured me, I'm coming to the end of my days. But while I still have the strength, I'd be happy to teach you the trade!"

"And Fianchetto would be an ideal place for the horses too," said Grandma. "Not long ago a few houses were left empty. We could renovate them, and one of them has a stable too, with grassland and pastures, and we're only a few hours walk from the castle. It'll be easy to visit Lady Alma, if she happens to be in residence, and she can take a carriage to see you whenever she wants!"

Everyone took to the idea, and slowly plans were made for the future.

The time had come to say goodbye. There were more hugs, tears, and handshakes. Alma naturally promised to return to the dominion in a few days, to get down to the work of governing the place. Lord Dharma asked if he could stay in the castle to organize his papers, pack his effects and ensure that he left Chesslandia in the best state possible. Alma agreed.

When everyone had said goodbye to each other, Alma, Bella, Felix and Drifter set off to go home, after their journey of several days.

"Mum and Dad will be crying their eyes out!" worried Bella.

"If you ask me, the police will be looking for us," added Felix.

"I'm going to get a walloping back home..." mumbled Drifter. "Nobody will believe this story. They'll think I was just wandering around."

"You have no cause to worry. Everything will be fine!" Lord Dharma reassured them. "All you have to do is rely on Lady Alma, hold hands and walk through the portal!"

The children were slightly apprehensive, but they went towards the castle gate hoping for the best. The others followed close behind them. After waving one last goodbye in front of the castle portal, the four children held hands. Then slowly and steadily they stepped onto the road leading back to the other world. Alma suddenly instinctively knew what she had to do. When they were under the vault over the portal, she made a wish. Silently, she commanded with all her might that they should arrive back in the storm, at the same place and time from where they had left. That way, people living in the real world wouldn't notice that the children had slipped away and had adventures in another dimension.

"Get ready for rain!" shouted Alma, as they stepped under the portal.

Felix was about to say that half an hour earlier the sun had been blazing away, but he had no chance to speak: the next moment an icy wind and pouring rain whipped round him. They stopped dazed for a few moments. The storm was still raging in the park. They were in the middle of the zebra crossing, embarrassed and confused. In a few moments they were soaked through. Alma was the first to come to her senses.

"There's a bus shelter over there, on the other side!" she shouted. "That's where we were heading!"

Drifter realized that he was clutching a skateboard under his arm. He glanced sideways, and next to Felix he saw Bella's bicycle, dripping wet.

"Bring the bike! Run for the shelter!"

They rushed over the crossing and took refuge under the plastic roof of the bus stop. They didn't have to squeeze under the shelter for long, because the sudden storm was easing off. The wild pounding of the rain quietened to a gentle patter, then stopped completely. In five minutes the cheering light of the afternoon sun came out from behind the clouds.

"So, do we go home now?" Bella looked at Felix.

"Yes, I think Gran will be there soon," he nodded. "You know, Mum and Dad are at the wedding this evening."

"Oh yes, I'd forgotten! That means it's still Saturday, does it?" said Bella glumly, but she soon brightened up. "But then tomorrow is Sunday, which means we go to the riding school!"

"Do you think I could come with you?" asked Felix doubtfully. "I'd like to give riding a try!"

As Bella nodded with a sparkle in her eyes, Drifter turned to Alma.

"And I'd like to learn how to play chess. What do you think, do I have a chance?"

"Sure!" said Alma. "I think you'd be good at it. Come to my

house tomorrow, and I'll explain the basics."

"And will you teach us too?" chirped Bella.

"Of course!" said Alma, laughing. "And I hope you'll come back with me to Chesslandia. Stella will be there, and Katalina and the others. And I really don't want to go on my own."

"We will come!" stated Bella firmly. "We'll ride horses and play chess together. Who knows, I might even succeed you on the throne! Bellia would be a good name for the dominion!"

"Suits me!" Alma held out her hand, then all four of them set off home. They uttered few words on the way, as they all silently turned over the events of the last few days in their minds. Sometimes they caught each other's eyes, and smiled. Meanwhile the clouds had receded from the sky, and with the warm sunshine it wasn't long before the weather-beaten warriors were home and dry.

APPENDIX

THE BATTLE – MOVE BY MOVE

1.	e4	c5	13.	Bd2	dxc3	25.	Be3	Rb7
2.	Nf3	d6	14.	Bxc3	Bg7	26.	Bd5	Rb8
3.	d4	cxd4	15.	Rg1	0-0	27.	Rc7	b4
4.	Nxd4	Nf6	16.	gxf6	Qxf6	28.	b3	Rb5
5.	Nc3	a6	17.	Qe3	Kh8	29.	Bc6	Rxf5
6.	Be3	e6	18.	f4	Qb6	30.	Rxc8	Rxc8
7.	g4	e5	19.	Qg3	Qh6	31.	Bxd7	Rcc5
8.	Nf5	g6	20.	Rd6	f6	32.	Bxf5	Rxf5
9.	g5	gxf5	21.	Bd2	e4	33.	Rd1	Kg8
10.	exf5	d5	22.	Bc4	b5	34.	Qg2	
11.	Qf3	d4	23.	Be6	Ra7	Black resigns		
12.	0-0-0	Nbd7	24.	Rc6	a5	1-0		

8...g6

12...Nbd7

15...0-0

18...Qb6

29.Bc6

34.Qg2

WHY DID BLACK RESIGN?

Black's situation is hopeless. He loses his pawn on e4 in the centre, and afterwards the white queen threatens his king. The game could have turned out differently: 34...Qg6, to which White would give check, 35.Rd8+. The king then tries to escape 35...Kf7. Now it is time for White to take a pawn, moving 36.Qxe4. The queen in the centre is in the strongest position; it is there that the piece has the greatest power. But the move Qe8 threatens checkmate. Black would try to find an escape route for his king on g7 by moving 36...Bh6, but this would only be short-lived, because after 37.Qe8+ Kg7, Alma would give checkmate with 38.Qf8.

Chess masters 'surrender', or resign as we say, if they see they no longer have any chance of avoiding defeat. And Lord Dharma knew that in the position where he surrendered it was impossible to save the game. Black had lost the battle!

34...Qg6
35.Rd8+ Kf7
36.Qxe4 Bh6
37.Qe8+ Kg7
38.Qf8#

This game was actually played by Judit Polgár, the best woman chess player of all time, against Viswanathan Anand, who would later become World Champion, in Dos Hermanas in Spain in 1999. The game can be played interactively on Judit Polgár's webpage: WWW.JUDITPOLGAR.COM

THE RULES OF CHESS

Based on *Chess Playground* by Judit Polgár and Zsófia Polgár

The **KING** can move one square in any direction.
The **KING** cannot move to a square:
- that is already occupied by a piece of the same colour,
- that is threatened by a piece of the opposite colour,
- that is next to the opponent's king.

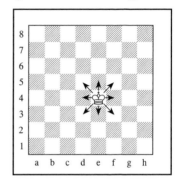

The **QUEEN** can move any number of squares, either in a straight line or diagonally, in any direction.

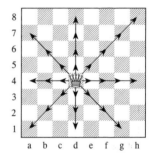

The **ROOK** can move any number of squares vertically or horizontally.

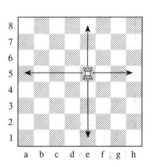

The **Bishop** can move any number of squares in a diagonal line, forwards or backwards. The **Bishop** always moves to a square of the same colour as its starting square at the beginning of the game.

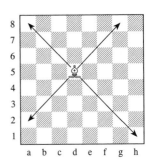

The **Knight** moves in an **L** shape, two squares in a straight line then one to the side. This is the only piece that can jump over other pieces of its own or the opposite colour.

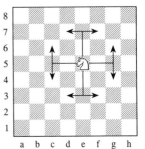

The **Pawn**, when it first moves, can move either one or two squares forward in a straight line. After the first move, it can move one square forward to an empty square in the file where it stands.

Except for the **Pawns**, every piece captures a piece of the opposite colour by making its normal move to occupy the square the captured piece was on. When the **Pawn** captures it moves diagonally forward one square. The pawn cannot move backwards or capture backwards!

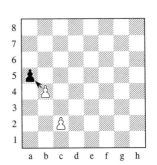

Promotion

When a **Pawn** reaches the 8th rank of the board (or, for Black, the first rank), it must be promoted. The player can choose to promote it to a queen, a rook, a bishop, or a knight (but never a king and it cannot stay a pawn).

En Passant

Capturing 'en passant' (a French phrase) is only possible if the opponent's pawn has moved two squares forward from the starting position, and if our pawn is immediately next to it. This capture can only be made immediately after the opponent pawn's move.

Castling, Check and Checkmate

Castling can happen in either direction. The king moves two squares towards a rook, the rook jumps over it and moves to the square next to the king. If this requires the rook to pass over one square, it is called castling short; if it passes over two squares, then it is called castling long.

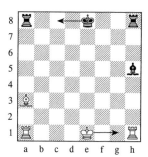

It is not possible to castle:
- if the king is in check,
- if there is a piece between the king and the rook,
- if the king would be in check after castling,
- if the square over which the king passes is under attack,
- if the king has already moved during the course of the game,
- if the rook involved in castling has already moved during the course of the game.

But it is possible to castle:
- if the king has been in check during the course of the game, but did not move and is not in check immediately before castling,
- if the rook involved in castling is under attack.

The king is in check if one of the opponent's pieces attacks it. The king can never be captured.

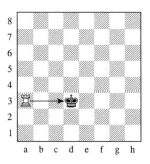

The player must always get the king out of check by doing one of the following:
- moving the king,
- capturing the threatening piece,
- positioning another piece between the threatening piece and the king, unless the threatening piece is a knight!

If the king cannot avoid check, it is in checkmate.

THE BEGINNING AND THE END OF THE GAME

The square a1 is always black. In the starting position the queen always stands on a square of her own colour. White makes the first move, then Black and White take turns.

When the king is in check and cannot escape, it has been given checkmate, or mate. The opponent has won, and the game is over. If a player thinks that the situation is hopeless, he can surrender, known as resigning.

A draw by stalemate happens when the king of the next player to move is not in check, but the player cannot make any move that is in accordance with the rules. A game is also a draw if neither player has the material strength to give checkmate.

The next player to move can claim a draw if the same position is repeated three times during the game, or if during 50 consecutive pairs of moves there has been no capture and no pawn move.

The two players can also agree to call the game a draw, when one player suggests a draw and the other player agrees.

CHESS NOTATION

If you want to play out the chess games and puzzles in the book, it is worth knowing the system used for notation of chess games.

King	♔	**K**
Queen	♕	**Q**
Rook	♖	**R**
Bishop	♗	**B**
Knight	♘	**N**
Pawn	♙	—

8	a8	b8	c8	d8	e8	f8	g8	h8
7	a7	b7	c7	d7	e7	f7	g7	h7
6	a6	b6	c6	d6	e6	f6	g6	h6
5	a5	b5	c5	d5	e5	f5	g5	h5
4	a4	b4	c4	d4	e4	f4	g4	h4
3	a3	b3	c3	d3	e3	f3	g3	h3
2	a2	b2	c2	d2	e2	f2	g2	h2
1	a1	b1	c1	d1	e1	f1	g1	h1
	a	b	c	d	e	f	g	h

1. The pieces are shown with capital letters: **K, Q, R, B, N**
2. The files are shown with small letters: a, b, c, d, e, f, g, h
3. The ranks are shown with numbers: 1, 2, 3, 4, 5, 6, 7, 8

First we write the name (or the abbreviation) of the piece. Every piece has a letter. The pawn can be written as P, but we don't usually write this. After writing which piece is moving, for instance, the queen, Q, we look for the name of the square it moves to, and write that after the letter Q.

For example, Qd5 means that the queen moved to the 5th rank on file 'd'. We don't need to write where it moved from, only where it moves to. For example, e4 means that a pawn moves to square e4.

If two pieces might be mistaken for each other on the same rank or file, we can indicate which one is moving. For instance, Rad1 means that of the two rooks on the 1st rank, the one on file 'a' moves to d1.

The Sign of a Capture: X

For example, Rxf5 shows that a rook captured an enemy piece in file 'f' in the 5th rank. exf5 means that a pawn captured an enemy piece, moving from file 'e' to square f5. This order only changes when a pawn is promoted: first we write down where the pawn is promoted and then which piece it becomes. For instance d8Q means that the pawn in file 'd' reached the 8th rank and was promoted to a queen.

Castling short: 0-0
Castling long: 0-0-0
Check: +
Checkmate: #
A good move: !
A poor move: ?
White wins: 1-0
Black wins: 0-1
Draw: ½-½

Each pair of moves in numbered. When White moves, we write 1., and then the move, for example, 1.e4. If Black's answering move is given immediately, then we write 1.e4 e5. If we interrupt the notation (to make a comment) then later when we continue the notation of this pair of moves we put three dots after the move number 1 then write Black's answering move: 1...e5

Example of the notation of a short game:
1.e4 e5 2.Nf3 f6 3.Nxe5 fxe5 4.Qh5+ Ke7 5.Qxe5+ Kf7 6.Bc4+ Kg6 7.Qf5+ Kh6 8.d4+ Qg5 9.Qxg5# 1-0

Move the knight on b1 to d2. Check. Black responds by moving the king to d4.

Give check again with the knight, move it to b3. The black king retreats to c4.

Dispose of the rook on a5 by capturing it with the knight. The black king moves back to d4.

The other knight deals the final blow, moving to f5. Checkmate!

SOLUTION TO THE PUZZLE ON PAGE 170

First Alma moves the rook on c4 to c8, offering this valuable piece to the opponent's rook. He responded by capturing it immediately.

Then her rook on d5 went to face the firing squad, moving to d8. Black captured this rook too, with his own piece.

Alma moves the white queen across to g8, to be next to the black king. Check.

Black has no other choice but to capture her.

Now it is the turn of the white knight, which jumps to f7, and wins the game. Checkmate.

SOLUTION TO THE PUZZLE ON PAGE 181

Felix the rook, strikes the black rook on e7, who is a soldier attacking with a sword.

Then he moves back for a moment to the black king...

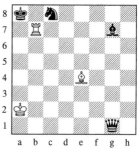

...but then he rushes off to eliminate the black bishop standing on g7.

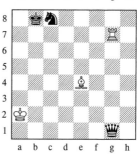

Finally he strikes the queen (or commander) swinging his broadsword on g1.

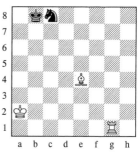

"As I see it, we didn't manage to give checkmate," Felix said, shaking his head. "Although we are definitely winning..."